Freddie Stockdale wa̶ ̶ ̶ ̶ ̶ ̶ ̶ ̶ ̶ ̶d read law at Cambridge. He ̶ ̶ ̶ ̶ ̶ ̶ ̶ ̶ck, and has three sons by a previous ma̶rriag̶ ̶ ̶ ̶s in Lincolnshire and runs Pavilion Opera; has dea̶lt̶ ̶ ̶ ̶ques; and is the author of *The Opera Guide* and *Figaro Here, Figaro There,* a diary about presenting opera on the road. *The Bridgwater Sale* is his first novel. His second novel, *Criminal Conversations,* is now available as a Doubleday hardback.

ex libris

CARMEN   GLAESSL

THE
BRIDGWATER
SALE

Freddie Stockdale

BLACK SWAN

THE BRIDGWATER SALE
A BLACK SWAN BOOK : 0 552 99546 0

Originally published in Great Britain by Doubleday,
a division of Transworld Publishers Ltd

PRINTING HISTORY
Doubleday edition published 1993
Black Swan edition published 1994

Set in 11/12pt Linotype Melior by
Phoenix Typesetting, Ilkley, West Yorkshire.

Corgi Books are published by Transworld Publishers Ltd,
61–63 Uxbridge Road, Ealing, London W5 5SA,
in Australia by Transworld Publishers (Australia) Pty. Ltd,
15–25 Helles Avenue, Moorebank, NSW 2170,
and in New Zealand by Transworld Publishers (N.Z.) Ltd,
3 William Pickering Drive, Albany, Auckland.

Reproduced, printed and bound in Great Britain by
Cox & Wyman Ltd, Reading Berks.

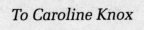

To Caroline Knox

CHAPTER ONE

The great lamps were hot and blinding, burning my eyelids, and for an awful moment I was tempted to scream. From behind them I could hear the sounds of people moving, whispering, and it didn't help to know that a TV camera was recording my ordeal.

The grip on my arm tightened, and I knew they were waiting for my answer. The silence was hot, sweaty, threatening. I could see one woman's eyes fixed on me, her jaw jutting forward and her teeth clenched in the drama of the moment. She had a horse face, with a fringe that straggled over her skull and stuck to her forehead. I decided to speak.

'It's against you, madam. Fifteen thousand pounds bid ... in the corner. Fifteen thousand bid, fifteen thousand,' I intoned. We were all destined for the local television news, so I had to give them what they were expecting. 'Fifteen thousand for this very fine pair of Holland and Holland shotguns. Mr Sarti's personal guns. Engraved with scenes from *Scheherazade*. Unique in the world of sport. Who'll go sixteen?'

I looked round confidently, the picture (I hoped) of a man on top of his job – six foot, fourteen stone, a positive bastion of respectability, forty years on the hoof and ready for the market, you might say, except for one irony: I happen to be the auctioneer. Of fine art, that is, rather than fatstock. Local director of Merrywethers, purveyors of fancy commodes and portraits of other people's ancestors to the nobility, the gentry, the upwardly mobile, indeed to anyone whose credit is good in the high street of the county town of Berington, that ancient haunt of haberdashers and cutlers in the rural county of the same name. Indeed, not to shrink from my own eminence, I combine the titles of local director, London director, main-board director and Consultant in Tapestries – a galaxy to swell any man's self-esteem. Or would be, if only the company were not threatened by the state of the market.

But enough of me. We were gathered together to disperse the assets of Gabriel Sarti. A year before, he was (if you read *The Sunday Times*) the twenty-seventh richest man in Britain, sometimes to be found in his castle in Scotland, or his *palazzo* in Venice, or his Manhattan duplex on the Upper East Side, but mostly ruling his empire (ladies' toiletries) from Gumby-in-the-Vale, his newly refurbished Jacobean mansion twenty miles north of Berington, ancient seat of the Gumbys whose last relic, Dapper Gumby, sold the house to pay off his asbestosis debts at Lloyd's. (There's a snag to that story. He took the purchase price in preference shares in Sarti Consolidated.) Anyway, to bring you up to date, when Sarti shot himself in Annabel's six months before, a rather different picture emerged. *The Sunday Times* had to downgrade him hurriedly to a position among the low sixty millionths – indeed, not to beat about the bush, he and his company were well up in the minus order.

Now we were selling his chattels. And I don't doubt we'll be selling what's left of Dapper's heirlooms in due course. Such is life (and death) at Merrywethers. Undertakers dispose of the body for a fixed fee, we deal with the possessions at an agreeable twenty per cent plus expenses. And if the market's weak? Why, we buy them ourselves and store them till trade picks up.

The grip on my arm was Robert's, Robert Head my principal assistant, thin, thirty, a little overawed by the swagger of today's customers and the television lights.

'I've got Sam Dickenson on the line. He's bidding.'

'Sixteen thousand,' I cried. 'Sixteen thousand by the desk.'

The toothy woman waggled her head.

'Seventeen,' I said, raising an eyebrow at Robert who

was talking softly into the receiver of the red telephone below me. He nodded.

'Eighteen. Eighteen thousand.' Somewhere fingers snapped. A tall dark girl at the back of the room was gesticulating. I looked across. She was pointing at a young man who was shyly raising one questioning finger. Even without my glasses, I could admire my resident porcelain expert, Mary Sykes. I looked at the man she had spotted.

'Are you bidding, sir?' He might have been picking his nose. He blushed and nodded.

'Twenty-two thousand!' I was in a bullish mood, and I couldn't see him contradicting me. 'Twenty-two thousand! A new bidder at the back.'

Several people turned and stared at my young benefactor, whose jaw had dropped. He half stood up.

'Twenty-two thousand.' I bared my teeth at him in genial menace, and he sat down again.

Robert, beside me, listened to his telephone and shook his head. The horsey woman in front was pretending to read her catalogue as if it had never crossed her mind even to consider bidding for this lot.

Bang! The young man had begun to show fresh signs of restlessness so I brought down the hammer with a resounding thud.

'Congratulations,' I said, pointing him out to our eager salesgirl, already sniffing her way down the aisle in pursuit of a signature. 'A bargain, I should say.'

Mary was glaring at me. The bidder wiped his forehead with a red spotted handkerchief.

'Lot seventy-three,' I said with a nonchalant smile. 'One Cartier shooting stick, slightly bent.' On we went, scattering the private life of our late client throughout our islands. It's an ill wind. The pensions funds may be in shock, and half the Sarti family on bail, but today at least Merrywethers' tills are ringing healthily. Yes, we were all engaged, Robert, Mary and I, in operating the tinsel roundabout of Vanity Fair, auctioning off the treasured contents of one half to feed the aspirations of the other in a satisfactorily perpetual circuit. On, on we raced.

'Twenty-five thousand pounds, twenty-five for this splendid set of Sèvres? Do you want it, sir? It's against you. Twenty-eight thousand I'm bid. Are you all done?' I can't help sounding like a nanny. You have to chivvy them along, otherwise the deliberately soothing luxury of Merrywethers' Grand Auction Hall would lull them to sleep instead of into calculated acquiescence.

'All finished at twenty-eight thousand pounds?'

'Over there,' whispered Robert, tugging at my sleeve.

'Thank you.' I beamed at a thin girl who had waved her catalogue, glossy in scarlet and gold, the Sarti racing colours. 'Thirty thousand and worth every penny.'

Once the sale was over, I ran across to the Castleton Arms for a couple of sandwiches and a pint of Guinness. Then on with the day's work. Merrywethers have their main offices in Mayfair and Fifth Avenue, but for historical reasons (a strategic takeover in the thirties) they also maintain a major presence in Berington, my patch. We have a staff of sixteen. There's Robert who masterminds the household auctions, Mary who's in charge of staffing and who specializes in porcelain, and me, the boss and general dogsbody combined. We still have half a dozen young things on the front desk, local yuppies with family connections who will have to be sacrificed if the market doesn't strengthen, a couple of porters cum security men, two secretaries, a telephonist and, crucial to our welfare, Mr and Mrs Gaskin. He, an ex-sergeant-major in the Coldstream Guards, functions as Cerberus, while she, hiding a heart of marshmallow beneath a stormtrooper's exterior, keeps us supplied with coffee, cakes and gossip.

The building itself is an old warehouse, relic of the days when the Great Eastern Canal, which still washes our back wall, was a national route for trade. Renovated at the turn of the century, and recently redone by a London firm, it provides our offices, our saleroom, several storerooms and an upstairs flat for the Gaskins, all underneath one towering roof and right on the high street between Boots the Chemist on one side and the National Westminster Bank on the other.

Returning from the pub, I pushed through our glass doors, winked at Gaskin who saluted smartly, and plunged past the counter. Beyond, the long corridor, lined with old auction notices and a couple of Rowlandson prints, was warm and inviting. I could smell Mrs Gaskin's coffee as I hurried towards the imposing door of my office. A square room with a dilapidated partner's desk, a couple of comfortable chintz armchairs, an Act of Parliament clock and my much-prized Piper watercolours of St Amedroz, Berington; this was my sanctuary from the bustle of our front counter.

The telephone rang intrusively. 'Is that Mr Griffin?' It was a woman's voice, loud and assertive.

I admitted as much.

'*The* Mr Griffin?'

'Well – I like to think so.'

'My husband has inherited some very important *objets d'art*.'

Oh, no! Monday afternoon and we were straight into pot lids. I'd better explain. Merrywethers are the up-and-coming auctioneers. Christie's get the snobs, Sotheby's the shits, and we go for the ones who actually want to work for the art's sake. The second-eleven teams, Garrisons, Phillips and Bonhams, lurk in our wake. Now you know everything.

'We were told to come straight to you, Mr Griffin. My husband's cousin – Lady Plumby, you know . . .?' Why *would* I know? But I've got the picture. Social antennae to the fore, flatter the brutes and I may get to sell the contents when one of them pegs out. Or at least that's what the rule book teaches us.

Through my glass porthole, courtesy of some crazed interior designer, I could see Mary at the front counter talking to a man with a brick-red face who was holding a lump of twisted metal. Even from behind I could see she was angry. She was pushing back her hair with both hands.

'So you will come and have lunch?' said the metallic voice on the telephone.

'Lunch?' My mind had wandered.

'Yes.' The voice sharpened. 'Thursday fortnight? That will give you lots of time to look over the other things.'

'Lovely,' I said. 'Thank you so much.' She still hadn't even given me her name. 'I should absolutely love to.'

Monday. And a wasted afternoon – the afternoon fixed by Terry Burton for his quarterly 'chin-wag'. He's the chairman's sidekick, a sort of elongated pink vulture, all legs and malice, working his way up the company until he can feed on us. By contrast the chairman, old Alan Merrywether, is good news. He hides a very astute business brain behind his cheery persiflage. The company was falling so far behind you would hardly have heard of us twenty years ago; but this year we sold the first Old Master to breach the magic fifty million mark. Next year, who knows, we might win the annual auction house turnover stakes, thanks to the Merrywether marriage. To explain—

'Hello?' It's the telephone again. 'Yes? He'll be late?' Well, thank God for some good news. That was Terry Burton's chauffeur ringing from the car to say they're stuck on the motorway. Anyway. Alan Merrywether, the chairman, married in the distant past a massive creature called Lady Moorea Bracy. What no-one could have predicted was that her brother Tom, now rejoicing in the title of Duke of Bridgwater, was six months ago to be unexpectedly bequeathed the entire Gimpal collection: sixty years' accumulation of the cream of seventeenth- and eighteenth-century European paintings. Heaven knows he's got enough space to hang them, even with a good assortment of plunder himself, but the rumour is he's going to sell. And if so, and if we, being 'family', handle the sale, then Sotheby's and Christie's will be left far behind.

'John!'

'Mary!' She's very pretty, very tall and very married.

'There's a man out here I'd like you to talk to.'

'Not the man with the bent barbecue?'

She shook her head impatiently, brown curls everywhere. 'He says it's an Alexander Calder.'

'I'd better have a look.'

Well – of course it wasn't, but you have to be kind. I picked it up, turned it round and sniffed it. I put on my special expert's voice: 'Aha.'

He looked up, gratified.

'Ah-aa.' I stroked an outer escarpment. 'A magnificent creation,' I said.

He nodded vigorously and said, 'The man in Tours says it is a very late Calder.'

I rather liked the idea of the old boy reverting to the habits of the playpen. But I shook my head. 'No, I think this is rather more interesting than that. I think—' I bent down and squinted through it, catching sight of the office clock.

'What's the matter?' he asked, startled by my cry.

I had promised to ring my wife at two, and it was nearly half past. 'I hate to say it, but I do think you should take this to Christie's. *At once*. Their chap Gresham is the leading expert in this field. But don't let him fob you off with a superficial glance. This piece needs research, with a capital R.'

'That's terribly kind of you.' He appeared genuinely impressed, and added, 'I've also got a Rockingham dinner service in the car. What should I do with that?' I took him by the arm. 'Oh, Mary here will be *much* the best person for that.' Indeed, she was already beckoning to old Gaskin. I left the proud owner beaming and ran back to my desk.

'Darling?' I said anxiously.

'It's half past two.' Barbara, my wife, sounded characteristically cross.

'Yes, I'm so sorry. What . . .?'

'Some of us have work to do, you know.'

'I got stuck. What . . .?'

'I couldn't sit here all day on the off-chance.'

'I'm really sorry. What did you want to ask me?'

13

'I haven't got time now. I'll be back at teatime.' The line went dead.

I sat staring at the Piranesi print on the back wall. It reflected my mood – dark and complicated. There was a flurry of bustling in the hall and a shadow filled the doorway.

'And how are we today?' Yes, it was, of course, Mr Terry Burton, assistant to the chairman and arch assassin of the Merrywether empire. He stank of Eau de Gorille.

'Who are you talking to?' he asked abruptly, fiddling with his gold and black signet ring.

I realized I was still holding the telephone. 'Oh, no-one.' I put it down. 'My wife.'

'Selling the Sheffield plate, is she?' I smiled to acknowledge the passing of a poor joke. 'However,' he went on, 'it's good to find that you talk to each other. The chairman was rather worried about you both. One hears things.'

'Did you have a good journey?' I asked brightly.

'Ghastly. I don't know why we keep this office in Berington. It's an awful trek.' He stretched himself across a chair. 'I've asked that sexy bit outside to brew up some strong tea.'

'Mary Sykes,' I said, 'is our porcelain expert, not our skivvy.' But as I spoke Mary hurried in with a steaming mug. She handed it to him and his enormous manicured hands folded over hers, prolonging the exchange to the point of nausea.

'Thank you so much, my dear.' He was positively leering.

Perhaps I ought to explain that he is thirty-two, wears white socks, beige cardigans and is taller than I am. Taking a cigar from my box, I bit the end off and deposited the bits in the ashtray. Mary, a militant non-smoker, glared at me and walked out.

'How many of those do you smoke?' Terry asked, watching me light up.

'Half a dozen a day. They soothe my nerves. Would you like one?'

14

'You don't seem to get many calls,' he said suddenly.

'No,' I agreed. It varies. 'But I think this office has the best results records outside London.'

'Mmm.' He was looking at me curiously. 'I never have understood why you allowed yourself to be buried out here.'

I shrugged. Why should I bore him with the benefits of woodland peace over city clangour?

'You've heard about the chairman's brother-in-law, Tom Bridgwater?' he went on.

'I heard there was talk of a sale.'

'Is this office bugged?'

'Of course not!'

'Have you checked?' His eyes had become cold and still.

'No,' I said slowly. 'I haven't.' He took out a small black notebook and wrote something on an inside page. Considering the struggle I'd had to set up the recording of some telephone conversations with a Hong Kong dealer last year, bugging hardly seemed likely. But Terry's paranoia made me nervous. 'Do you think I should?' I asked.

He looked up and nodded. Then he leaned forward and whispered, 'Tom Bridgwater is very ill.'

'Oh, I'm sorry.'

'Sorry? You realize what that means?'

'No,' I said stubbornly, even though I could see his point: if the old man were to die before selling, then the choice of auction house would fall to his executors, whoever they might be, and Merrywethers might not get the business.

There was another long pause while he sipped the tea, and made another note. 'Shall you miss Mrs Sykes?'

'Shall I . . .?'

'It's really her I've come here to see. Van Zwanenberg is being given early retirement.'

I sat for a moment and stared at him, trying to conceal my feelings so as to mitigate the satisfaction that he was already exuding, surrounding him in an invisible cloud of ill-will. Both statements were shocking, the first for me personally, the second for the firm. Basil van Zwanenberg was one of our greatest successes. The chairman had poached him from a Swiss company ten years ago, and his European contacts had brought us some of the best porcelain sales ever held in London.

'But he can't be more than sixty,' I said, 'if that.'

'It just shows,' Terry said. 'Time catches up with all of us.' He looked me up and down in a distinctly unflattering way. 'Mary Sykes will be able to handle the job, we think.'

'This has never been discussed with me,' I said.

'Oh?' Terry spotted a blemish on one of his fingers and paused to apply himself to it. 'Well, that's why I'm here. Do you think she's not up to life at head office? What specific complaints have you?'

'None,' I snapped. 'None at all. Mary is excellent and will do Basil's job very well if that is what is needed. It's just rather a shock. The chairman said nothing about it last week.'

'No,' said Terry. 'He's had a lot on his plate lately. You've to come to London for an emergency board meeting tomorrow at nine. We won't talk of this until then. Meanwhile I am to tell you that he is not satisfied with figures here.'

'But . . .'

He held up one hand. 'Please let me finish. He knows you try your best. Personally I think you've lost your edge. This is a business, you know, not an extension of your London club. We need more sales. Here is a list.'

I took the piece of paper and studied it: Colonel Chaucer, Passenham House; Mrs Jeremy Granger, Littlethwaite Hall; Lord Tottenham, Wedderburn Woodhouse.

'This is wrong,' I said. 'These people have always used the opposition, and always will.'

'Nevertheless,' he replied, and stood up, 'your job is to recruit them. Have a party. Use a bit of black propaganda. Try to find that old aggression they keep telling me about. Anything that comes to mind. But *do it*.' He was gathering up his papers and walking to the door when I spotted another snag.

'But they're all very very old.'

He turned and stared at me scornfully. 'That, my friend, is the point.'

Perhaps I *had* lost my edge.

CHAPTER TWO

Resisting the urge to smash something (a habit particularly to be discouraged in auctioneers), I tried to settle back into my work. But the thought of life here without Mary to talk to, to discuss the daily events with, kept distracting me. Should I really be chivvying old people on the edge of the grave?

There was no reply from Barbara at teatime, so I spent my last hour in the office checking the latest valuations – the nuts and bolts of our business. Whether for probate or insurance or, best of all, for a prospective sale, it keeps our eye in having to estimate the value of the vast assortment of valuables (not to mention junk) that our clients possess. Paintings and tapestries, silver and porcelain, carpets and furniture – the background to their domestic life forms a colossal worldwide market that ebbs and flows according to unpredictable moons. With the Japanese no longer representing the real market strength, the emphasis is on good quality pieces where the supply is limited and the provenance impeccable: eighteenth-century English furniture, the top Dutch and Flemish Old Masters, that sort of thing. Guardi is in, so are the Pre-Raphaelites. Large second-rate works are definitely out. Try telling that to a man who has always looked on his Hoppner group as the family insurance against a bad harvest! But the daily work lies with silver teapots and old wardrobes. It's Aunt Dorothy's *chaise longue* (slightly distressed) that pays the rent.

But valuations also have to be watched. They are the single biggest category of art market fraud, far outweighing the occasional (and usually unsuccessful) attempts to pass yesterday's brown varnished copy as a centuries-old masterpiece. Imagine you want to transfer a million pounds to your friend. Assuming he has something worth a million in his house, an obliging expert values it at two million. You buy it for that sum so that when you subsequently sell it you have a useful capital gains tax loss while he in the meantime has the cash. With a little creative accountancy, he should be able to keep most of the proceeds, and that's just one of the simpler ones.

I was on the last of my figures when Mary knocked on my door.

'Come in.' She did so and stood in front of me, five foot eight of feminine beauty heavily camouflaged within a severe suit of red and black woollen check. Her eyes, through their long curling lashes, looked troubled. The air around her had a delicate hint of Chanel.

'Why is your telephone in pieces?' she asked.

I fiddled with two of the smaller ingredients in an attempt to appear competent and in control. 'Oh – just checking for bugging devices.'

'And—?' she persisted.

'Well . . .' I shrugged. 'It won't quite seem to fit together again.'

She smiled. Why does one fall in love? I had always believed that hopeless love was a self-inflicted injury for idiots. No-one in their right mind commits their senses to another without encouragement. And Mary was entirely innocent of encouraging me in that way. And yet . . . ! I loved her, judged by any of the conventional signs: the warmth in her presence, the soothing effect of hearing her voice in a crowd, the thrill of her smile flashed across the auction room, the painful seeking out of her silhouette among the throng, the dampening depression of her absence, the pulse of sexual excitement when I could see her body, supple and slender, moving within a summer dress. Today's outfit would have anaesthetized a rapist, but still I could feel an idiotic smile parading across my ill-disciplined face. To her I was an amiable colleague, and she treated me with all the kindness that

19

was so typical of her, and which only exacerbated my helpless and hopeless ardour.

Why shouldn't a man make friends with a woman? What, for example, did she think of me? Ostensibly I was her superior, although I can't say I ever looked on our working relationship in that light. We were colleagues, pooling our talents and exercising them together for the benefit of Merrywethers. I had an additional administrative function that involved supervising her, but surely she should see beyond that. But see what? A man nearly ten years older than her, overweight, overlined and over the hill? I hoped she was complimented rather than offended by my obvious admiration – she must, after all, be very used to male attention. And we could laugh together. Surely that was a good sign? I passed a hand over my face, hoping to erase the tell-tale expression I knew it held.

'I want to ask your advice,' she said. 'As usual.'

This was very flattering. I wouldn't mind her advice on one or two points. 'Won't you sit down?'

She settled into an armchair. 'Terry Burton wants me to move to Mayfair.'

'I see.' Did I mention she had a wide mouth, its dark lips shaped voluptuously round a gleaming glimpse of teeth?

'It would be an amazing promotion,' she went on. 'And I'd have six months with Basil before he goes. What do you think?' She fixed her eyes earnestly on mine.

'I don't see how you can turn it down,' I said. 'But what about George?' George, of course, is her husband, a contemporary of mine at school, married on an impulse within three weeks of her graduating from the Courtauld, a big man with big appetites. He owns and farms 3,000 acres immediately to the east of the town and is always grumbling about his wife's job.

'That's the point,' she said. 'He could never move, and the children are so settled, too.' She had two, a boy and a girl, but I could never remember their names. She doted on them. 'I'd get an allowance for a flat,' she said in a matter-of-fact tone.

I raised my eyebrows. That wasn't company policy. Terry must have been muscling in on the personnel budget as well. There wasn't any doubt about Terry. No-one doubted that he was heading for the chairmanship, and no-one doubted that he would ruthlessly undermine and destroy anyone rash enough to pose a threat to him. He knew it. They knew it. I knew it. And yet, in a way, perhaps he would deserve the prize, since he worked so assiduously to increase Merrywethers' prestige and profits. Whether this was to increase the value of his ultimate goal, or whether it was his nature to work hard at anything he took on, hardly seemed to matter. Merrywethers employed over 750 people. He propelled each department forward by the threat of turning his attention on to their activities. No wonder the chairman relied on him. And one day would fall to him.

I sighed and stubbed out my cigar. Mary watched the sodden end smouldering away among the mound of ash, her lips drawn back over the little pointed teeth in a rictus of involuntary distaste.

'It's so unfair,' she said. I nodded, then paused. 'What is?' I asked.

'Well – you know – men can pursue their careers and everyone applauds, while women get criticized for neglecting their families.'

'Aren't you happy here?'

'Yes, of course I am. It's great to be a member of your team. You've taught me so much.' Her reply was too quick, too much the automatic response to obvious fishing. But I was determined to build on it, cautiously.

'Do you have to give an immediate response?' I asked.

'The implication was that I do.'

'Well, don't. If they really want you, they'll wait. If they don't, you're losing no points by staying here doing excellent work. I've got to go to London tomorrow for the board meeting. Let's talk about it again when I get back.'

She nodded and smiled, her eyes puckered by inner anxiety.

Old Gaskin was locking up and the others had already

left. I watched Mary as she went downstairs to check the safe and then I drove through the town and out on the Market Plumby road towards my house.

It had been a long, hot summer and on the clay fields great cracks had opened, running criss-cross among the stalks of corn. The little river had almost dried up again and even the water hens, drifting among the reeds, looked oppressed. Higher up the hill the crops in the sandy fields were obviously in trouble. The beet was yellow, its leaves hunched in withered folds, the thinner soil exposed to the evening light.

I stopped just before our turning to smoke a last cigar and enjoy the peace of the countryside. Within half an hour the scene had changed again. The rich glow of another summer's evening that had picked out the golden cattle as they circled, slowly but with such plodding purpose, had gone. A new light, dim and yet so penetrating that it threw the details of the long grey front of our house into sharp relief, had spread from the west, sending deep shadows of an almost theatrical midnight blue striped across the pale dusty stone.

As I turned into the drive I passed a red car coming out: Bertie Russell – my wife's lover, though I pretended not to notice. My wife was in the kitchen. She looked smart and fresh, her thick black hair as glossy and sleek as usual.

'You never rang back,' she said sourly.

'Yes, I did,' I said. 'I rang three times at teatime.'

She stared past me. 'This heat is unbearable,' she said. 'It's too hot to think.'

She made me some tea and we sat in silence for a few minutes. A bit of family history may explain my *froideur*. Barbara is my cousin as well as my wife. In some ways we're rather alike, except that she is slender whereas I need a good tailor to disguise the dimensions. We loved each other, I'm sure we did, and when I proposed in the heat of the moment, the words whistling out like a dying man's confession as we celebrated Christmas under our grandfather's billiard table,

22

the future looked pretty good. But we were so young, so innocent of everything except gymnastics. Our subsequent years together lacked the mature consideration that greater experience might have taught us, had we not been banged up together in a marriage cell and thus denied individual development. Now our house is our Passchendaele, a series of interconnecting trenches, sodden with her angry tears and enlivened only by the occasional crackle of sniper fire when one of us scents the chance of an easy score. I don't blame her for seeking reinforcements, but she *does* blame me for increasing her guilt by not minding. 'To understand all is to forgive all.' I'd like to meet the clever-clogs who thought that one up. It may be true, but it doesn't help the pain.

'Bertie dropped in,' she said with an inconsequential air.

'Yes, I passed him on the drive.'

There was another silence, while she stared at me curiously and I watched the steam coming up from my cup.

'He's going to America for a month,' she said.

'I'm sorry.'

She didn't reply.

'What did you want me to ring you about this morning?' I asked.

She got up and started tinkering with some knives on the trolley. Then she said, 'I wonder what it would have been like if we had had any children.'

'Noisier?' I suggested, and immediately regretted my flippancy.

She was rubbing one of the knives, polishing away some invisible blemish.

'I've got to go to London on the early train,' I added. 'I may have to stay the night.'

'Do you want me to pack some things for you?'

She came and stood beside me, one hand on the table.

'No, thanks.' Of course I could identify an offer of affection, but it came from too far off, dimly reverberating through the chasm of time, a distant echo of lost dreams.

'Would you like to have dinner by the fire?' she said.

'Yes, let's.'

Unexpectedly, she bent down and kissed me on the cheek.

'You're very sweet to me,' she said.

I shrugged. She smelt of Bertie Russell's aftershave.

CHAPTER THREE

Merrywethers' London headquarters is a splendid Edwardian baroque fantasy just off Berkeley Square. Hidden inside the extravagances of empire building there lurk the modest remains of three Georgian town houses, knocked together and then joined on, by a glass and concrete extension at the back, to two more Victorian houses in the street behind. Quite a chunk of real estate if all else fails and containing most of our central office together with a specialist saleroom and a set of splendid viewing rooms. These culminate in the Red Damask Gallery where the daily dramas of the big sales unfold.

Outside it looks like a robber baron's idea of an Italian palace – which is what it was. The chairman's grandmother was the only daughter of E.V. Draycott, the man who built the Minnesota railroad. Up till then the Merrywethers had been barrow boys in Hereford Street market. Overnight, or at any rate once E.V. saw signs of grandchildren, they set up in a grand way. Now it's a major corporation, but still privately owned by a series of offshore trusts and administered in the Bahamas, so the lure is in the salaries, not the prospects of equity appreciation. And there's been plenty of money for all of us until recently, financed by heavy borrowing. But if the flow of sales continues to abate the banks may throw us out on to the street.

I stopped the lift at the ground floor, only because I like the bustle and the smell of the different departments. I like belonging to such a heaving, chattering, bustling throng – for a day, that is – then I like getting back to the peace of the Berington office.

The ground floor houses the front counter, arrayed this

morning with patient customers clutching indeterminate pieces of art – here a violin case, there a jewellery box, clasped in both hands by a woman with a hungover, anxious face. The girls behind the desk are scrubbed, orderly and sexless, like dental receptionists. A porter ambles past with a new batch of catalogues for the book-stall. The green baize door behind him swings shut, closing off the cavernous storerooms with their acrid smell of glue and sweat.

'Morning, John! What are you doing here?'

It's Rodney, the French furniture expert, the Queen of Mayfair as the chairman tolerantly calls him behind his back.

'Some board meeting, I think.'

'Not discussing my rise, by any chance?' The polished but ageing face was alarmed behind the chuckle.

'Not this time, Rodney.'

'Have you a moment to glance at the Bréauté Table? It's just arrived.'

'I'd love to,' I said, 'but later. You did really well to get that.'

He beamed, then he took me by the arm and whispered in my ear: 'You've heard about Basil?'

I grunted, unwilling to get drawn into a subject I knew too little about.

'It's that naughty Terry, you know,' he went on. 'That boy! He needs a good slapping!'

'You go ahead, Rodney,' I said, laughing and return-ing a wave from Elizabeth, the chairman's secretary, who crossed at the top of the staircase carrying a silver teapot.

'Plastic mugs is all we get,' Rodney called after me as I ran up the stairs.

'Ah! Griffin!' This from Lord Darlington, our token peer. Every auction house has one; it looks good on the writing paper and reassures the punters. Some have several. We think that's a bit flashy – or maybe the chair-man couldn't face two Lord Darlingtons. He's thickset with curly grey hair, large blue eyes and a rather sallow complexion. Someone told me once that he brought in a lot of clubland business, but if so it comes by some imperceptibly subtle process. He very rarely speaks at meetings and spends all day in a tiny office on the top floor which he nominally shares with our two absentee directors based in New York.

'Exciting times!' he said, rubbing his hands together.

'Yes, indeed,' I agreed, and hurried on to where I could see my old friend, Ralph Tritton, the expert on Old Masters, coming out of the computer room.

'Ralph!'

We shook hands and he took me into his office, a sunny room hung with icons.

'We've ten minutes,' I said, looking at my wristwatch. 'So tell me about Basil.'

Ralph is an old man now. He was elderly even when I attended his Courtauld lectures. His red face is cratered with the lines of laughter and chagrin, but the white hair is still thick and abundant. It's a face to warm to.

'Oh, dear!' He laughed. 'It's a monumental cock-up, that one. Rasputin's been at it again.' This was his private name for Terry, and wholly appropriate. Terry is dangerous. Scion of one of the tougher Gateshead Comprehensives, he got a scholarship to Oxford. After that he spent two years at the London School of Economics and walked straight into the chairman's office. He's a natural born predator – no chairman should be without one.

'But why?' I asked. 'Basil's done good work. He's got a lot of mileage left in him. We need him.'

'Rasputin wanted him out. There's dirty business somewhere. He kept undermining Basil, moving his secretaries, allocating odd jobs. I tried telling Alan, but you know what he's like.'

I nodded. The chairman uses Terry to do the hatchet work, and thus he puts himself in his power. It didn't seem to make much sense.

'You were right to settle for your own private fiefdom in Berington,' Ralph said. 'The atmosphere here isn't what it was.'

There was a knock on the door and Bonas, the managing director, alias the Screaming Skull, a tall, thin stooping man with no hair, appeared.

'Are you coming or not?' he asked, giving me a perfunctory nod and his ghastly graveyard grin.

'We're coming, we're coming!' cried Ralph, slapping me on the back and reaching for his stick.

'Good,' said Bonas, and preceded us down the corridor, his dull grey suit in marked contrast to the vivid blues and green of the carpet and walls. Alan Merrywether was sitting in a red velvet throne at the head of the table. It was always supposed to have been the only unsold lot in his grandfather's first big sale. Certainly it was the outward and visible sign of chairmanship – rickety but gorgeous with its gilded wood and snarling dragon arms.

'Good to see you, John!'

I smiled back cheerfully; he was a very sympathetic figure with his broad white face sticking out of a mass of green tweed. My first job had been in his office and he had always been fun to work with. Terry Burton was on one side of him, Elizabeth on the other. There were only four other directors present, Bonas, Lord Darlington, Ralph and me. The rest must have been abroad trawling for business and cultivating their connections.

'Do we have anything as grand as an agenda?' The chairman peered about him, and Elizabeth passed him a pair of bifocal spectacles which he carefully perched on his nose. 'Aha!' The piece of paper in front of him had swum into focus.

'Apologies.' Terry read out the names of the six missing board members.

'Minutes of the last meeting. Must we?' The chairman gazed round plaintively. Jack Bonas read through the minutes while Lord Darlington looked at the painted ceiling. It was not a good example of its kind, hideous cherubs and very plain nudes, but it was better than magnolia emulsion.

'Item three. The sale coded Jasmine. Terry is going to speak on this.'

28

Bonas stopped, disconcerted, because Terry had stood up, marched across the room and flung the door open. This would have been more absurd if there had not indeed been a figure standing there.

'Is that you, Bryant?' said the chairman sharply.

'Yes, sir,' the figure replied before Terry closed the door in his face.

'I asked him to stand there, Alan,' said Terry, returning. 'I wanted to check he was in place.'

Ralph stared at me and I stared at him. We said nothing.

'Well, Terry? Fire away with what you've got.' The chairman sounded impatient now.

'You all know that Tom Bridgwater is dangerously ill,' said Terry, and for a moment I thought he was going to smile. 'We need this sale. Some of you' – here he paused and looked at a point slightly to the left of my head – 'may not realize how badly. The Gimpal collection is conservatively valued at . . . what would you say, Ralph? Six hundred million pounds? The Getty is bound to be after the Titians and the Rembrandt Guild portrait. We know the Met has had its eye on the Tintoretto Parables for years. And the Louvre will do anything to get the Fragonards. *Anything.*' Another pause while we thought on this. Murder? War? Terry was enjoying himself hugely. 'Now in different circumstances, I think we could have been sure it would have come through us. Indeed, Tom spoke to me about it when I was racing with him at Whitsun.'

'Yes,' interposed the chairman. 'He *even* mentioned it to me.' Golly. Was this a rift? Was he actually being ironical at the expense of his pet piranha?

'Your brother-in-law,' continued Terry smoothly, 'felt we could get him the best price, regardless of any other consideration. He really doesn't want the bother of yet more pictures. But if he should die—' Lord Darlington, next to him, shifted uncomfortably in his chair. 'If he should die, the decision will then be with his executors, given the awkward situation.'

'Do we know who they are?' put in Bonas.

Terry made as if to defer to the chairman, but the latter waved his hands.

'We do,' Terry said.

'Are you going to tell us?' Ralph Tritton asked.

'Sir John Best and Colonel Bracy.' Now this was mixed news. Colonel Bracy was a nice ineffective old buffer, a cousin of the family, who lived in Albany and sent us Old Master drawings from time to time to pay his club bills. But Sir John Best, senior partner of Dangerfields, the institutional solicitors, was a rather different matter. His would certainly be the dominant voice. And he was not known to be a supporter of Merrywethers. Which implied the reverse. Like our competitors, we reserve our choicest invitations and most lavish parties for the 'Filthy Fifty', the top institutional advisers who administer the major estates – the lawyers, accountants, investment bankers. This group – there are forty-eight on our Platinum List, encompassing London, Geneva, Frankfurt and New York – bring us, year on year, nearly forty per cent of what we call 'cover items', the really big picture or jewel that raises the tone of the whole sale. Dangerfields are among the top five solicitors in London, and John Best *never* accepts our invitations. This could have been the result of scruples, but Bonas reckoned he felt closer to our competitors, notably Garrisons. We sat and considered this in silence.

'Obviously any overt move on our part at this moment could be considered to be in very poor taste,' said Bonas.

'Obviously.' The chairman nodded, massaging the back of his neck.

'So what can we do?' I felt it was time I made my presence felt.

'Oh, you're there, John, are you, behind all that smoke?' Terry's voice sounded genuinely encouraged, and the others laughed.

'It can't be good for you, my boy,' said the chairman kindly. 'You ought to try chewing gum. My wife swears by it.' It was a grisly thought.

'What news of your nephew?' I asked. It was time to divert them away from me and towards Tom Bridgwater's heir.

'Ah,' said the chairman. 'Well. There you are, of course.' And the others showed their silent agreement. Ralph sucked in his cheeks and made a strange whistling sound through his teeth. Bonas coughed softly as Lord Darlington stared at the pattern of the carpet. Only Terry put his thoughts into words.

'Completely cuckoo.'

'Have you seen him?' the chairman asked.

'No-o,' was the reply. 'But one of our contacts had a talk with Dr Milligan and he said there was no prospect of improvement.'

I'm afraid this was no surprise. We all knew that Lionel Bracy, heir to the Bridgwater millions, was a manic depressive to the point of coma. He spent most of his life in St Seraphina's, that rather charming Gothic fantasy on the Sussex Downs, coming out very occasionally to show the flag while positively rattling with pills to maintain his equilibrium. So much for the benefits of great wealth. Hence the significance of the executors. Hence this meeting.

'Terry thinks we should go on the offensive,' said the chairman, interrupting our reverie. 'Come on, my boy, give us your five-point plan.'

Terry's long blond face, with its depressingly healthy colour heightened by an innocent blush, swivelled to take us all into its authoritative gaze. 'Well,' he said. 'I think the Bridgwater collection is achievable, but only if we approach it in a committed way.'

'Meaning?' I said. He ignored me.

'The power lies between Tom, who is dying, his trustees who may be inclined elsewhere, and the heir, your nephew.' This with a razor-beam smile at the chairman who was nodding attentively. 'Who is temporarily' – he raised a bossy finger – '*temporarily* confined. I think we may assume that the chairman and I together can deal with Tom, if he rallies. I think I can deal

31

with the heir, although I would rather not be pressed on details. Do you object, John?'

This because I had let out an involuntary snort at the idea of Terry's likely method of dealing with the heir, attracting a sharp look of disapproval from Lord Darlington. I lifted one hand in a gesture of peace, and he continued.

'The real threat lies with the trustees. May I speak off the record?'

The chairman nodded and Elizabeth obediently laid down her pencil, placing it carefully and symmetrically along a line of her thick pad.

'I have engaged Trinity and Samson, a company you will all be familiar with, to make discreet enquiries on our behalf. Their results will be circulated on a need-to-know basis.'

'Trinity and Samson?' said Ralph. 'I thought they were divorce-court specialists.'

'They—' began Terry, but his reply was drowned by a sudden convulsion of coughing from Jack Bonas. I thought he'd been looking rather pale. But now his face was suffused with blood as he bent over the table, his shoulders shaking with the paroxysm.

'I'm so . . .' He started coughing again. 'So sorry.' To my alarm I could see that there was blood, dark, angry blood, on his handkerchief. Then, just as suddenly, he subsided.

'They deal with any matter of great delicacy,' Terry continued, as if the interruption had never occurred.

'What do you think of that, boys?' chuckled the chairman, gazing round at our faces. I fumbled with a match so Ralph led:

'What are "discreet enquiries"?'

'Digging for dirt,' smiled Terry, showing his teeth. They are white and even, but come accompanied by too much gum.

'For blackmail?' asked Lord Darlington.

'Gentle pressure, more likely.' This was the other side of the chairman, his voice studiedly neutral but allowing us room for no indulgence in heroic high principle.

Bonas wiped his mouth. 'This is new territory,' he said.

'Not for our opponents,' replied the chairman briskly. 'We all know why the Port Talbot jewels went elsewhere.'

The room fell silent. Pot lids and Aunt Dorothy's *chaise longue* seemed far away. And far more attractive.

'Are you asleep, John?' The chairman was looking at me. 'You don't like this?' he persisted.

'Not much. Any more than I like being asked to badger my oldest neighbours out of their homes so that we can filch a 20-per-cent share of what's left of their heirlooms.'

'Then what are you doing in this business?' he snapped. Fighting talk.

I shrugged. 'It's possible to fight a battle without resorting to germ warfare.'

'It's sales that pay your wages, not day-dreams,' cut in Terry, smiling ominously.

Bonas nodded, flinched and held himself very still.

'Ted?' The chairman turned to Lord Darlington.

'Yes,' he said. 'Yes – I'm for it. I think Terry's approach is good. We owe a duty to our employees to go on the offensive.'

Oh God! Counter principles.

Ralph Tritton nodded too and we moved on to probe the finer points of the pension plan.

As we were leaving, the chairman asked me to stay behind. I thought Bonas looked sympathetic, but the others avoided my glance.

'Your office figures are holding up,' he said when we were alone.

'Yes, they are,' I agreed. 'Mary Sykes is a great asset, and I shall be sorry to lose her. You must be sorry to lose Basil.'

He didn't respond to this. After a few minutes of rustling through papers, he said, 'Terry is doing a first-class job this end. It's a cut-throat business and next year may determine the next twenty as far as we are concerned.'

'I'm sure you're right,' I said. 'I never feel entirely easy when Terry's within reach of my throat.'

The chairman frowned. 'You're the only main-board member based outside London or New York,' he said. 'I'd like to think you were still in tune with what I'm trying to do.'

'We used to have a policy of no poaching. We have our clients, our opponents have theirs. New business is fair game, but the people on the list Terry gave me the other day . . . to take just one example: the Chaucers have always used Sotheby's. It's pointless and wrong to pester the old man. We wouldn't like it if they started wooing the Castletons.'

'I'm only thinking of your future, John.' The voice had changed, become silkier. 'Perhaps the pressures seem less urgent from a rural perspective?' He raised an ironic eyebrow. 'When I go,' he went on, 'there will be changes. I think they will be more Terry's way than yours.'

'I understand what you're saying.'

'And you can see that Jack is not a well man. That's the place I always assumed you were heading for.'

I stared at the table non-committally. No-one refuses promotion, or ignores its prospect, but I liked working with Jack Bonas, and I certainly didn't want a bigger salary at the expense of his health.

'It may be you're a bit too precious for the top table,' mused the chairman, stung by my lack of response. Still I made no reply. Then he said: 'How's Barbara?' A loaded question, casually put.

'In excellent form, thank you,' I said, meeting his grey gaze with total imperturbability.

'Good, good.' He looked unconvinced. 'Now I must leave you.' He hustled me to the door shouting, 'Good-bye! Goodbye!' as Elizabeth ushered me down the corridor.

I decided to lunch at my club. Hope, the porter, had been there all my life.

'It's a great life if you don't weaken,' he gasped as he took my coat.

'How's the asthma?'

'Thriving. Madam well?'

'Yes, she sent her love,' I said, knowing it would please him.

'She's too good for you, sir.'

'I think she'd agree with you,' I told him as I saw a familiar stooping figure with long dank hair crossing the hall.

'Charlie!' He turned and smiled. Charlie McGregor might be my chief opponent in the auction stakes, but he was also my oldest friend, a fellow survivor of the school near Reading where we had both studied Herodotus under the lash of Dr Robert Jenyns, otherwise known to us as Der Führer.

'Are you lunching?'

We went into the dining room, a tall, red room hung with long state portraits lent by a Scottish member.

'Are you together, gentlemen?' lisped the steward, a plump little man with glowing cheeks.

'Not the way you mean, Iain.'

Iain shook his cheeks delightedly and led us to a table. 'Treacle tart is on today,' he whispered. 'The members are going mad for it.' I gazed round curiously but the room seemed a haven of order.

'So,' said Charlie, when we had ordered. 'Will you get the Bridgwater sale?'

'That depends if there is one.'

'Leukaemia's a bloody thing to have, even at that age.'

'I think it might reasonably come to us,' I said. 'After all, he is the chairman's brother-in-law.'

'His father always used Sotheby's. Dukes don't change, that's what we were taught.'

'So how did you get the Port Talbot jewels?'

'We reckoned that was fair enough. Anyone willing to go to bed with Mimi Port Talbot deserves something pretty generous. That's why we employ old Tony. He's never turned up his nose at a dowager yet.' Tony

Sheepshanks was notorious for his lubricious way with old ladies. I drank some wine as I thought about it. Ugh!

'We're thrilled to be recruiting Basil,' Charlie said casually.

'He's coming to you?' I was astounded.

'Yes.' Charlie was positively chortling. 'He couldn't stand your awful Terry badgering him. He says he's retiring, but actually he's joining us. I think we'll have to send Terry a present, don't you?'

'Couldn't you take Terry as well?' I suggested.

'Aha!' he said. 'So he's after you now, is he? Yes, please.' He helped himself to some parsnips and then the gravy. 'I don't know if we'd have a place for you. I don't want you pinching my job. You'd better consider Garrisons, although they'd pay you less and you'd have to move back to London. But perhaps you should anyway?' His expression was cautiously sympathetic. 'No,' he went on, 'Terry's far too valuable to us where he is. We reckon Merrywethers is at double or quits; if you do get the Bridgwater sale, you can afford Terry. If not, with your rate of borrowing, you'll all be back in the Portobello Road.'

Too many of my auctioneer friends had travelled that same route for me to smile at this. When business is booming and new world records fill the headlines, why not hire an extra expert in *cloisonné*, say, or a marquess's heir where the cash flow is known to be shaky? For when records are being made everyone flocks to the market-place. One man suddenly perceives his familiar possession not as a pretty landscape any more, but as hard currency losing interest for every day it stays on the wall. But markets, by their nature, vary and when suddenly they drop, great is the rage of the potential seller, for whom that picture, now that it has been mentally transmogrified into hard currency, can never regain its place in his heart. There it hangs in mute reproach. 'If only I'd sold it earlier,' he moans, anxiously scanning his scarlet bank statements. Poor, despised daub! And a fall in the market shows up with even more and painful clarity in the auction house accounts. Twenty per cent of nothing is nothing. The new ones go first.

'Sorry, old boy. *Cloisonné's* out for the moment. Next year, perhaps.' 'Thank you for being with us, Lord Brook and Belville. Of course you will keep your privilege for selling through us at twenty per cent discount.'

Then the older men.

'Forty years! Is it *really*? That's a wonderfully long time. You'll be pleased to have more time with your family. Accounts will sort out the details.'

But there's always one or two senior ones who go too, just to remind the troops that no-one is immune. For me the precipice loomed irrespective of trade. I had Terry on my scent.

CHAPTER FOUR

Two weeks later I drove over to lunch with the woman who had rung me the day of the Sarti sale in her pretty whitewashed village house in Plumby Puerorum. She looked like a round little partridge, but walked with a slight limp as she passed from one piece of furniture to the next, placing a cautious hand on each. The house was beautifully cared for and filled with an agreeable smell of fresh polish.

'And *what* do you think of this?' This is, of clients' questions, the one I dread most. It implies a special significance in an object that is almost always a dud. And yet! Perhaps it does have something special that one misses at one's peril. ('Merrywethers' man got it hopelessly wrong, but we got a million through Christies!') I stared at the source of these misgivings. It was a shabby, black lacquer cabinet, four foot high on stencilled black legs with a curly top. Two drunken doors gaped on their twisted hinges to reveal a mass of little drawers inside. My instant reaction was that it would look particularly good on top of a bonfire. However, business is business, so I walked round it murmuring appreciative gobbledegook. 'Nice patina, sturdy construction, crisp moulding, finely aged.'

My hostess vibrated with suppressed excitement. 'Is it worth an awful lot?'

Got it in one, I thought. It truly is an *awful* lot.

'It's eighteenth-century Japanese. I think we would catalogue it as a prayer cabinet. You see, they used these drawers for individual requests. They were very popular with nineteenth-century collectors. Do you know how you got it?'

'It was in my husband's aunt's boudoir. It came with these *objets d'art*.' Yes, indeed. We'd spent the whole morning listing paperweights at £200 a throw.

'Well, for insurance for replacement I would think five thousand pounds.' (That's a safe one.) But she came straight back at me.

'What reserve would you recommend for the saleroom?'

'Ah, well. Er.' This would be trouble. 'I don't think I would.'

'No reserve *at all*?'

'Not if you wanted to be sure of selling.'

'But we need the money.' It always comes down to this in the end. First comes the gracious tour, the hints of family connections, the anecdotes of how this plate or that saucer came from Tottering Towers, the mystical family seat in the palmy days before the Ark. But before you leave the ugly truth will out. 'We need the money.' And it's my job to find it. And to find it accurately. Because if the old family rocking-chair makes a penny less than I've recommended, the whole world is to be told of my iniquity.

'How much are you looking for?' I asked. 'Altogether?'

Her pretty plump face became puffier as one by one its individual muscles gave up in despair. Her eyes twisted this way and that. Oh, no! She's going to cry and I've only got one handkerchief.

'Forty thousand pounds!' And then it all came out: her husband's gambling, her daughter's mishap. This is the world of family secrets, incontinently evacuated to the sympathetic man from Merrywethers. 'God,' it has been maintained, 'tempereth the wind to the shorn lamb.' Sometimes it seems that there must be a veritable hurricane before such mediation.

'Well,' I said encouragingly, 'you obviously do need the money. Let's have another look round.'

Up into the attic, once more round the bedrooms, into the basement. There was nothing. The whole lot would scarcely fetch £40,000 and then they'd be without even a bed. I could hardly suggest putting a match to the place for the insurance.

'Do you mind eating in the kitchen?' she asked.

'I much prefer it,' I answered truthfully, remembering the dreary rituals of countless chilly dining rooms, brought back from the dead to impress the casual visitor.

We had a rather good lunch – salad, steak and kidney pudding which she had made herself and some Stilton washed down with an Australian red wine.

'That was delicious,' I said, smiling at her sad face.

'Coffee?'

'Yes, please.'

'Do you smoke?'

'Do you?' I parried. She smiled guiltily.

'Only when my husband's away. You see,' she went on, 'I'm rather addicted to these.' And out of the bottom drawer she pulled a blue packet of Gauloises. 'I'll have to open the window. Philip goes crazy if he thinks I've had one.'

'Then I should love to smoke one of my cigars,' I said. 'You can blame it on me. This will cover anything.'

We lit up together as she made the coffee.

'I don't have an ashtray,' she said. 'I always use this,' and she put a pretty little bowl between us. I dropped my ash in it.

She told me about her son in Hong Kong and I told her about my father's time there during the war. It was most companionable.

'Tell me about your wife. Philip says she is superb on a horse.'

'Yes,' I said, distracted by the idea. It had been watching her as a schoolgirl, flying over the Lincolnshire dykes on a black stallion, that I had felt my first pangs of desire for my enigmatic cousin. The Burton may not be the Galway Blazers, but there are enough woods in that country to provide cover for hunting's most traditional pastime, the brief absence of two of the field 'earth-stopping', as my grandfather would charmingly

40

categorize his own all-too-regular disappearances. 'Yes, she has always looked her very best on a horse.'

'It must be exciting to be married to such a striking woman,' she said, meaning to be polite.

I was silent.

'I'm so sorry,' she said. 'Have I offended you?'

I started laughing, and she relaxed. 'What have I said?' Really, I could have kissed her. 'I'm going to ask you to make a great sacrifice,' I said.

'What on earth are you talking about?' She stared at me. This is one of the perks of my job: the chance to help people unexpectedly.

'I want you to part with your ashtray.'

'Oh,' she said, uncertainly. 'You can have it if you want.' She pushed it towards me, as if to emphasize the gift. Our ash, mine dark and solid, hers in silvery flakes, mingled promiscuously in the blue and red bowl.

'No, no,' I said, pushing it back. 'We'll sell it for you. I've only ever seen one other, in the collection of a Dutch diplomat. He specializes in this period.'

'You mean . . .' She was puzzled and embarrassed. 'You mean it's worth something?'

'Oh, yes,' I said. 'It's called "Intermediate" because it came between the two dynasties at the end of the seventeenth century. You'll certainly get your forty thousand pounds. Probably double.'

'What!' she cried out. 'What?' She had dropped her cigarette and it lay smouldering on the table. I leaned over and propped it up in the bowl.

She sat very still, gazing at it. 'My mother's little bowl?' Suddenly tears began spilling down her cheeks. 'My mother's little bowl?'

'No,' I said firmly. 'Your ashtray. And don't let your husband forget it!'

CHAPTER FIVE

There was a message from London when I got back to the office. Would I ring Elizabeth, the chairman's secretary? And Mary was at my desk, checking another valuation. She seemed worried.

'All well?' I asked.

'No. Robert's miles too optimistic on the Madder Hall furniture. I know it's his field. But I also know the house and this is wrong.' Robert is the third of our triumvirate. Each of us has general expertise, but he specializes in furniture.

I had a quick look. Typical country house pictures, a Gainsborough, two Cuyps, a set of Wilson landscapes and a really good Zuccharelli that I knew the National Gallery had their eye on. The figures were on the high side, but nothing outrageous given the present trends.

'The pictures seem OK.'

'Yes, so's the china. But look at the furniture.'

I turned to the furniture pages. The dining room entry appeared normal. I hadn't visited the house for some years but I could remember a decent set of Hepplewhite chairs. Drawing room: two Louis-Seize commodes, £80,000; yes, they were stamped Topino, so that wasn't too unreasonable. Bureau *plat* by BVRB, £400,000.

'The bureau *plat* is too high now that Sabat's out of the market,' I said to support her.

'But it's nineteenth century,' she said.

'What?'

'It's not stamped. He's just attributing it to Risenburgh. And he must know he's wrong. It's a very good copy but it would never have been intended to deceive.'

'Are you sure?'

Her eyes met mine. They are light brown, flecked with green and grey. They are more beautiful than any bureau *plat*.

'Of course I'm sure,' she snapped, made uneasy perhaps by the enormity of what she was suggesting.

'Where is he now?'

'He's shooting with the Hendersons today. And he's spending tomorrow valuing two houses on the other side of Market Plumby.'

'Well, keep it here. I'll talk to him next week.'

'He was very insistent they needed the valuation tomorrow.'

'I see.'

'There's something else wrong,' she said. 'Look at the hall table.'

The entry read: 'George II side table, verde antico top on lion legs with acanthus moulding. By William Kent. £75,000.'

'What's wrong with that?'

'John Battle made it for them twelve years ago. They gave the original to their elder son.'

'How do you know?'

'He was my boyfriend at the time.'

'Oh, dear.'

' "Oh, dear" is an understatement.' But she was more relaxed now. She had made her point, she was no longer alone.

'Let me ring Elizabeth and then I'll talk to the Kembles with you on the extension. Stay here,' I said as she got up to leave me.

'Merrywether and Company,' said the operator in Mayfair.

'May I speak to the chairman's office, please?'

'Putting you through, Mr Griffin.'

'Elizabeth?'

'Oh, there you are, John. You've got to go to Bridgwater tomorrow.'

'Is it vital? I'm booked to do three valuations.'

'You'll have to send Mary or Robert. This is urgent.'

'I see.'

'No, you don't. The chairman's brother-in-law died this morning. The chairman is staying there. He wants you to go and make out you have an urgent problem that couldn't wait. He'll pretend to be angry, but you must insist. After that, you play it by ear.'

'I see even clearer.'

'That's my boy.'

She rang off. Mary was watching me. 'What now?' she asked.

'Can you do three valuations for me tomorrow?'

'If I must. I'll have to take Rosie with me as it's our nanny's day out. Why are you so upset?'

I shook my head impatiently. Her future was with the new Merrywethers – scrabbling on the coffins of its friends to earn a bit more money to boast about in a press release. My disease was contagious and would harm her. She was pouting. I'd never seen a real pout before. The effect was rather nice.

'I like your pout.'

'Are you calling the Kembles or shall I?' she said, ignoring my compliment.

I consulted the client list and dialled their number.

'Madder Hall,' said a firm neutral voice.

'May I speak to Mr Kemble?'

'Whom shall I say is calling, sir?'

'John Griffin, Merrywethers.'

I could hear a measured tread receding down a stone passage. Then returning.

'Mr Kemble is just coming.' Then a click.

'Mr Griffin?' A rich, fruity voice.

'Mr Kemble? Hello. Yes, it's John Griffin here. We're working on your valuation.'

'I thought Robert Head was in charge of that.'

'Yes, but we all work together here.'

'Is anything wrong?' His voice was very sharp, too sharp. Mary was listening on the other headset and our eyes met.

44

'No, I'm sure not,' I said calmly, 'but it will be a few days more. There was a note that you needed it urgently and I thought I'd better let you know as Robert is away for the rest of the week.'

'I do need it urgently. I wouldn't have asked Merry-wethers to do it if Head hadn't said I could have it tomorrow. What the devil's the matter?'

'I don't think anything's the matter. We should be able to deliver it to you next Wednesday. We just need to do a bit more research.'

'What on?'

'The Zuccharelli for one thing. It's one of the best examples still in private hands.'

'Oh.' He seemed relieved. 'Well, it's the furniture figures I need tomorrow. Those I must insist on having.'

'Any particular reason?' I asked. Mary's eyes bulged with anticipation.

'What's that to do with you?' Now we're getting to it. Oh, Robert! What have you been up to?

'This is a professional valuation. We can't put our name to a figure unless we believe it can be substantiated.'

'Meaning what?'

'Nothing, except a little extra research. I'm sure you wouldn't want us to mislead you.'

'I wish I'd known you were going to take so long. I could have gone to Garrisons.'

'If it's so urgent, and you can tell me why, I could send Mary Sykes over tomorrow to give you some unofficial figures.'

'Why can't Robert Head come? He's the man I deal with.'

'Unfortunately he's out of the office.'

'Well, send the bloody figures next week, then.' Suddenly he was shouting and then the line went dead.

We sat in silence. I picked up the telephone again.

'Mrs Gaskin? Could we have some China tea, please. Yes, for Mary and me. Thanks so much.'

I sat and thought.

'I'm afraid it must be a valuation for a private sale.

Authenticity kindly supplied by Merrywethers,' I said. 'Large and fraudulent profit for the Kembles, something tasty for Robert, all the risk for us. Oh, God! What do we pay Robert?'

'Forty thousand and a car, plus bonus,' Mary said. 'Same as me.'

'Isn't it enough?'

'Nothing is ever enough if you want more.'

What was she implying?

'Well done for spotting it.'

'What will you do?' she asked, not looking at me.

'I don't really know,' I said. 'What would you do?'

She raised her face and frowned. 'You've never asked me that before.'

'Well, I'm asking you now.' I felt slightly threatened by her appraising stare. I was beginning to tire of being thought outmoded because I took time to consider before reacting.

Mrs Gaskin brought in our tea; milk and sugar for me, slices of lemon for Mary. She had also slipped a couple of pastries into the order, laid out on a plate with forks and napkins.

'You're spoiling us,' smiled Mary.

Mrs Gaskin grinned back, her last two remaining teeth a terrible warning against too many sweet things. 'Someone's got to, my dear.' Who knows why stuffing people with indigestible cake should be seen as a favour? But we ate them obediently.

'Where are you going tomorrow?' Mary said, amid crumbs.

'Bridgwater.'

'Do you think we'll get the sale?'

I shook my head. 'I've no idea. I hope so, if they do sell, but I'd rather see the collection kept intact. Old Gimpal was a great expert, you know. It wasn't a case of taking whatever Wildensteins and Agnews didn't keep for themselves. He went out and researched his field, picked his pictures and then waited until they came up. But once available, he would do anything to get them. He sold both his houses to buy the Velasquez, leaving Mrs Gimpal in a boarding house in Brighton until he could afford to buy somewhere else. They had no furniture – just pictures from floor to ceiling. A real enthusiast.'

'You'd better not say that in front of Terry,' she said. 'Or the chairman.' Or her?

'No,' I agreed. 'Terry'd like everything split up for sale. Again and again! By the way, what have you decided about London?'

'I'm still thinking.' She changed noticeably, becoming more buttoned up in her manner, her eyes again evading mine.

'Have you talked to George about it?' I asked casually.

'Oh, God, no!'

'So . . .?'

'So nothing. I must get back. I'm taking the children bowling, and we like getting there before the rush.'

CHAPTER SIX

The next morning I dressed early and tiptoed past Barbara's bedroom and made myself some coffee. It was still dark outside and the lawn was white with the first frost of autumn. So many hopes had died in this house that it was difficult to feel cheerful, even when the early sunlight began to play upon the dead trees on the opposite hill. It gave a startling yellow glow that accentuated their gaunt silhouettes. Turning from the window, I put the kettle on.

'Why are you making so much noise?' She had come downstairs silently and stood before me, looking reproachful but undeniably desirable, even more so without her make-up.

'I've got a long drive. I hoped you wouldn't hear.'

'You know I never sleep. Why didn't you ask me? I would have cooked your breakfast.'

'I really didn't want any.'

'Will you be back tonight?'

'I expect so.'

'Just so long as I know.'

'I could stay the night in Somerset if you like.'

'No!' she said. 'No! No!'

'I just thought . . .'

'Well, don't. That's all. Don't.'

Then she went back upstairs, and I walked out to the car.

I've always been a sucker for architectural landscaping. Five miles west of Bridgwater you become aware that Man has been at work. Suddenly all the farmsteads start looking immaculate. The woods have a sculptured feel, sweeping up the hills and round their slopes in soft, contoured planting. The cottages shared the same coloured paint and the same ornamental plaques above their doorways. The road becomes an avenue, crossing another the same. There on the left is an obelisk, here on the right the trees part to reveal the portico of a Grecian temple. Yes – Arcadia has been re-created. A vast, triumphal arch of golden stone looms ahead, flanked by two matching lodges. This is Bridgwater Park, where time stands still. Men work here, decay and die, but the heritage, the idea, lives on.

At the gates, a confident-looking man held up a hand. 'Can I help you, sir?' Meaning the opposite.

'Yes, thank you. I'm going to see Mr Merrywether up at the house.'

'Is he expecting you, sir?'

'Yes.' I thought I could risk that. A symmetrical answer to his first question.

'Straight on and you'll see the house down past the lake.'

'Thank you so much.'

It would have been a miracle if I'd missed it. Five storeys of Elizabethan prodigy building in good, solid, local stone, it dominated its valley with effortless confidence. The scarlet and silver striped flag was flapping at half-mast as I drove up. By good fortune the chairman was standing on the steps with two other men. I guessed they would be the two executors. They stared at me as I got out.

'John?' His tone was surprised, hostile.

I hurried forward, holding an empty briefcase, the picture of apologetic concern. 'I'm awfully sorry to bother you.'

'What the devil are you doing here?'

The other two were looking confused.

'I'm afraid we have to talk urgently.'

'You'd better be right,' he said stiffly. 'Oh, I'm so sorry. You may not know Colonel Bracy.' I shook hands with the older man. 'Or Sir John Best.' The latter stood slightly apart and just bowed. He was smaller than I

49

expected, short, stocky and with a sallow boyish face.

'Good morning to you,' he said crisply. 'We'd better leave you to your business affairs.'

Colonel Bracy was gazing at the chairman's impassive face. Then the two of them walked on down the steps and off towards the stables.

'Come in, John,' said the chairman loudly. 'What on earth can be so important?' And we passed through the heavy door and into a hall where a huge fire was spitting and crackling behind a steel mesh curtain.

'How did you get past the lodge?' he asked abruptly.

'I said I was expected.'

'Let's go in here, where we can be private.'

Once in an immaculate little lacquered library, he closed the door.

'So?' I asked him. 'What's up?'

'Best is insisting on selling through Garrisons. He told me yesterday – as a courtesy, he said. We need to work fast, and Terry's in Zurich. If they get this sale instead of us . . .' His voice trailed away.

'Any reason given for not using us?'

'None to me. Though he must have said something to Bracy. Who, by the by, is no match for him.'

'I see.'

'Any suggestions?'

I sat and thought. The only thing that mattered was to prevent a firm commitment at this early stage. 'They're determined to sell?' I asked.

'Oh, definitely. They want the cash, and the heir can hardly make a decision without two nurses. It's not as if the pictures are old family property. They could get them all exempted, of course, but they don't want the worry of it. And it means everything else can be kept intact or extended. There's talk of looking for another estate nearer London for the dowager. I don't know if you know why Gimpal left it all to Tom?'

'No, I don't,' I replied. 'I assumed it was to give the collection a good home.'

'It's much more romantic than that. I didn't know

myself until this week. Tom was the Polish liaison officer with British Intelligence in the war. Gimpal's mistress was stuck in Warsaw and Tom got her out. She lost a leg in the process and we lost a couple of agents, but he got her out. This was the unexpected pay-off.' He laughed. 'Tom told me when he was dying. He thought it would amuse me.'

'Have they talked to Garrisons?'

'No,' he said, after a pause. 'No, I don't think they have.'

So, I thought, there's still a chance. 'Would they deal with Bernard O'Connor or with Rupert Englefield at Garrisons?'

'That's an interesting question. Why do you ask?'

'Because,' I explained, 'Bernard couldn't offer the sort of special deal they'll ask for without consulting the board. Rupert Englefield could. It's his boardroom responsibility. After that, they'd be committed.'

'Englefield's a friend of Best's. I think he'll deal direct.'

'So,' I said. 'First we've got to delay that call.' There was another long silence while he stared at the books and I thought of the options. Odd how millions could rest on a single telephone call.

I stood up.

'Where are you going?' he demanded.

'I can't stay long – it'll be obvious. But I know what to do.'

'Which is?'

'Get Englefield out of the way.'

'You're getting as bad as Terry.' He looked startled.

'Don't worry. I shan't have him assassinated. Try to keep Sir John away from the telephone until tomorrow. I'll do what I can.'

'And how do I explain your visit?'

'Tell them that I caught a junior partner fiddling a valuation.'

'God forbid!'

I made no comment. On the way out, we met the others coming back.

'How did you get past Danvers?' Sir John asked me sharply.

'Is that the man at the gate?'

'It is.'

'I'm afraid I lied. I told him I was expected.' I smiled apologetically. 'Obviously I was plausible.'

'Obviously,' the other replied dryly. 'Does your profession call for much mendacity?'

'No more than others,' I said and moved away, hoping to escape.

'I believe you run the Berington office,' Colonel Bracy said.

I turned. 'Yes, I do.'

'You know my nephew, Bertie Russell, I think.'

I listened to the name of my wife's lover with no reaction. The three of them watched me walk to the car and drive off as if I hadn't a care in the world. What is it about wounds that leads even good-natured people to probe them so remorselessly?

To say that I had a plan would be a gross exaggeration. But clearly contact between Best and Englefield had to be delayed as long as possible, in the hope of something positive presenting itself to our side. To my surprise I found myself rather enjoying the situation. Perhaps I *had* stagnated in my rural idyll. Certainly I liked the idea of showing we could manage without Terry's schemes.

It was after three when I reached London, but that miracle of modern science, the radio telephone, had enabled me to establish three facts: the Englefields were spending the evening at Covent Garden, he was away from his office all afternoon, but he had a meeting scheduled there for tomorrow morning. The immediate danger, therefore, was his home number. I got Elizabeth to ring it on a spare line and keep the receiver off. If he had a second line, we didn't know it. Perhaps Sir John didn't know it either.

When I reached Mayfair I took the chairman's space in the staff car park and ran up the stairs.

'Any other instructions?' asked Elizabeth as soon as she saw me, in a rather scratchy voice.

'Yes,' I said, still panting. 'Cancel the chairman's schedule for the next week.'

'Even the Prime Minister's dinner party?' she said drily.

I paused for breath. 'No. Everything but that. But he's going to be busy. Is Terry back?'

'Not yet.'

'Let's keep it that way. Don't tell him I'm here. Don't let him in. I need peace and quiet.'

She smiled. 'I know what you mean,' she said.

Then I rang Isabel. Isabel Courtauld is to gossip what Wisden is to cricket. She *knows*. And she's always right. It's an instinct, an obsession. People tell her things because they know she really wants to know. Years ago, before my marriage, we had been close. One unexpected weekend doesn't constitute an affair – we were too young, and too incompatible. But it did cement our friendship. And I love her sense of style, the way she sways her hips and sends her long red hair flicking round her neck with a single glossy toss of her head.

'Isabel?'

'What do you want now?' Her voice sounded husky. 'You haven't rung in months.'

'Information. Who is Rupert Englefield sleeping with?'

'Well, it's not me. I can tell you that.'

'So who is it?'

'Why do you want to know?'

'Because.'

'That's not good enough. Not after all this time.'

'All right,' I said. 'I promise I'll explain. But not now.'

'I don't know why it matters. You couldn't possibly know him. But I think it's someone who works at the V. and A. called Graham.'

'Which department?' I asked.

'How the hell should I know?'

'OK. Now, even more crucial, Mrs E.'

'That is *really* asking.'

'Why?'

'Because she's my best friend,' she said slowly.

'I never knew that.'

'Well, you know now.'

'So?'

'Look, John, nobody knows. She's a sphinx. She's never, never indiscreet.'

'Ah, but you know, darling. You always do.'

'I know about Bertie.'

'Oh, come on, Isabel,' I said angrily. 'The whole world knows about Bertie. Tell me about Mrs E.'

'Not over the telephone. Do you want to meet me for a drink?'

'Yes.'

'Would you like to come to *Lohengrin* at Covent Garden tonight?'

'Why? Have you got tickets?' Luck is an extraordinary thing. At least I could keep an eye on the Englefields.

'Yes.'

'Then yes, please.'

'Good. I'll tell you in the interval. Will you pick me up? It starts at six thirty so be here by five forty-five. Bye.'

CHAPTER SEVEN

I just had time to ring home and then Mrs Gaskin to say I might be away for the weekend. Neither call was reassuring. Barbara snapped my head off and Mrs G. told me that Robert had been trying to reach me all day. 'Tell him to see me on Monday morning at nine,' I said, and left a message for Mary to ring me at the company flat. The Kemble valuation was secure in my office safe and couldn't go out without my signature. I still could hardly believe it of Robert. I had trusted him without reservation. It's not easy to admit to being a bad judge of character. I suppose it's because I find it so much more comfortable to accept the pretty parcels people make of their self-presentations than always to be examining the entrails in search of a baser truth. At least I knew I was on firm ground with Mary. There was so much to admire in her generous and reliable nature.

The chairman's office had a shower, and I used it. This was the life, if only temporarily. Then I drove to St James's Place and picked up Isabel. She was still attractive, but with a rounder, more careless look than when we had been together. Two husbands had deserted her, but neither had left children as consolation. Now she drifted from lover to lover, her real interest being the troubles of others and their frantic attempts to keep sorrow at bay.

'You're looking wonderful,' I said, burying a kiss in the dense red hair that smelt deliciously of coconut.

'Well, you're looking perfectly frightful,' was the response as she got into the car. 'And why this prurient interest in the Englefields?'

I had already decided to be frank. 'The Bridgwater pictures.'

'You mean the Gimpal collection?'

'Yes.'

'I've always wondered if that Polish tart was worth it.'

'How on earth did you know about that?' I asked, remembering the chairman's confidential manner.

'About Ivana? I though everyone knew about Ivana. Look out!'

I swerved to avoid a bicyclist with no lights and then we were there, in the shadows of the great cream-coloured theatre.

'I'll drop you and park in the Strand,' I said.

'Why don't I come with you?'

'Because I want you to get rid of that coat and buy a programme.'

She got out and I rejoined her in the lobby where she was talking to a blond woman in a tight black dress.

'Here we are. I don't think you know each other. John Griffin. Antoinette Englefield.'

She was much younger than I had pictured, with sharp cheekbones and a strong chin that gave her face the architectural beauty of a Gothic cathedral made out of marble. We shook hands and she smiled gravely, acknowledging my stare as a compliment.

'Isabel has often talked about you,' she said. 'You are not what I expected.'

Try translating that one! Anyway I rallied as best I could, as shortly afterwards her husband hurried in, tall, immaculate, a little too soigné with his diamond studs.

'Sorry I'm late. The bloody telephone's out of order.' We knew each other by sight – indeed, he had offered me a job at Garrisons fifteen years ago.

'Alan must be mad to let van Zwanenberg escape,' he said as we queued for the stalls.

'I'm very sorry myself,' I agreed. 'He's such a nice man to work with.'

'I wonder who'll sell the Gimpal pictures?' he said casually.

'I think we're all wondering that.'

False bravado would count for nothing with him. Then we separated, for they were with a corporate party while Isabel and I were alone, though in better seats, right behind the conductor, so we could see the orchestra passing round cans of lager and packets of chewing gum.

The lights dimmed, a wave of applause and then that mystic first chord. Isabel and I sat side by side, not holding hands as we used to but surely she was as alive to those memories as I was. When the curtain lowered for the first interval, she turned and said, 'I was once as trusting as Elsa. But with men it's always less important.'

'That wasn't the way with us,' I reminded her.

'No.' She smiled, then we both laughed, twenty years draining our pain of all but a not-unpleasant aftertaste.

'So tell me,' I persisted.

'They're only three rows behind.'

'*Tell me.*'

'Sir John Best,' she said at last. 'Why on earth are you looking like that?'

'Ah,' I said. 'I see.'

'Do you never say anything else? Without doubt you're the blindest man I've ever met. Women deceive you at every turn and all you ever say is "I see"!'

'But in the end,' I said with invincible good humour, 'in the end, I do see.'

'And what do you see now?'

'I see the Gimpal collection coming nearer and nearer.'

'That must be a *very* encouraging sight,' said a deeper, softer voice behind me. It was Antoinette Englefield, who had made her way over to us and was smiling at Isabel. 'Rupert tells me he offered you a job once,' she said to me.

'Yes. I'm afraid I was foolish enough to turn it down.'

'Perhaps he will offer it again.'

'You're wearing Fracas,' I said, caught by her undeniable allure.

57

'Are you Merrywethers' specialist in scent?'

'No, but my wife once spilt a bottle in my suitcase. I've never forgotten it.'

'And where is this wife?'

'You mustn't bait John,' cut in Isabel. 'His women give him an awful time.'

'Are there so many?' Her lips were full, and painted a soft pink.

'I need a drink,' I said, on an impulse. 'Can you escape?'

'No,' she said. 'No, I cannot escape,' and she moved very smoothly, sliding as it seemed, through the throng towards her group who were laughing at something her husband had said.

'Satisfied?' said Isabel icily.

'More than that,' I replied. 'I owe you a very substantial favour.'

'I'll settle for dinner,' she said, cheering up at the thought of food. Nothing changes, I reflected, eyeing her ample proportions. 'And you needn't pull a face like that,' she snapped. 'You don't look as if you're on hunger strike, either.'

When the opera was over we turned down memory lane and dined at Rodolfo's, a garlic-ridden little French restaurant off Connaught Square. The waiter recognized my name and led us straight to one of the brown boarded alcoves hung with indiscreet scenes of nineteenth-century Paris. On the way we passed the familiar sign which said in French: 'Don't trouble to shout at the proprietor, his wife takes care of that.'

'How are things with Barbara?' Isabel said.

'Bad.'

'Oh, well.' She sighed and sipped the champagne we had once enjoyed. 'I never did think you suited each other. No mirror image there, I used to say.'

'Your judgement in these matters is known to be impeccable,' I found myself replying and for a moment we stared at each other with unexpected hostility. Then she laughed and patted my hand.

' "It is better to travel hopefully than to arrive",' she quoted. 'Nowadays I protect myself by ensuring that I remain totally uninterested in the destination.'

'You just enjoy the rides?'

'Precisely.' She laughed again, but I shook my head. Mary's face swam through the murky depths of my mind, obliterating my brief interest in Antoinette's lips.

'So what have you been up to?' I asked politely.

'I've just come back from Aspen,' she said. 'Before that I was in Holland, staying with the Amerongens. Gop is furious, because his uncle who made an absolute fortune buying up Rotterdam in the war has left it to the government rather than to him.'

'But Gop's quite comfortable, isn't he?'

'No-one's too comfortable to take thirty million guilders.'

'Cor!' That's ten million quid. 'And he left it to the Treasury?'

'No. That's one good thing. It's to go on art purchases.'

'Aha! That's more like it.' I grinned. 'Gop would just have invested it. It'll do more good in the sale rooms.'

'Are none of you ever satisfied?' she asked as the first course arrived.

'Never,' I said, and turned my attention to my plate of snails.

After dinner I drove her home. As I watched the door close behind her, I reflected that I was well on my way down the disreputable path mapped out by Terry Burton.

The company flat had only one book. While doubtless exhaustive on early Jewish genealogy, it was entirely silent on more recent events. So I rang my elder brother, my mentor and occasional confidant.

'Have you any idea what time it is?' he demanded.

'I know. This is frightfully urgent.'

'Well?'

'Could you please go downstairs and get the latest *Who's Who*.'

'*What?*'

'Please.'

There was a silence, then he picked up another receiver.

'I can't believe I'm doing this.'

'Look up Best, Sir John.'

'The solicitor?'

'That's him.'

'Got it.'

'Is he married?'

'Yes. Married. Brenda, only daughter of John Hamish Batt. He has four children and his hobby is fencing.'

'Married how long?'

'Fifteen years.'

'Address?'

'Old Rectory, Harting Hampden, Basingstoke.'

'What's that? An hour from London?'

'Why don't you ring the bloody AA? It's three in the morning, John.'

'I'm very grateful. Go back to sleep.' I rang off before he could reply. I sat and thought of the consequences for all those involved for nearly an hour. Then, burying my conscience, I dialled another number. It rang and rang. I just waited. Finally a male voice answered.

'Bridgwater Park.'

'I'm sorry to disturb you. I have an urgent call for Mr Merrywether.'

'I'm only the nightwatchman, mate. I've never even heard of him.'

'I'm sorry,' I said. 'But I know he's in the house and I must speak to him.'

'Hold on, then.' I could hear him grumbling to himself. I waited for a long, long time.

Suddenly the earpiece exploded. It was the chairman.

'Who is this? What do you want?'

'Where are you?' I whispered.

'In the library. And speak up. I can hardly hear you.'

'Wait for the receiver to be replaced,' I said.

And, sure enough, we could dimly hear the man returning to the other telephone.

As he picked it up I said, 'Thank you, I've got Mr Merrywether on the line.'

'Cheers,' said the other, and there was the click of the extension closing.

'You've got to talk to Colonel Bracy first thing. Tell him that John Best is sleeping with Rupert Englefield's wife and that there'll be an almighty scandal if Garrisons get the sale on his say-so. Which there will, if Dempster picks it up.'

'Christ! You're sure of this?'

'Yes, but Bracy must be discreet. All he's got to do is stall.'

'John Best is a lucky man.'

'I know. I met her tonight.'

'It doesn't mean we'll get it.'

'No, but it'll hold things up long enough to think of something else more watertight.'

'Well done,' he said. 'This is more like the old days,' and rang off. At backgammon the dice always even out in the end. The same is true of cards. If this holds good in the ordinary way of things, I had used up a fair supply of my favourable chances in the last few hours.

And a few principles, too.

There was nothing more I could do. The next step was up to the chairman. I couldn't sleep, so, without thinking, I drove home in the early hours. And, of course, there was the familiar red car parked outside the house when I arrived. I started to reverse as quickly as I could but the gravel had done its worst. A shaft of light flooded out from Barbara's window and I could see her silhouetted against it.

I drove back up to the door and parked beside the other car. The front door was bolted, so I went round to the back and let myself into the kitchen.

Presently Bertie came downstairs.

'Barbara's very upset,' he said.

'I'm sorry,' I said wearily. 'I didn't think.'

'No,' he said. 'It wasn't very thoughtful.'

'She said you were going to America.'

'Not till tomorrow night.'

'Do you want a cup of tea?' I asked.

'I must say you're very cool.' He sounded aggrieved.

'Well, of course, you're not the first.' It wasn't true, but I couldn't resist it. The effect was satisfactory. He said nothing for a while, then: 'I wish you wouldn't talk about it like that.'

'I shall never allude to it again.'

'I'm sorry,' he said after a pause.

I just shook my head.

'It was ending anyway,' he muttered.

'Yes,' I said. 'It's been ending for a long time.'

'No, you don't understand,' he said. 'I mean between Barbara and me.'

'Oh, I'm sorry.'

'Are you always so detached? She says you love her.'

'I do, but I'm very tired.'

'Well, I'm off,' he said, looking and probably feeling rather foolish. He offered me his hand. It would have been pointless to ignore it. It was damp and disagreeable to touch. I let him out of the front door and stood on the step while he drove away. Barbara was, no doubt, standing a few feet above my head. We must have presented a curiously vertical view of a splintered marriage.

I went upstairs to pack. She came and stood in the doorway.

'Are you leaving too?'

'I think so.'

'Why did you come back?'

'I was too sleepy to think straight.'

'Would you like some coffee?'

'No, thanks.' There was nothing that I felt able to accept from her any more, however generous her impulse. It was as if I was consciously fending off the grappling hooks of the past.

'Where will you go?'

'I'll write.'

'Are you very cross?'

'No.'

62

'It wasn't much fun.'

'Perhaps not.'

'No, I mean with Bertie.'

'Ah.'

And with that the conversation, and the marriage, finally ended.

CHAPTER EIGHT

'Has Robert arrived yet?'

It was Monday morning and I had breakfasted well at my new base, the local inn. It was difficult to know precisely what to do about Robert. My inclination was to dismiss him, without discussion; but the more I thought about it, the more I kept reminding myself that I had recruited him and that perhaps his failings could be turned to Merrywethers' advantage in their new atmosphere of guerrilla warfare.

'Not yet, sir.' Old Gaskin is a wonderful survivor, six foot six of muscled Guardsman, reduced now to a hobbling giant but still able to lift a Dieppe cupboard. Mrs Gaskin dotes on him. Everyone does. Always smiling, always cheerful, he's a model for all time.

I heard the outer door open. It was Mary, her hair untidy, with a pile of folders.

'Working over the weekend?' I said lightly. 'What about your poor family?'

'I had to do this,' she said. And put the files down with a slap. 'Robert's valuations over the last year.'

'And?' I looked up at her, registering the determined set to her mouth.

'Three.'

'Serious?'

'Yes. I'd never have spotted them if I hadn't known what to look for.'

'Which was?'

'Single items in his specialist field which we mightn't ordinarily query: a Langlois commode, a pair of statues by Clodion and a Chippendale bed.'

'Any connection with the Kembles?'

'Yes,' she said. 'One is for his cousin. I expect they're all tied in. He could hardly suggest it himself.'

'But you mean once he has done it for one family, they might drop a hint to someone else?'

'Yes,' she said. 'Precisely that.'

'Oho.'

'What's that supposed to mean?'

'I'm trying to stop saying "I see".'

She laughed a little grimly. 'It's much too late for that.' She looked hard at me. 'You seem strained.'

'I am strained,' I said defensively.

'In so far as?'

'In so far as I'm lodging at the King's Head.'

'Oh.' For a moment I hoped she was going to make some physical gesture of sympathy, but she turned away towards the window. 'How lucky you have no children,' she added.

Mrs Gaskin put her head round the door. 'Mr Head is here.'

'Thank you, Mary,' I said, and as she left Robert stormed in. I waited for his outburst.

'You *know* I've had Mr Kemble chasing me all weekend. You *know* that valuation was a rush job.'

'Come and sit down,' I said. 'And let's talk about it.' He seemed almost to be squinting with the strain of these complex interior feelings that must be warring within him.

'We'll lose all our bloody business at this rate,' he blurted. 'Or don't you care? Terry says you don't care.'

'What would Terry say about these, then?' I pushed the four folders towards him. It took him only a quick glance to see the point. His face went very pale, almost grey. Then he made an obvious effort. Could he try to talk his way out? No. It was too much, with the four in front of him. He laid out his hands in a gesture of part surrender, part supplication.

'I needed the money,' he said. So it was to be self-pity

and feeble self-justification; I think I would have preferred straightforward bluster. But I was surprised to find myself entirely free from civic outrage.

'How much did you get?' I asked.

I could actually see him calculating the least he could plausibly say. 'You wouldn't believe me.'

'Probably not.'

'I'll pay them back,' he gabbled. 'I can borrow from my father. The only big deal was a sale to Thorpes. I got five per cent, nearly eight thousand pounds.' It seemed pitifully small. 'I'll do anything to avoid a scandal.'

'It may not come to that.'

'Ah,' he said. 'I suppose a scandal would hurt you as much as me. Everyone says you've slowed down to the point of immobility.'

I smiled at this.

'It's not *funny*.' Suddenly he was shouting. 'It's my career at stake.'

'Yes,' I agreed. 'Though you wouldn't necessarily go to prison.'

'Prison?' He was appalled. '*Prison?*'

'It *is* fraud, but it's also your first offence,' I said, then added, 'I assume?' I raised my eyebrows. He nodded, dejected but angry, offended even.

I got up and walked behind him. Immobility indeed!

'It's just between you and me at the moment,' I whispered. 'I will have to see how you go from here. I'll make a decision later. As a matter of fact,' I went on, 'I might be needing someone not averse to using his imagination.' He turned in his chair and stared at me. I gave him my version of Terry's chilling smile. 'But not immediately.'

He still stared. His lower lip was trembling.

'I'll sit on this for the time being.' I took the folders back in rather a deliberate fashion. 'In the meantime, you'll have to rework the Kemble valuation. And pitch it right. He'll be more inclined to chase you even harder now, but I'll cover your back.' He got up, anxious to leave the room. 'And Robert,' I called to him as he reached the door, 'be prepared to use your imagination *for* Merrywethers instead of against us.' I put the folders on one side, ready to deal with as soon as I had time to consider their details, but the next hour rushed by as telephone calls came faster than we could field them.

The chairman wanted to know why his appointments had been cancelled.

'So you and Bonas can put together a package for the executors,' I explained. 'You know, the usual thing – guarantees, exhibitions in New York and Paris. The others'll be doing the same.' The family connection seemed to have closed his mind to the concept of business as usual.

Then Terry, in uncharacteristic congratulatory mood. 'You did a great job. We never picked up Mrs Englefield. Thanks, Johnny.' I was rather touched, though annoyed that the chairman had told him. 'How about that list?' he asked.

'Good heavens,' I said, 'I haven't even thought about it.'

'Just do it, John.' Click! I smiled ruefully. Then it was Isabel on the line.

'You bastard! You absolute bastard!'

'What's the matter?' But I could guess.

'It's all over the world, that's all. I wonder you didn't ring the *Daily Express*. Antoinette is totally devastated.'

'Why?' I deliberately made myself sound bored, cold. 'Why is a bit of gossip so damaging? No-one suspects her of sleeping with her husband. She must be allowed some fun.'

'They have a very good relationship.'

'Her and that camp old queen?'

'He's not a camp old queen, and you know it.'

'I'm really sorry, but I had to use the information. You surely couldn't have thought I was asking for purely private consumption.'

'Oh, I see. It's my fault now.' She sounded very angry.

'No, Isabel. No. I'm truly sorry and the responsibility is mine. But I still don't see why the fuss.'

'Did you know John Best is married?'

'Yes.'

'Did you think about his position?'

'Yes.'

'So – why?'

I thought for a moment. I had felt the need to check this very point. I made myself articulate the unflattering truth. 'Because my job, and Merrywethers, matter more to me than Lady Best's feelings.'

'Or their children's?'

'Or their children's.'

She rang off.

Then another voice. 'It was you, wasn't it?' It was Antoinette Englefield.

'Yes,' I said. 'I'm very sorry.'

'Just for those silly paintings.'

'Those and other things.'

'Things that matter to you.'

I didn't know how to answer that. There was passive acceptance in her voice, and it was her very docility that stripped away the self-assurance I had used on Isabel, leaving me face to face with self-contempt.

'It's a terrible thing you've done,' she said after a pause.

Then she too rang off.

It doesn't do to wallow in misery, neither one's own nor anyone else's. So I looked up Colonel Chaucer – the first name on Terry's list – in the telephone directory and dialled his number.

'Yes?'

'Colonel Chaucer?'

'Yes! Yes!'

'It's John Griffin here. We met shooting with my brother last year.'

'I remember you.'

'I wondered whether I could bring a friend over to see your Tischbein. He's giving a lecture in Amsterdam and yours is the only important one he hasn't seen.'

'Oh, God!'

'I realize it's a tremendous favour to ask.'

68

'No, no, I'll be glad to see you. You must come and take lunch with me. When did you say you'd be coming?'

Aargh! I had hoped we could leave this open. Who knew what Hans was up to? I hadn't been in touch with him for months.

'Friday week?' Worth a try.

'Friday week,' he said. 'Come at twelve forty-five.'

It took ten minutes to get through to the Rijksmuseum.

'Hans?'

'John Griffin?'

'You know you've always wanted to see the Chaucer Tischbein.'

'I have indeed. They've never even allowed it to be photographed.'

'Can you do Friday the fifth?'

'Why the urgency?'

'Because I think he might sell.'

'Why do you say that? I was talking to your friends in Bond Street last week. They say he will never sell.'

'Have I ever misled you?'

'No,' he said, 'but the old man does not deal with your firm.'

'Do you want to see it or not?'

'Yes, John,' he said. 'I will come to see your new client.'

'Good. I'll meet you at Heathrow. You've got to be landed before ten, so it's an early start. But we'll talk before then.' It was too easy.

Then I rang Mrs Granger, the second name on the list.

'Hello-o-o?' It was a very quavery voice.

'May I speak to Mrs Granger, please?'

'This is she.'

'My name is John Griffin, Mrs Granger. I'm afraid we haven't met, but I'm doing some research on Thomas Chippendale and I wondered whether you would allow me to take some photographs of your mirrors.' Not a very subtle approach, I'm afraid.

'Are you the man who works for Merrywethers?' she asked.

'Yes. As a matter of fact I am.'

'I'm afraid we've always dealt with Christie's. Thank you for ringing.'

'But—'

'*Good*bye.' Her fluty voice allowed no room for argument.

And as a matter of fact, I sat back well satisfied. Why should she change the habits of a lifetime? If she was happy with her contacts, I was very happy with mine. I just hoped *our* old ladies would show equal alertness and determination.

I decided to leave Lord Tottenham, the third name on the list, for a quieter day and I put Robert's folders back in the safe for tomorrow, hiding them under some other papers.

The King's Head, and a whisky and soda, was altogether a more tempting prospect.

CHAPTER NINE

I think it's time I said rather more about Mary. If I'd been younger, I would have sold my soul for her; as it was, I could watch over her impassively. In appearance she was, as I have said, tall and dark, with a pale ivory skin, wide, inviting mouth and a Mephisthophelean lift to her eyebrows that gave an intriguing suggestiveness to her natural gaiety. And her eyes? Oh, yes, I have gazed at her eyes when I have thought myself unobserved, mesmerized by their shifting shadows of green and brown and grey, their faintly oriental slant and, above all, the warmth and kindness in their expression. On reflection, I think I would have to say that her eyes are, to me, the most beautiful that I have ever seen. But best of all, we are so much in sympathy with one another, sharing (or so it seems to me) the same pleasures, even companionable silences when there is nothing that needs saying.

At this stage, I had made three judgements on her character. I knew that she had worked hard at learning our trade and at applying it. I believed her to be committed to her role as wife and mother, or perhaps to her image of what this should be since I had noticed that she seemed to pay more attention to her children in her conversation than in her actions. And I had learned to be alert to her sudden temper, of which, to the careful observer, she gave a rich variety of storm signals. Impatience could be diagnosed from a sharper note in her voice, the tapping of the scarlet nails or, in extreme cases, in her eyes flickering from side to side. Strong disagreement produced a warm flush about her cheekbones, an unfortunate trap for the susceptible. But the invariable portent of real anger was a vague but repetitive brushing movement in which, with both hands, she would scrape her hair back behind her ears. Whatever the turmoil within her head that produced this reflex, it would very soon afterwards be released in unexpectedly savage words. She never raised her voice but irony and cruelly accurate barbs did the work as well as any bombast.

On Tuesday morning we were both booked to value a client's house. I was having breakfast in the pub dining room trying to remember if there was anything I had left undone when I looked up to see her walking across with her usual jaunty stride.

'Like some orange juice?' I asked, pulling out a chair.

'Have we time?'

I ordered some and she gave me a piece of that double-edged news to which all auctioneers have to become used.

'Mrs Spencer has died.'

'Are you sure?'

'Oh, yes. One of the grain salesmen told George this morning. He lives in the same village as her doctor. She died at dinner last night.'

I was sorry, because Mrs Spencer was a friendly old lady who had been especially kind to Barbara and me when we first moved into the county. But my professional interest was naturally calculating the probable sequel. She had a married daughter in Australia and a bachelor son teaching at Cambridge. She had always made a point of sharing things equally between them, involving me in such divisions of paintings and china on several occasions. I was pretty sure the property would be sold. And the good news in this was that the house was large enough, Mrs Spencer was rich enough, and that generations of Spencers had lived there long enough for the contents to fall into the golden category of an important sale on the premises – magnet to 'vanity fair' and international dealers alike. No grubby map with compass points, no specks of gold in a Klondike stream could have published wider the message of buried treasure than the announcement of a proper gilt-edged country house sale.

All over the country (and abroad) people consult their diaries and calculate their capacity to bid. From old curtains and new china to the grandest of Louis commodes, everything fetches a better price with that glamorous extra tag, the latest old mansion to be sold up. No matter if some pieces came from Harrods the week before (and some owners are not even above buying in a little second-hand junk as a speculation), 'This and this I bought from Castle Wobbling' is a marketable remark. And my job is to sell it into the mouth of the highest bidder. Assuming that I get the job, of course. Which you can't in this business, not till you've got a written contract.

'We must warn the office.'

'Don't worry,' she said. 'I've left a message on Robert's answering machine and I dropped in to alert Mrs Gaskin on the way here.' See what I mean?

'Wonderful,' I said, finishing my coffee. My car was parked round the back, and I felt suddenly ashamed of its muddy appearance and astringent ashtray atmosphere.

'Where are we going?' She was sitting beside me, her long legs drawn up uncomfortably.

'Do you want me to put the seat back?'

'No, I'm fine,' she said, twitching her skirt to cover her knees.

'Norton Park,' I said, to answer her question. 'New clients. Mr and Mrs Tredinnick. Moved here a year ago. New money, I think. They want a valuation of any items over two thousand pounds, excluding silver which is being done in London.'

'Anything interesting?'

'Probably not. He talked a lot about comparing our terms with the others'. Heaven knows how he chose, because we're all the same more or less. There was some talk of family connections with someone. You know. The usual garbage.'

'Can we get away for lunch?'

'Yes,' I said, glancing at her. 'Yes, I'm sure we can.'

'I want to talk to you about something,' she said, looking straight ahead through the misty windscreen.

'Fine,' I said and turned the car into the driveway, a nice concave balustraded green with two matching stone lodges, the whole image marred by a new sign with the words 'NORTON PARK' in script. Below was printed, 'Tradesmen by appointment only'.

'Lucky we've got an appointment,' Mary said as we wound up the drive neatly planted with old limes and oaks. One last corner, and the house stood in front of us – a pretty seven-bay Georgian house with a pediment sporting an elaborate coat of arms. On either side, two contemporary wings with hipped roofs and cupolas extended the façade. A large red Bentley was parked immediately in front of the door. I parked beside it and Mary walked to the door and rang the bell.

By the time I had joined her, a little woman in tweeds was shaking her hand.

'And you must be Mr Griffin,' she said to me. 'Oh, good. Here's Puffy. Really, darling, it's very late to be in your dressing gown.'

'How do you do! How do you do!' Her husband, a round little man with a purple face, bowed to Mary and then extended his hand downwards and at an angle to me, so that I practically had to go down on my knees to take it. It was soft and flabby, but I like to think that my face showed no expression beyond polite expectation.

'I mustn't hold you up. You've got a lot to do. Would your secretary like a cup of tea?' It seemed that he was incapable of looking Mary in the face, for his pop-eyes roved restlessly around but away from her.

'Thank you, no,' said Mary, totally unmoved. 'Shall I start in the dining room?' she asked Mrs Tredinnick, who looked anxiously at her husband. Decisions were apparently his province.

'Start where you please,' he snapped. 'We can't offer you, mm, either of you, lunch as we're going over to the Beringtons. My wife's cousins, you know,' he added.

Well, I did now.

74

'All right! All right!' He waved a pudgy hand at the hall and bustled upstairs, leaving behind him a distinct smell of talc.

I spent the next hour patiently detailing the ground floor. As a matter of fact, there was nothing of any great value, although in any large house the total inevitably creeps up unless the place is empty. I had found nothing over £5,000 when Mary and I met at the foot of the stairs.

'How are you doing?' I asked her.

Her mouth turned down expressively.

'No time to gossip!' shouted our genial host, leaning over the stairwell. He was wearing a startling green and yellow check tweed waistcoat and trousers, and was busily threading a gold watch chain through the button-hole. 'You'd better have a good look at these pictures on the stairs.'

We steadily continued our work, and then he was with us again, this time with the jacket on as well. In a way he looked very smart, but the effect was just a little too contrived, a little too outré. I wished I could have observed his entrance at the Beringtons' lunch party.

'Now don't forget that tapestry. I bought it at Belton, you know.'

'It's splendid,' I said. It was: a pretty hunting scene with a château, Oiron by the look of it, in the background.

'Do you know what date it is?' he asked, winking at his wife who had come along the corridor to join us.

'Yes,' I said. 'I do. But I'd like to hear Mary's opinion.'

She walked over, felt its stitch, turned the corners over to examine the reverse and then stepped back to get a general view. She turned and smiled.

'Well, my dear?' Mrs Tredinnick was looking impressed.

'If John knows,' Mary said, 'it means it's either a genuine 1642 Lefèbvre, one of the set "Les Chasses" which the brothers designed for Fontainebleau, or it could be one of the nineteenth-century Gobelin copies. *Just* as important,' she added hastily when she saw their expressions.

75

'They were produced for the Troisième Empire. Since John didn't need to look, and since I couldn't find the red Lefèbvre signature stitch, I'm going to plump for Troisième Empire.' She glanced anxiously at me. I positively beamed.

'Not bad for a "secretary"!' I said. 'I do congratulate you on spotting it. It's a very specialized piece.'

Puffy looked as if he was going to explode with suppressed rage at the demotion of his household treasures. 'Are you going to be much longer?' he squeaked.

I looked at my watch. 'Another hour should do it.'

'But I've got to put the burglar alarm on!'

I know one shouldn't laugh, so I assumed a solemn expression and promised to hurry. We tore through the bedrooms where there were one or two good satinwood pieces, and within forty minutes we were out of the house and waving goodbye to Mrs Tredinnick as we bowled off down the drive.

The Three Goats is a ramshackle old inn a few miles south of Norton. Still retained by the local landowner, and run more or less as a social club for the estate staff, it has managed to resist the dreary changes foisted on us all by the big breweries. Consequently we found a roaring fire and comfortable chairs in the panelled bar – panelled, I should emphasize, in oak stained a cheerful mahogany, with none of the obligatory black, white or red colour schemes of Olde Englishe 'hostelries'. I went through to the public bar to order the house specialities: game pie followed by treacle pudding. I caught the landlord's glance at my waistline and we both smiled.

When I went to join Mary beside the fire, she was looking at a rumpled photograph of her children which she carried in her handbag.

'To go or not to go?' I hazarded.

Her shocked face turned sharply and she seemed almost afraid.

'How did you know?'

'Because,' I said patiently, 'we discussed this before.'

'Oh,' she said, her face relaxing. 'Oh yes, we did, didn't we?'

I had ordered some claret and there was a pause while this was delivered. I sipped mine – it was excellent – then saw that she was crying. She was sitting there, quite silent, with large single tears dropping slowly from her eyes and then trickling past her nose and down to her chin, where they were collecting like liquid icicles along her jaw.

I put out my arms and pushed my chair back, and she came and sat heavily on my lap with both arms round my neck. She sobbed and sobbed. The couple opposite had almost finished their lunch. A few minutes of this and they tiptoed away, but not before the man had winked at me in sympathy and the woman shot me a look of angry distaste. Did she think I had caused this inarticulate grief? Did she know how much I was enjoying the warmth of Mary's body, the scent of her skin rising from between her breasts? Then, just as abruptly, Mary got up, drew out my pocket handkerchief, blew her nose very loudly and went back to her chair. Still without speaking she took a gulp of claret. The game pie had mysteriously appeared during this drama, and she attacked it with enthusiasm. My appetite had gone, leaving in its place a dreary ache, the need to hug her again, a sense of inner emptiness that food would be altogether unable to assuage.

'Eat up!' she said, scraping up her gravy with a great lump of brown bread. 'It'll get cold.' I had another drink instead.

'You did well getting that tapestry,' I said.

'Thank you,' she said gravely. 'Now I think I can talk.' Again her expression changed to an introspective intensity. 'I've got to talk to you. You're the only one who might understand. You're so kind.'

I was beginning to get the idea. Trouble at home – a lover – I really didn't want to hear, but clearly I was going to.

'Tell me,' I said. 'I promise not to say a word.'

77

'No,' she said. 'I know you won't.'

There was nothing new – there never is. I don't think anyone divorces unless it's the only conceivable alternative that they believe remains. How much heartbreak would be avoided if only people shunned marriage except on the same principle. Men rarely admit to making the wrong decision; their explanation is more likely to be some change of circumstance. But with women: what a panoply of poor excuses for that first error: I wanted to get away from home, I thought he would change, he was the first one to ask. *He was the first one to ask!* How's that for a reason to marry! What a depth of insecurity is thus revealed. Why not, 'I loved him'? Or is there some feminine resistance to admitting that their love, like men's, can wither of its own accord?

'George was so persistent. He kept saying that I would learn to love him as much as he loved me. And I did love him, in a way.'

Poor George. Poor trusting, arrogant, immature George. He was just the same at school. It is said that no-one works harder for their money than those who marry for it. Perhaps no-one suffers more from love than those who marry without its reciprocating warmth.

'And your friend?' I crossed my fingers, praying to be told to mind my own business.

Her eyes met mine, and there was a pride in her expression that tore at me. 'I've got to speak about it or I'll burst,' she said. 'And I'd rather tell you than anyone else. You're so much more of a friend than a colleague.'

Oh, thanks, I thought sourly.

Then she said just one word: 'Terry.'

Terry! TERRY!

'I see.' ('Oho' wouldn't have said the half of it.)

'You know,' she went on, 'I've never had a moment's pleasure with George. He's so selfish. Can you believe this? Whenever we make love, once he's finished, he breaks away from me without a word, goes into the bathroom, washes himself and then just comes back and goes to sleep. That's it! That's the whole of it. What do you think it makes me feel like?' Her mouth screwed itself up in disgust, then relaxed, became rapturous. I tried to close my ears, to think about treacle pudding, anything.

'Whereas Terry . . . Oh, John! He's so – so different!'

'You must be easily pleased,' I murmured.

She stared at me and raised her eyebrows.

'Try telling that to George!' Her laugh grated. It managed to be both coarse and scornful.

I didn't want to know this. I wanted to keep my illusions intact, poor innocent day-dreamer that I was.

Terry! With this beautiful creature! And I knew, which she didn't, that Terry was sexually impartial as to gender. His antics with the younger Mayfair porters were no great secret. It just wasn't interesting, so I had never thought of discussing it with her or, indeed, anyone else. So there I was, boiling with rage and jealousy and with no room for manoeuvre. I had to hide it.

'Are you really so shocked?' Her voice, always soft, had shrunk to a tiny murmur. Another trickle of tears was tracing its way past her quivering mouth – the mouth that I longed to kiss. I wiped them away with my repossessed handkerchief.

'No,' I said. 'Of course I'm not. But I'm sorry for you. So very sorry.'

'And poor Terry,' she said. 'It's *so* hard on him, seeing me going back to George. I keep telling him that I sleep in a separate bed, that I won't let George near me, but he tortures himself.'

'And is that true?' I asked.

'Oh, no,' she said. 'I have to think of the children. George would be unbearable if I didn't keep him satisfied. But Terry believes me. I've learned to be very convincing.'

With both of them? I poured myself some more claret. A pint of whisky was what I really needed.

'What are you going to do?' I asked.

'Carry on as best I can.'

'Does George know?'

'Yes, I'm afraid he does. He pretends not to mind but he does, poor man.'

'How did he find out?'

'He kept asking me. And in the end I sort of half told him. We've always been totally honest with each other. I couldn't bear the deceit.'

Oh Mary, I thought, have you never heard of the generous lie that conceals the cruelty of the truth?

'How are your children?' Anything to change the subject. She smiled as she thought of them.

'Robin's fine. He goes away to boarding school next year and he's really excited about that. Rosie guesses, I think. She keeps watching George and me, and looking sad. I long to tell her that I do have some happiness.'

'I wouldn't do that.'

'Oh, but I think that she'd be pleased. Pleased for Terry and me.'

'I wouldn't bank on it,' I murmured. 'Children are very self-centred. And quite right too.'

Her fingers began to drum, and a trace of colour appeared. 'As you haven't got any,' she said sharply, 'you can't begin to understand.'

It was a fair point, and the treacle pudding brought the conversation to a temporary halt.

'Aren't you hungry?' she asked between mouthfuls.

'I'm trying to cut down,' I said.

'Yes,' she said, eyeing me up and down. 'It might be wise.'

I shrugged. I wanted to get away from Terry, from the Three Goats, even from Mary. There was no point now in discussing her prospective job, since clearly it hinged on her emotional decisions, and we drove back to the office in opaque silence.

CHAPTER TEN

Late that afternoon the telephone rang again.

'Yes?'

'Will you accept a transfer charge call,' asked a metallic female voice, 'from a Cambridge call box?'

'Yes, I will.' This is absolutely typical, I may say. The richer the client, the more likely they are not to carry coins.

'Mr G-Griffin?' A hesitant voice, one that I had been hoping to hear.

'Professor Spencer?'

'Yes. How did you g-guess?'

'I was very, very sorry to hear about your mother. She was always extremely kind to me.'

'Thank you,' he said. 'It has been an awful shock. Worse than I expected.'

'Does your sister know?' I asked.

'Yes, but she's not coming back for the funeral. She has family problems out there.' He sounded bemused, alone.

I waited.

'We, that is I, would like you to handle the sale,' he said slowly, searching for each word.

'Naturally,' I replied, 'I would be very happy to do so. Not least because I know the house and its contents so well.'

'How would you approach it?'

'You would certainly get the best price from a house sale on the premises,' I said.

'Oh, dear,' he said. 'Is that absolutely necessary? I had hoped for a general dispersal through your private sales.'

'The difference will be several hundred thousand,' I

said. 'At least. Such an important house collection hasn't been on the market for at least two years. There will be considerable interest. As a matter of fact,' I added with native cunning, 'I believe your mother would rather have enjoyed a sale *in situ* – like that very funny jamboree last year.' I was thinking up my next argument, but he didn't take long to agree.

'I believe you're right.' A pause. 'Yes!' he said. 'Yes, let's do it. What do you want from me?'

'Just a letter confirming your instructions.'

'Have I g-got your address?'

'Sixteen High Street, Berington,' I told him. 'Leave the rest to us.'

'Thank you,' he said, and then again: 'It's been an awful shock.'

My next call was to Ginger Corbett. He's our country house sale supremo, the spider at the centre of an intricate web. We may make our basic living through valuation and middle-range sales, but our publicity, essential for attracting new clients, comes from the mega-buck Impressionist sales and from that magnet to everyone's nostalgia and greed, the sale of the contents of a grand country house. It's got something for every-one: malicious interest for the locals, mementoes for friends, grand associations for the small buyer, reliable provenance for the bigger fish, but, above all, there is the chance to uncover a forgotten masterpiece. Every expert believes that he has a chance in the bran tub – some neglected object, disguised by grime, which will make his fortune and his reputation.

'Did you hear about David? He bought an early Stubbs at Dorset Towers. Merrywethers had catalogued it as "School of Ward". The Dorsets are suing, but David's sitting pretty.'

This, of course, cuts both ways. The next house may go to one of our competitors, until they make a howler. No-one *means* to, but it does stimulate the bidders next time round.

'Ginger?'

'Johnny!' I hate being called Johnny. I don't know why. Some echo from the forgotten past?

'I've got a good one for you,' I said, anticipating his delight. Prematurely.

'Have you spoken to Terry?' was his cautious response.

'Terry?' I said. 'Why should I speak to Terry?' The man was beginning to haunt me.

'Oh.' He sounded confused. 'I thought all country house sales had to be cleared through Terry's office.'

'That's news to me. Just get weaving and I'll deal with Terry.' The whole company was at risk of going down the spout and we were being given extra bureaucracy!

There was a pause. 'If you say so,' he said, with audible reluctance.

Something is going to have to be done about Terry, I thought. 'The house is called Trent Hall. Mrs Spencer was an old friend of mine. It's a good example of late Carolean with a touch of the William Kents. We'll need the full team.'

'Any cars?' (His obsession.)

'Could be. There's certainly a carriage.'

'Give me a quick rundown.'

'Paintings range from Murillo up to early twentieth-century portraits – you know, Boldini, Augustus John. Some good silver, mainly English furniture but one or two Dutch pieces. Good Rockingham and Meissen. *Very* good watercolours. We'll need Dr Rheinhardt to look at the medieval books and Basil for the porcelain.'

'Basil's gone.'

'Already?' I was shocked.

'Yes, he walked out yesterday. He rang me to say goodbye.'

'But this is madness! It's his speciality.'

'They say you've been sitting on his replacement.'

'That's rubbish.'

'Well,' he said. 'You know Terry.' Yes, I thought. I do.

'Any guns, or armour?' he asked.

'Not that I've noticed.'

'Two days?'

We can sell roughly 600 a day starting at ten thirty a.m.

'No, indeed,' I said. 'Three, even four unless we ship some of the specialist stuff south. There's some jewellery which might go better in Geneva.'

'Cor!' he said. 'You do know the house well. I'll start ringing round. But mind you clear me with Terry. I don't want my exit visa too.'

I slammed down the receiver.

'Hi!' Mary had opened the door and was standing smiling at me. 'Can I have tomorrow off?' she asked.

'Yes,' I said. 'I'm sure you can. Where are you going?'

'Terry's taking me to meet the new Duke of Bridgwater. You know, the heir. Somewhere in Sussex.'

'That'll be fun. I wonder what sort of food they serve in lunatic asylums.'

'Oh, no!' she said. 'We're taking him out to a restaurant.'

'Good luck,' I said, disliking the 'we' and not knowing how to disguise the fact. I could feel my face taking an independent line in expressions. She stared at me then walked out, closing the door softly.

I rang the London office. 'Mr Burton, please.'

There was a click. 'Mr Burton's office.' A voice I didn't know, a new secretary, perhaps.

'Is he in?'

'Who may I say is calling?'

'John Griffin.'

There was a long pause.

'I'm afraid Mr Burton is in a meeting. Do you want to call back later?'

'Perhaps he might call me?' I suggested.

'Just as you like,' she said sweetly, and the line went dead.

I sat and meditated. Finally the call came.

'Johnny!'

'Terry.'

'What can I do for you?'

'Nothing, but I'm setting up a major country house sale and—'

'Not so fast,' he interrupted. 'You're doing what?'

'Setting up a major country house sale,' I repeated, slowly, for the brain-dead.

'Not your province, old boy,' he said. 'Don't you read the inter-office memos any more?'

'No,' I said. 'They're not intended for main-board directors.'

'Oo-oh?' he said. 'Main-board directors are too grand to read, are they?'

'Terry,' I said, 'I'm sure you do a great job. But you are not, as yet, chairman. Country house sales in this area are my province, not—'

He had hung up.

I put the receiver down slowly, gazing bleakly at the stormy weather in Piper's watercolour opposite.

CHAPTER ELEVEN

A week later I met Professor Spencer off the Cambridge train. Berington Central Station is an engaging essay in Bates Motel Gothic, all colonial clapboard and staring black windows under steep tiled French roofs set with spikes and gingerbread. The doors creak, and the timbers glower. I love it. It was one of those bright October days when the sun seems specially blinding, and the leaves drift across the paths in their bright decaying colours. There was the delicious scent of an autumn bonfire, with pale wisps of fragrant smoke, the fugitives that warn of winter's approach.

'John G-Griffin!' the professor said, shaking my hand warmly. 'I haven't seen you for years.' He was a tall, spindly man, with rimless spectacles and a rather feminine gentleness in his movements. His thin, yellowish face was settled into a grave smile, carefully thought out, perhaps, as comprehending both our renewed acquaintance and its doleful cause.

'How are you, Professor?'

'Oh, Bernard, please.'

'Very well,' I smiled. I'd forgotten, as one does, but Bernard seemed entirely appropriate.

We drove peacefully through the marshes and then up into the little hills where Trent Hall, foursquare and defiant, stood in its own valley with the estate village nestling up against the park walls, and a fine crocketed church spire poking out of the woods on its left.

Smoke was curling up from one of its chimneys and it seemed both welcoming and alive, with its crisp white window frames and warm weathered brick. Just selling the Murillo would deal with the estate duty. I had spent two hours on the telephone with the local solicitors, establishing the background facts on finance. Perhaps they should have been more discreet, but Jim Plunkett, a garrulous old friend of my father's, hadn't been able to resist a chance to gossip. Mrs Spencer had, as I would have foreseen, been meticulous in her arrangements for her own passing. The estate had for years been in the hands of London solicitors as trustees, while she paid a market rent out of her substantial portfolio of shares, including, to my surprise, a major interest in Gallico, the West End picture dealers. As we drove down the village street, admiring the perfectly preserved Georgian façades with their orderly gardens and then turning in to the swaggering pillared gates, I couldn't help reflecting that this sale, so profitable to us, so unnecessary for my passenger, was another deliberate step away from sylvan England towards the New Age of the balance sheet. I wanted to ask him to reconsider, to keep this idyllic world intact. But I didn't. Idylls are for those who don't have to earn their living.

As we reached the front, a door opened and Horrod, the butler, squat and beaming, came ponderously down the steps to greet us.

'Good morning, Mr Bernard.'

'Hello, Horrod. All well?'

'Yes, thank you, sir. Good morning, Mr Griffin.'

He came here, I believe, after the war. Indeed I think he was old Major Spencer's batman. If so, he must have been very young then, or older than he looks now.

The hall was misty with smoke from a vast fire hissing quietly to itself in the hearth and all around us yellowed portraits of Spencers past provided the unmistakable evidence of an imperfect chimney.

'What time would you like to lunch?' Horrod asked my client as we stood for a moment.

'One o'clock, I should think,' the professor replied. 'What time is it now?'

'Midday, sir. Mrs Farmar is very anxious to see you when it's convenient.'

I left them to it, because I had much to do. Trent Hall was built by Sir Orlando Spencer in 1688. Some have claimed to trace the spectral hand of Sir Roger Pratt in its design, but as William Talman was working in the neighbourhood for the Beringtons he is more generally given the credit for its tall proportions and dignified façades. Like most houses of that date, it has a central hall leading, through gilded doors enhanced in the next century by pillars and a pediment, to a double-height saloon, the ceiling gaily painted in the Italian style with a classical scene of delicate depravity. To left and right, divided by staircases, lay four sets of apartments for Sir Orlando, his wife and the grander guests. Over the years, however, these rooms had been commandeered for communal use. The family had prospered in the eighteenth century. A prudent marriage to the heiress of a Barbadian sugar king had brought a larger estate in Oxfordshire followed by an earldom. The Regency earl had harboured strong suspicions of his wife's familiarity with their future sovereign. These suspicions hardened into certainty when he woke one morning to find himself Marquis of Oxfordshire.

It was Trent Hall's good fortune that his son, notable for his coarse red features and considerable girth, chose to rebuild on the other estate. The pleasant manor house outside Banbury was torn down and a succession of architects collaborated in producing a Jacobethan extravagance now the headquarters of an international computer company. The second marquis was also the last. With no direct heir, the Oxfordshire estates were quietly sold and a distant descendant of old Sir Orlando inherited Trent Hall, untouched by the new money but still supported by its ancient lands. Disdaining Mr Gladstone's offer of a new barony, he settled back into the comfortable obscurity of rural life. He was Bernard Spencer's great-grandfather.

My first task was to go through the rooms, noting

the rough number of lots per specialist. The attic and basement were as yet unexplored when Horrod came to find me at five o'clock to say that tea was available in the boudoir.

'You must be very sad to see the place being sold,' I said.

'Yes,' he said, 'and no.' With his bald dome of a head set with grizzled curls, he looked like a Roman Emperor without the laurel leaves. He had a large bent nose, and his eyes twinkled with a mischievous glee completely at odds with his ponderous walk.

'Really?' I was confused.

'Yes. I'm sorry that Mr Bernard doesn't want to continue here. It's a lovely house and we hoped he would settle. This house needs children. We all do.'

I nodded non-committally.

'But then again,' he said, 'no, I shan't be sorry to retire. The major left Mrs Horrod and me very well provided for. Of course we stayed on for Mrs Spencer, as we would have done for Mr Bernard, but we bought our little house in Torquay when the major died. So now we can retire there.'

'Torquay's lovely,' I said encouragingly.

'Do you know it well, sir?'

'Not terribly,' I replied. I'd never been there in my life. 'But I always think of it as nice and warm with lots of flowers.'

'Yes,' he said. 'We're on the Welbeck Road if you know it, just past the Co-op.'

We were slowly making our way down the east stairs when I stopped abruptly. 'You carry on,' I said. 'I just want to check something.' We had walked past a large bronze bust. An old panama hat was tilted irreverently on its head, and a vase of dying roses partly obscured it. And yet. I moved the vase, itself a nice piece of Chelsea porcelain, and took off the hat. The face was Olympian in its demeanour, but there was something in the modelling, something about the breastplate that rang a bell. I had already noted it down but now I put an asterisk against it with the initials P.Z. – for Pico Zust, a Swiss medievalist with a shattering laugh who freelanced in the recherché.

If my immediate idea were to be right, this would be the centrepiece of the sale.

'Tea?'

Bernard was sitting in front of a gleaming tray of silver kettles. He looked uncannily like his mother. Clap on a grey wig, and she'd be there.

'Yes, please,' I said, picking up a tiny sandwich oozing with anchovy paste.

'Help yourself to milk and sugar.'

I did.

'You must wonder why I'm selling,' he said after a while.

'Yes,' I said. 'It must be rather a wrench.'

His face was bent over the water jug, flickering in the light of the little blue paraffin flame. 'What you see is a fine house full of beautiful objects,' he said.

I nodded, my mouth full of sandwich.

'What I see—' He looked up, and there was a new tense expression. 'What I see is room after room of loneliness, a building bursting apart with melancholy memories. How do you remember my mother?'

'She was charming to me,' I said. 'Very kind, very thoughtful.'

'Oh, yes,' in a bitter tone, 'she was always charming. To us as well as to you, to her g-guests, to our friends. In public. In private. She never varied. Nor did my father. To them I think we *were* g-guests. Two more to be charmed, to be made comfortable. But there was no love. No caring. Do you know what I believe is the g-greatest g-gift you can give?'

I shook my head.

'Time,' he said, and nodded energetically, spilling his tea as he did. 'Time. It doesn't matter how many presents you g-give a child, it's your time that counts. Not this modern concept of "quality-time".' There was a magnificent sneer in his voice. 'But ordinary time, time to stimulate confidences, time to spend on quiet companionship. Wait till you reach the attics. You'll find our parents g-gave us everything but time.' He poured himself some more tea, slopping the milk in the saucer. 'It's no coincidence my sister lives in Australia. She deliberately chose the furthest place to g-go, to g-get away from all this.' His emphatic gesture took in the fragile furniture, crowded with figurines, the little gold mirrors and the thick chintzy sofas piled with cushions. It was a supremely feminine room, bright and warm and pretty. You'd have thought that no-one would have felt excluded from its seductive softness.

'Won't you be keeping anything back?' I asked quietly. My own childhood had been such fun that it was hard to judge what he was saying other than as a report from an unknown country.

'Yes,' he said, laughing. 'I'll keep the furniture in Zellie's room. She was packed off to the attic as well.'

I remembered Zellie, a frail little woman with a French accent and an alarming squint who used to appear at occasional meals.

'She looked after me,' Bernard explained, 'after Nanny Fisk died.'

I got the impression this had been an improvement.

'I'll never forget Zellie,' he said. 'Never.'

For a moment I thought he was going to break down. Poor man. And yet also rich. Very rich indeed if we did a proper job for him.

'G-God, how I hate this house!' he said, standing up suddenly. 'I'm g-going back to Cambridge. Can you drop me at the station?'

'Of course. I've got to go to London tomorrow. May I come back next week to continue?'

'Yes, yes,' he said. 'Talk to Horrod. He's in charge now.'

'So you'll be selling the house as well?'

Yes, John Griffin never sleeps.

'Eh?' His eyes were far away. No doubt he was rocking in Zellie's lap.

'The estate? Will you be selling it?'

91

'Yes,' he said. 'I was hoping that you . . .?'

I smiled reassuringly. 'We can handle all that for you.' Seven thousand acres, or so I believed. Not even Terry Burton could have given birth to Merrywethers Estate Agency, all of two minutes old, with such lack of fuss. 'No problem.'

CHAPTER TWELVE

I set off towards London and rang the chairman from the car.

'John?'

'Yes. Sorry to bother you but I need your help.'

'Indeed?' His voice was cold.

'You may have heard that Trent Hall has come to us.'

'Terry and I want to discuss that with you.'

Meaning Terry.

'Well, before you do I should like you to hear about it from me.'

'I'm afraid I haven't time for office squabbles now. I'm dining with the Prime Minister,' he said, managing to sound hunted and grand both at the same time.

'Can we meet tonight?' I made myself sound determined.

'*Tonight?*'

'There's a lot at stake.'

'Good God! What's happened to office hours?'

'I wouldn't ask if it wasn't important.'

'Oh, all right,' he snapped. 'What's your club?'

'Blunts'.'

'I'll meet you there at eleven thirty.'

When I went in past the porter's lodge, Hope didn't even look up from his newspaper. I shrugged my shoulders. His adoration of my wife was beyond me. Too bad. Hall porters are the best informed people in the world. They have nothing to do except listen to gossip.

'Come here and have a drink.' It was Charlie McGregor and he sounded drunk.

I sat down near the bar beside him. He poured me a glass of champagne from a nearly empty bottle.

'I suppose you've tied up Trent Hall?'

So he's not that drunk, I thought. I smiled cautiously. 'We may be handling the sale.'

'Not if Gallico's have anything to do with it.' He started laughing. 'I probably shouldn't tell you this, but old Gallico took the first flight today to Sydney. The Spencers have a forty per cent investment in his business. He reckons the daughter – what's she called? Millicent – will spot a good deal when she sees one, or her husband will.'

'How do you know this?'

'Ah!' he said. 'It's Rupert Englefield's idea. He's got a down on you, that's for certain. That's how we picked it up.'

'Meaning what?'

'Meaning just that and nothing more.'

This auction business isn't what it was. I drank the champagne. It was still cold. He must have drunk most of the bottle in the last ten minutes.

'So how are you, Charlie?'

'Bloody awful,' he said.

'What's up?'

He gazed at me blearily for a long time. 'How do you keep so cheerful?' he asked unexpectedly.

'Me? Cheerful?' Frankly, it hadn't occurred to me.

'Yes, you. You're always so bloody buoyant. I can't think why.'

'Hello-o, gentlemen both!' It was Iain, the steward, bustling through the door with a freshly filled coal scuttle for the fire. 'Can I get you another bottle, Mr Charles?' He smiled with delighted complicity. He's a nice man, who genuinely enjoys seeing people taking pleasure in their eating and drinking. Given this generous impulse, his job is ideal for him. He can minister to those appetites which he evidently shares. And in an all-male club, he does not have to witness the outward and visible signs of those other appetites that, by nature, he does not share.

We were well into a battle of backgammon when the chairman breezed in.

'Hello, Mr Alan, sir.' Iain came rushing up to take the chairman's overcoat. 'Been dining at Number Ten, have we?'

'Thank you, Iain,' said my imperturbable employer. 'I won't ask how you know.' He turned a chilly eye on to his country employee. 'Can we talk somewhere quiet?'

'Do you know Charles McGregor?' I asked, as Charlie made some token attempt to look as if he might be about to stand up.

'Yes, indeed,' breathed the chairman, with a grisly false bonhomie. 'Yes, *indeed*.'

I took him upstairs to the committee room, a narrow lobby hung with cartoons of past members.

'Fraternizing with the enemy?' he enquired, raising one eyebrow.

'Charlie's an old friend,' I said. 'And it's good to keep in touch.'

'In case you need a bolthole?'

'Alan,' I said, and I can't pretend I've ever felt easy addressing this much older and alarmingly charismatic man by his Christian name, 'with you and Terry sniping at me, I need all the alternatives I can find.'

He subsided with a groan into an armchair. 'I've drunk far too much port,' he said. 'I knew it was a mistake. So' – turning to face me – 'what's so important?'

Where to start?

'I want to leave aside the question of Terry's attempts to hijack country house sales. It's obviously absurd, doesn't add anything tangible to his prestige or self-esteem, and simply clogs up a system that works well as it is—'

'I thought you said you wanted to leave it aside,' cut in the chairman, smiling at last, one hand massaging his temple.

'Yes. Because it is a silly diversion from the real issues.'

'Which are?'

'The art market is in a state of hypertension. It could go any way. There are six firms battling it out for a market

95

that can only sustain three, and the fighting is getting dirtier. I've found I can live with that, up to a point. But you have got to call a truce on civil war within Merrywethers. To survive as a front player, we've got to get the Bridgwater sale, and we've got to build on our existing sales base as well. I've got this house sale,' (he raised his eyebrows) 'Trent Hall, the Spencers' house, and it's got seriously good stuff, including something really important unless I'm very wrong. The heir wants to sell the whole thing. Eight years ago that was seven thousand acres. It probably still is. I told him we would handle that.'

The chairman started to protest, so I held up one imperative hand to halt him. I had been mentally reviewing the possibilities all day.

'Wait. Wait till I explain. We set up an estates division, based in London; use Lord Darlington's room, for example. All you need is a manager and a secretary. Half the agents in London are working on reduced wages. I could get you a good man by lunchtime tomorrow. So could Terry, or anyone else. It's a buyers' market. And there is an almost immediate half-million pounds in commission to clear up the cash flow within three months.'

'Seven thousand acres!' he said. 'Who's going to buy that?'

'How about the Bridgwater Trustees?' I suggested with a grin. 'They'll have the cash and they want a smaller house for the dowager duchess. Keep it in the family.'

'Yes,' he said. 'Ye-es. That's rather a neat idea. For the dowager.'

'But you have *got* to neutralize Terry,' I said firmly.

He stood up. 'Don't come down with me. I'll think it over.' And with that he left.

When I went down, Charlie was dozing by the fire.

'Good night, ol'boy.' He raised a languid hand.

'Good night.'

'Good night, sir.'

'Good night, Iain.'

96

Hope was studying his paper as I passed the lodge. 'Good night, Hope.'

He gave a sort of wheezing grunt. I was too excited with my own thoughts to care. There was no denying that having Terry on my back was a vitalizing tonic.

CHAPTER THIRTEEN

I had set my alarm for seven to meet Hans off the Rotterdam plane. I had a quick bath before driving to Heathrow. As it happened, his flight landed early so I found his conspicuously tall figure pacing anxiously up and down the terminal lounge.

'My dear Hans.'

'John Griffin. This is a surprising trip.' We shook hands. 'We will make some enemies if this succeeds.'

We both laughed. Ours is a world where enemies are far from rare.

'How is Barbara?' he asked, as we dipped under the Hatfield underpass and accelerated into the Cambridge-shire fens.

'We're no longer together.'

'I am sorry for that,' he said. 'She was a pretty girl.'

'She still is,' I said defensively.

'Too good for you, perhaps,' he said.

'That's what they all say.' I thought of old Hope, sitting angry and disappointed in his glass cabinet at the club like a beetle in an entomological display. 'And Lilian?' I added, deciding to strike back.

'Too good for me!' He was positively chortling. 'Oh, so much too good for me!'

Passenham is a little village thirty miles south of Berington. We turned into the manor drive at exactly a quarter to one. Colonel Chaucer was standing on a circle of lawn in front of the rambling stone house, poking at something in the grass with his walking stick. He had a brick-red face with one of those moustaches which grow out horizontally in stiff white bristles of superb discipline.

'Voles!' he said as we walked over from the car. 'God damn them. They're impossible to kill.'

'This is Dr Grottingen,' I said. 'Colonel Chaucer.'

'How do you do, Colonel.'

'How do you do, young man.'

Hans beamed. He's at least fifty, but with the seamless good looks of a man insulated from the world's drearier cares.

'Have you come to see my Lolita?' the colonel continued.

'Your Lolita?' We must have both looked uncertain, because the old man shouted with laughter.

'Yes. The little hussy! I've always called her that. My old mum hated her. The little witch! Come and see.'

He took Hans by the arm and propelled him through the low dingy hall and past a stuffed bear into a dark room overflowing with papers. On the desk, on the chairs, on the sofa, all over the floor, mounds and mounds of papers were spread willy-nilly, at all angles, a picture of total confusion.

'This is my filing cabinet,' he explained breezily. 'Now what do you think of her, eh?'

'Good God!' I said. I'd heard the gossip, but this was my first visit to the house.

Over the fireplace hung the portrait of a beautiful girl. Painted in pastel, it had a luminous softness which contrasted with her brazen look of coquetry. She was begging for attention, promising impossible delight. Her lips were half open with just the hint of a pink-tipped tongue, her eyes were wide and taunting and her expression daring but afraid. One hand hovered at the knot securing her bodice.

'O-o-oh!' sighed Hans. 'It is. It is the Unknown One.' He sat down.

'The Unknown One?' I asked, puzzled by the expression on his face.

'Yes. I knew about her, but I only surmised that he had painted her. I knew about this picture, of course. But I never dreamt . . .'

'You like her, eh?' The colonel was simply thrilled by our reactions. 'Hot stuff. That's what my grandfather used to say. He bought her in Paris in the 'nineties.'

We gazed and gazed.

'All right, all right!' the colonel said. 'Now what about a drink?' There was a bottle and some glasses on a small card table. 'Gin do?'

There didn't seem to be much choice.

'No ice, I'm afraid,' he added. 'Fridge on the blink. But I've got bitters, or there's some tonic water in the kitchen.'

'Tonic for me,' I said.

'And the good doctor?'

But Hans was transfixed by the picture. He had gone up to it and was carefully examining it through a small lens.

'He doesn't drink,' I said.

'All the more for us,' said our host gaily, sloshing gin into two tumblers. 'Wait while I get your tonic water,' and he hurried off into the back of the house.

'John, my friend,' said Hans, 'this is a revelation. She was his great love. It's always been known that she existed. A single letter survives. He tried to commit suicide because of her. And you can see why!'

I stared at that uncapturable woman, the everlasting fugitive. What had life brought her? What was *her* end?

'Have you never seen a reproduction?' I asked.

'Never. I believe the Chaucers always refused. Certainly they have never lent her. Pico Zust saw her twenty years ago . . . to think he never realized what he was seeing! That *dummkopf*.'

'Do you want her?'

He turned to me, his eyes cloudy. 'Want her?' he whispered. 'I would give half my Rembrandts for this creature.'

'Only half?' I said laughing.

'All right! All but the Night Watch!'

'I will talk to our host. I doubt if he has room. But what in cash?'

He thought. There was a crash from outside followed by an explosion of sound.

'Damn and blast you, you silly little fool!' the colonel was shouting at someone. 'Why can't you keep out of my way?'

A red and white spaniel scampered into the room, its eyes dancing; then Colonel Chaucer followed, wiping his hands on his corduroy trousers, and the dog slunk into a corner beyond the fireplace, watching him with a mournful expression.

'All right, damn you,' he said. 'I'm sorry I shouted.' He put out a hand. The dog remained crouched and wary. 'I've said I'm sorry, damn you!' he bellowed and immediately the dog leapt up, rushed over to him and rolled on its back. 'There, there,' he said as he rubbed the dog's fluffy stomach. 'You silly bitch. You know I didn't mean it.'

There was the sound of someone sweeping up glass outside.

'I'm afraid it will have to be pink gin for you, Griffin,' he said. 'That was our last bottle of tonic.'

'That'll be fine,' I said.

'So. Isn't she a honey?' The colonel turned to Hans.

'Yes, yes,' he said, still recovering from the scene. 'A most handsome dog.'

'No, no, my dear fellow. Not Maisie, her – Lolita.' He pointed at the languorous beauty who had been sulking in her frame while attention was being diverted by Maisie the spaniel.

'Oh,' said Hans. 'I am so glad I came on my friend here's advice. I am so grateful to you for allowing this. We have nothing to compare with this.'

Aaargh!

I saw the colonel's eyes swivelling between us. 'Griffin's advice? We? Who's we?' He put down his drink with a distinct thud. 'I thought you were doing a thesis on Tischbein.'

'Oh, but I am,' smiled Hans, master of so many occasions. He slipped his hand around the colonel's

101

arm, risking grievous bodily harm. 'Come over here, my dear sir.' Against all odds, the colonel allowed himself to be led over like a lamb. 'Look at this delicacy of touch, this passionate craftsmanship.' The colonel took out a pair of half-moon spectacles and put them on carefully. Then he leant forward until his moustache nearly touched the picture.

'Hrrmph!' he said. And then a lovely smile slowly softened his face, and all the craters of its extended buffeting by the elements seemed seamlessly wiped away. For a moment, as if by a trick, I had the illusion that I was looking at a teenage boy.

'My word,' he said. 'You're right. It is fine work. But what a honey!' He moved away, taking off his spectacles and replacing them in a metal case which snapped shut with the finality of a mousetrap. 'And who do you say she is?'

'The Unknown One,' sighed Hans. 'They spent just one night together and he never saw her again. But again and again he refers to her, sometimes in his portraiture, sometimes in his conversation. Titi Amerongen kept a diary of the period. She was his confidante. I know it is. It is she.'

And he sat down with his head in his hands. The colonel coughed, and turned away uncomfortably. 'Do you want to – er – wash your hands, Griffin?' he said gruffly.

We left Hans alone with his emotion.

'Typical Dutchman,' whispered the colonel. 'Saw a lot of them after Arnhem. Terrific aesthetes!'

'What a wonderful view,' I said. We had crossed to the other side of the house and through a glass door I could see that the land dropped steeply away down to a river, half hidden in the trees but glinting in the sunshine. Beyond a round hill rose, crowned by a church with symmetrical steeper hills beyond it, wooded and glazed by the blue of the distance.

'That's not a view,' he said. 'That's someone else's land. Here. Here's the gents.'

I was still looking out across the little valley. 'I've

rather lost track of my bearings. What are we looking at?'

'That's the church at Stoke Spencer. Lovely piece of Saxon walling, you know.'

'Good heavens!' I said. 'Does the Trent Hall estate come down this far?'

'Yes,' he said. 'Look at this map.' There was a yellow parchment hanging in the cloakroom. 'Here's Passenham,' he said. 'Our land runs down to the river. We had some farms there.' He pointed to an area shaded in green. 'But my grandfather sold them to Osric Spencer. Here's Trent Hall. Their land has always been stretched out because they've got the Beringtons on one side and the Castletons on the other. Old Rupert Oxfordshire tried to plant an avenue right across the county. He bought up all sorts of bits of land to do it' – he laughed loudly – 'but we stopped the bugger.' He waved his hand towards two identical doors. 'Use the one on the left, the other one's had it.'

Lunch passed off without incident. It seemed that the colonel's wife had died some years ago. His only son was the agent of a big estate in Derbyshire, for there wasn't enough to occupy him on what was left of the Passenham estate, a home farm with a few dairy cows and some small let farms round the village. There were two grandsons at Eton.

'I don't know how Gerard can manage it,' muttered the colonel as the creaking housekeeper, trim in her faded black and white starched uniform, carried our plates away, one by one. 'No, you don't, damn you!'

Maisie, who had been watching the plates pass, each with a single chop bone, had stood up and walked towards the door. She stopped dead and turned her face towards him. There was something uncannily authoritative in her look, some undefinable challenge to his command.

'Oh, all right, blast you. Go seek!' Her face lit up and she scampered after the elderly servant, who we could hear grumbling to herself behind the dining room screen.

In the car driving south I had to listen to Hans's monologue on the poverty of his buying power.

'Yes, yes,' I said, 'I know. I sympathize. But do you want that picture?'

'John Griffin,' he said. 'That is *the* picture. I don't want your shiny Bridgwater pictures. I don't want any more Vermeers or Van Goghs. If I never buy another picture, I have to have that one.'

It is like love, this passion that grips collectors, both public and private, in the vice of desire.

'If it went to auction it would fetch many millions.' It was time to soften him up. Stage one: make them think big.

'Many millions?' he gasped. 'The last Tischbein only fetched half a million dollars.'

'Yes,' I said scathingly, 'a little portrait of a mincing schoolmiss. You'd be up against Mishuno Kato on this one.'

'Kato? You think he'd bid?'

'Yes,' I said. 'And he can't *bear* to be defeated. With the Getty and the Louvre, not to mention our own dear National Gallery backed up by the new minister, you'd be lucky to get it under ten million sterling.' *A la guerre comme à la guerre.*

'You're joking.'

'I'm not. You know I'm not.'

'Ten million sterling. Where would I get such a sum?'

'Give us back our Holbeins.'

'*Your* Holbeins!'

'You know what I mean. The Holbeins William of Orange pinched after Queen Mary died.'

'We settled that one in 1712,' he said, looking straight ahead and no longer smiling.

'I know, I know,' I said, patting his knee, 'they weren't worth fighting about then, and they aren't worth getting huffy about now.'

He smiled again. 'Anyway, I don't have control of the

Mauritshuis. Where will I find ten million?'

Now for stage two – show them that they *can* afford it!

'Talk to your minister.' Then I remembered what Isabel had said about someone's uncle leaving a fortune to the Dutch government to spend on art. 'Didn't I hear there was a legacy recently from the old scoundrel who bought up Rotterdam during the war? How much was that?'

He turned and stared at me. 'How did you know about that?' he asked quietly.

I grinned. 'News travels fast on the grapevine. Someone told me it was thirty million guilders. That would be, let me think . . .'

'Oh, yes,' he said stiffly. 'It's very neat. Ten million sterling.'

'There you are,' I said breezily. 'Give me a ring when you've talked it over.' Yet again Isabel's phenomenal accumulation of gossip had proved both accurate and valuable. Someone ought to syndicate her.

I had dropped Hans back at Heathrow after a quick snack on the motorway when my car telephone let out its shrill buzz.

'Yes?'

'Mr Burton for you.' A crisp feminine voice with loads of authority.

'Hello?'

'Johnny!'

'Yes.' I was feeling pretty crisp myself.

'We need to meet. Where are you?'

'Heading north on the M25.'

'You're not coming back to London?'

'No. I'm going home.' In a manner of speaking.

'Where will you be at nine tomorrow morning?'

'Having breakfast in the King's Head, Berington.'

'Good,' he said. 'I'll join you.'

The line went dead before I could protest.

CHAPTER FOURTEEN

Breakfast at the King's Head is an uproarious affair. Both the doors into the kitchen creak – or to be more precise, one creaks, the other groans. Add to this the giggling of the waitresses, two shapely twins with matching bobbed brown hair and huge black-rimmed eyes, and the barking of the proprietor's Jack Russell, and you have a cheerful level of background sound.

'This bacon is especially good.' Terry Burton, his mouth full of breakfast, had turned up at half past eight just as I was having my bath. His tie had a mauve background on which yellow elephants alternated with orange stripes.

'Did you drive all the way up this morning?'

'No. I took the opportunity to stay at the Bell at Aston Clinton,' he said. 'The chairman encourages me to enjoy the occasional outing.'

'Ah.' I attacked an egg. What new assault was he preparing to launch? The left-hand door creaked as one of the twins disappeared into the kitchen for some toast. The right-hand door groaned as she came back with it.

'Thank you.' Terry beamed at her, and she flushed a delicate pink.

'So to what do I owe this pleasure?' I said, speculating on what the chairman could have said to him.

'You mean, why am I here?'

'So to speak.' I waited for the declaration either of a war or a truce.

He pulled his chair closer. The stench of his readily identifiable cologne made me want to sneeze. 'It's Mary.' I was startled. 'Please don't interrupt. She told me she'd talked to you, and I don't want you making a nuisance of yourself.'

I put down my knife and fork. The succulent egg had suddenly cloyed. 'This is none of my business,' I began, but he raised a large silencing hand.

'I mean to keep her, you see.' His eyes were wide and rather crazy. 'She is just what I need.'

I had the feeling he was talking about his career rather than his bed.

'So what's the problem?' I said reluctantly. 'She's a great fan of yours.'

'Oh, yes,' he said with a sudden complacent grin that I didn't take to. 'We're amazingly compatible. It's astounding.'

'Astounding,' I agreed, and he looked up sharply.

'Meaning?'

'Meaning your uninhibited behaviour in and around The Wedge and Whippet,' I said smoothly, waiting for the backlash to this reference to his all-embracing sexuality. It didn't come. He nodded his head.

'Yes. I have been a bit indiscreet in that direction. But no harm done. Of course I had a test,' he added.

'A *test*?' I shouted. 'A blood test? To salve your conscience while you're threatening to spread the plague because of your archaeological approach to other people's drainage!'

He flushed. 'Listen,' he said. 'Your job with this firm hangs by a single thread. Mine is secure. So forget your prissy inhibitions. If you say one word to her about that, I'll have you dismissed within twenty-four hours.'

Just like that. Not even with a smile. The trouble is, I believe he could.

'Anyway, there's no point,' he went on. 'She's coming to live with me in London. She won't be impressed by her dear "friend" showing his jealousy by indulging in nasty innuendo.'

'But what about her children?' I half stood up, silencing the twins in mid-giggles. 'What about her children?' I repeated in a lower voice, leaning towards him.

107

'They'd come too, naturally.'

'I can't believe this.'

'Don't be absurd!' He gave me an impatient glare. 'You're stupider than you look. Older. Slower. But most of all stupider.'

I smiled at this, not because it was funny but because I had felt my mind experiencing the refreshing coolness of accelerating into a new gear. I was suddenly determined to prevent this. I was not going to lose Mary. But to succeed I knew now that I needed to be calm, and not only for now but for months to come. Nice John Griffin had just died; long live his alter ego, calculating John Griffin.

'Perhaps she doesn't want to go.' I tried not to sound too positive. It was early days to smite him on the chops.

'Of course she does!' he snapped. 'Very much. She wants to very much. She's said so.'

'So she's worried about the children?' I suggested with a cosy smile, watching that arrogant face showing the first real signs of uncertainty. I decided to cast myself as the friendly stooge, everyone's favourite confidant.

'Perhaps,' he said, 'but they'd be fine. It's better to get it over with now, before they can think for themselves.'

I considered the point. 'Yes,' I said. 'I think that is right. What are they now?'

'Rosie's six and Robin's eight.' He said it mechanically, like an enforced memory test. He raised his voice. 'Could we have some more coffee?' One of the twins scurried over, smiling slavishly.

'And tea for me,' I added.

'You've got my message?' he said. 'You understand?'

I shrugged my shoulders.

'She trusts you,' he said.

'Perhaps George does too.'

'Don't be ridiculous,' he said. 'That idiotic snob. He's utterly indifferent to anything but his cows.'

I'd often thought the same myself, but faced with Terry I felt a need to defend him.

'I'm not so sure,' I said. 'I just remember him at school. Marriage has changed him.' I took a sip of tea.

'Perhaps it will change me too.' Terry's smile was an open wound with its livid flesh and inner glimpses of undigested bacon.

'I doubt it,' I said.

'You don't like me very much, do you?' he said in a matter-of-fact tone, spearing another sausage.

I shrugged again. What was the point?

'Is it just my background or because you'd like to be screwing Mary yourself?' He laughed. 'I can certainly recommend her. She knows her way around.'

For me to laugh back, as I did, was a triumph of self-control. Such triumphs one can do without. To have plunged his head in the coffee urn while unravelling his large intestine would have given greater satisfaction. So much for calmness.

'Don't blush,' he said. 'It doesn't suit someone with your complexion. Still, if you don't want to talk about it I quite understand. I expect you're one of those men who like to feel protective towards a woman, carry her coat, that sort of thing. Take my advice, Johnny.' Here he leaned forward across the table, dangerously within range. 'Give them what they really want. And often.'

A pair of corn merchants at a table in the corner had stopped talking and were watching us.

'Now look, Terry,' I said, deciding to take the initiative, and ignoring his mocking grin. 'Actually I am quite sympathetic to your predicament. If I can help you both, I will.' He was watching me suspiciously. As well he might. 'I will even say that I believe that problems such as these are the *real* problems of life, as opposed to the relatively unimportant priorities of one's job.'

He opened his mouth as if to interrupt, then he shook his head. 'You don't understand how we feel about each other.'

Lovers! It's marvellous, isn't it? At the right moment they represent to each other the incarnation of every secret hope, the revelation of so much unlooked-for perfection. The whole world throbs with passion, illuminated by the dazzling golden light of love. And

109

to the rest of us? Two very ordinary human animals, with more or less of natural grace. Is it their eyes that are rosily deceived, or ours that are shadowed by the dust of disappointment?

'Well,' I said. 'However that may be, I want to talk about the Bridgwater pictures.' He nodded. This was a tack he could relate to. 'But first I want an end to this intra-company sniping. If I get a sale, country house or country kettle, I set it up, with or without Miss Snooty's permission.'

'Miss Snooty?' He looked momentarily puzzled.

'Your new secretary, or should I say personal assistant?' This time I gave him a real beam, crinkling the eyes and showing the teeth.

He raised both hands in a gesture of genial surrender. 'Consider it done.'

'Didn't the chairman say anything about this?' I asked on an impulse.

'The chairman?' He was genuinely surprised.

Thanks, Alan, I thought. Great support.

'Now to those pictures,' I said. 'You saw the new duke?'

'We took him out for tea,' he said. 'I've never seen anyone eat so many scones, and mounds of clotted cream. You'd think they were starving him.'

'What's he like?' I asked curiously.

'Greedy as a pig and mad as a snake,' said Terry, laughing. 'He likes me, though.' Christ!

'But what did he say?'

'Oh, he's quite sane about the pictures. He thinks it's a mega idea that we sell them. He wants to set up a foundation to study corn circles. That's his current obsession.'

'What? Flying saucers?'

'No,' said Terry. 'The Little People. Trampling our crops with many tiny feet. Plays havoc with the gross margins. He's rather into the farm accounts at the moment. He'd spent all morning with the agent from Bridgwater. No corn circles there, of course, *yet*. But it worries him. And he's much more normal. The new pills must be working.'

'I see.'

'Yes, so the sale is definitely on. He wants me to take him the inventory next week to start work on pricing.'

'Good luck,' I said, but this was good news. 'Well done.' Two friendly colleagues enjoying their work together!

'And your list.' He looked up suddenly, sharp and ready to attack. 'Have you dealt with it?'

'Yes and no,' I said. 'I have established contact with Colonel Chaucer, but Mrs Granger was no good at all. She might almost have been expecting me to call.'

'And Lord Tottenham?' Does he never forget anything?

'No. I'm stumped on that one. But it's at the top of my list.'

'I might be able to help.'

This was unexpected. 'Oh?'

'Yes,' he said. 'He rather took me up at Balliol, because I was a friend of his nephew's. He's asked me to shoot in a fortnight. He always asks me to bring a mate. I suppose you do shoot?'

I pleaded guilty.

'Come on, then. Get your diary out.'

I obeyed.

'Thursday the twenty-fourth.'

'Yes.'

'It's up at Tottenham. Do you know it?'

'I've seen photographs. Big castle with turrets north of Chesterfield?'

'That's the one. We get there Wednesday night in time for dinner. Two guns, but they'll provide a loader.' Oh good, I thought. Barbara used to load for me, but I could hardly ask her now.

'So we're all settled. Don't forget what I said. Oh, and thanks for the breakfast.'

He rose, winked at the twins and left. When I came out of the hotel, it was to see the back of his car disappearing round the corner on the London road.

CHAPTER FIFTEEN

'Of course I'm not leaving!' said Mary. 'It's utterly selfish of him even to suggest it.'

She was brushing back her hair with heavy, rhythmic sweeps of her hands and blinking rapidly. I nodded, expressing delighted solidarity, even if I was secretly staggered by this apparent inconsistency in her feelings.

We were sitting in the King's Head, having a quick cup of coffee before setting out to continue the survey of Trent Hall, this time with her to help.

'Doesn't he realize I've got a husband and children to think about? I mean, I ask you!' she said, turning angry eyes towards my hooded ones. 'Does he never think of anyone but himself?'

'Perhaps he thinks,' I felt my way cautiously, hopefully, 'that you actually want to go.'

It hovered on the edge of being a question.

'*Thinks?*' she exclaimed indignantly. 'He'll think anything that suits him! That's the trouble with people who live alone. They become unbearably self-centred.' She gave a great snort and put another sugar lump into her coffee.

'You haven't said you wanted to leave?' It was tentatively put.

'Well, what if I have?' she demanded. 'One can discuss things, can't one, without being crucified? George is no saint, but at least he doesn't whine.' It was awfully hard to imagine Terry whining.

'Terry loves you very much,' I said, against my true wishes.

'Faugh!' she said.

'Faugh?' I laughed. '*No-one* says "faugh" any more.'

'I mean *really*,' she said, ignoring me. 'It's utterly monstrous. How dare he be such a . . . such a *galloping* egotist? It turns my stomach.'

The twin by the coffee urn was trying to pretend not to listen, and failing.

'Come on,' Mary said. 'You've had quite enough coffee for one day. Let's be seeing this house you keep going on about. You're becoming the Trent Hall bore.'

I signed the bill and we set off. We were halfway there when I pulled up on the verge.

'Now what?' Mary was still fussing with angry thoughts of Terry.

'I'm sorry,' I said. 'But I can't drive past the last of the blackberries without a quick expedition.'

'Blackberries!' she said. 'Oh, good!'

We leapt out of the car and fell upon the thorny hedge, with its shining black and maroon fruits. The cobwebs still glistened with dew, and behind the hedge we could hear sheep calling to one another in the pasture.

'Isn't this fun?' I said.

Mary turned to me, her mouth stained with juice. Overwhelmed by a surging desire to kiss her, I moved towards her but managed to turn myself half away in time.

We stood there in silence.

'We'll be late,' she said, and her voice sounded as if from a long way off.

Without looking at her, I walked back to the car, seething with anger at myself. I had betrayed myself, and I felt I had insulted her. Would she think I thought she was available to any casual interest? She could not know how I felt.

Trent Hall was looking as welcoming as before when we pulled up below the steps. I could not imagine it as the bitter place Bernard Spencer had described. Its warm bricks were shining in the sunlight and Horrod, standing in the doorway above us, raised a genial hand in greeting.

'Good morning, madam,' he said when I introduced Mary. 'There's coffee in the library and luncheon will be at one.'

113

'Coffee's very bad for Mr Griffin,' she said, smiling at him. 'But I should love some. You get started,' she turned to me, 'I'll catch you up. Good heavens! Who's that?'

It was a portrait of an old man leering at us from a bath chair.

'Charles Augustus, Fourth Viscount Trent,' I read from the inscription.

'Is it by Hogarth?'

'School of, I think.' We separated. I returned to the bronze bust, though with my head still full of remorse towards Mary. The bust had its hat on again, and a fresh vase of small lilies was in front of it. Clearly life at Trent was not dependent on a Spencer being resident. I moved them back. It was a magnificent piece.

'Giambologna,' said Mary in a hushed voice behind me.

'Yes,' I said, and on an impulse I took her hand, hoping she would see this temporary touch as an inarticulate apology. Her hand was cool and comforting. She held mine firmly and without comment. 'That's the point,' I went on. 'Rudolf wanted him to work in Prague, but he never went there. Or that's what we've all been taught. But that's Rudolf to a T, isn't it?'

'Yes,' she said, feeling the patina with her other hand. 'That's the old brute, large as life. We used to have a copy of the Vienna de Vries of him in the dining room at home. I rather fancied him as a teenager. I think it was this nose.' Her finger ran speculatively down his face.

'Did Rudolf ever visit Florence?' she asked.

'It's not very likely.'

'So how?'

'Yes,' I said. 'How?' If the emperor had never been to Florence, and Giambologna had never been to Vienna, when and how did they meet? And meet they must have, for the proof, solitary but solid, was staring at us with the unmistakable eyes of its sitter, fashioned by the equally unmistakable hand of its creator. It

114

would be interesting to see what Pico Zust, the self-proclaimed Greatest Living Expert, made of it. Temporarily abandoning this historical adventure and letting go of Mary's hand, I led her up to the attics, which we explored like two children. Lumber rooms full of trunks, several servants' bedrooms which had been left neat and shiny with polish, their doors propped open to show that we were expected. Then we came to a long, low room packed with toys, a rocking-horse, a play-pen. At the far end an elaborate model railway was still laid out, but smothered in dust. A dozen trains, in deep green livery, were drawn up in ranks with the name 'Trix' emblazoned on their boiler plates.

An ottoman on being opened proved to be piled high with Dinky cars, every model that I had ever seen, and several examples of each. At the bottom I found an Austin shooting brake, misshapen and half flattened, as if its owner had taken a hammer to it in a fit of uncontrollable rage. In another corner, on a sofa, were lions, leopards, polar bears and a seal, all shapes and sizes, and a doll with its eyes gouged out.

There was a creak outside. Mary jumped.

'It's only me, miss.' An angular woman in a black dress stood in the doorway. 'I'm Mrs Farmar, the housekeeper,' the woman said. 'Mr Horrod said you would want the key to the glory hole.' She held out a massive iron key which Mary took. 'It's this way.'

We followed her down another arched corridor. There was a rusty sound as the key turned and there we were – in Aladdin's cave.

It was a vast low chamber, presumably above the raised ceiling of the saloon. A massive four-poster bed stood in one corner, swathed in dust-sheets. Along one wall were row upon row of pictures, stacked twelve deep and separated by old grey blankets. In the middle of the room stood several buckets, souvenirs of some storm, no doubt, as they were placed haphazardly beneath the cracked and stained ceiling. There was even a bath under one long fissure. A group of wheelchairs communed together to one side.

'Look,' said Mary. 'There's that bath chair.' Indeed it appeared identical to the one in the picture of the fourth viscount downstairs. Bronzes and marble busts were scattered on a dozen tables, and a magnificent French commode.

'There's something for Rodney,' I said. 'He'll love that.'

'But it's not original,' said Mary doubtfully.

'No, but I bet it's from Winckelsman. It's wonderful craftsmanship. And look! Here's the imperial cypher! Probably from the set made for Pierrefonds and never installed.'

'Would that be for the Emperor Napoleon the Third?' asked Mrs Farmar.

'Yes,' I said. 'Exactly.'

'He stayed here,' she said. 'It was the first place he came after he had to flee. There's a lovely picture of his wife downstairs. By Winterhalter. He was a friend of the last marquis, of course.'

I liked the 'of course'.

Mary called out. She had been pulling back some of the pictures and the one she held up was an oval flower painting, its glaze cracked through neglect.

'What is it?'

'It's Bosschaert. Here's the stamp of Peter Stas, and the Antwerp guild too.'

'I can leave you then,' said Mrs Farmar, smiling.

'Absolutely,' I said. 'This is our idea of heaven.'

We lunched in companionable silence, each full of thoughts about the treasures we had found and those yet to be discovered. One of the things I loved most about Mary was that she saw these works of art as exactly that, art, and not as sources of cash. We had never discussed monetary value once. She was not yet infected by Terry's virus, the chilly calculation of income and commission.

'That's not George the Fourth, is it?' she asked, interrupting my reverie.

'Who? Where?'

'Him. There.' She was pointing behind me.

I turned. Over the sideboard hung a long state portrait of a robust man swathed in red robes, his midriff slashed by a broad violet riband.

I laughed. 'No,' I said. 'It must be Rupert Augustus, the second marquis. But his mother was immensely obliging to the Regent, which is why he looks like that.'

'You mean . . .?'

'Well, that, or there is Goethe's Theory: *Wahlvervanschaften*. Elective affinities. That if you sleep with one person while dreaming of another, it is the latter that the child resembles.'

She laughed in a throaty, introspective way. 'I see,' she said. 'I see. It's a *lovely* idea.'

'I'm glad you like it,' I said, concealing a momentary spasm of bitter desire, and returned to the halibut.

When we had finished that evening, I dropped her at her home, a large square Georgian house set back from the handsome farm buildings that occupied her husband's working hours.

'Mummy! Mummy's back!'

Her little daughter came running out, shouting and laughing, but when she saw me, she stopped dead and her joyful face closed up into a sullen scowl.

'Rosie, darling,' said Mary. 'Come and say hello to Mr Griffin.' The child stood obstinately still.

'Hello, Rosie,' I said. 'How's that hamster?'

She muttered something inaudible, then turned and ran back into the house. Following her with my eyes, I noticed a familiar figure in the doorway.

It was George Sykes, deliberately half out of sight.

'Hello, George!' I called.

Reluctantly he came out of the shadows, tall and sturdy, his thick fair hair caked down with perspiration. A quarter of a century had left less of a mark on him than on me. He was still immediately recognizable as the cricket hero of the sixth form.

'Darling,' said Mary, rushing up and hugging him as he

117

waited for her, stiff and ill at ease. 'Have you had a good day?'

'Much the same as usual,' he replied. 'How are you, John?'

'We've had a super day,' Mary said. 'You'll never guess what we found.'

I shot Mary a warning glance. The name Giambologna needed to be kept under wraps at this stage.

'Oh, George wouldn't know the difference between Giambologna and jam tart,' she said gaily. 'Would you, darling?'

She put her hand up against his cheek, but he swung away and walked into the house.

'Robin!' she called. 'Robin!'

George turned on his heel and came back at her. 'It's his music lesson today *and* it's Gina's day off. Perhaps you forgot?'

'Oh, darling, how *awful*,' she said, casting a mock-sorrowful glance at me. 'Did *you* have to take him?'

'Yes,' he said. 'I did.'

'Never mind,' she said. 'I'll go and collect him' – looking at her watch – 'now.'

I waved goodbye and headed back towards Berington. I spent the evening answering the tactful letters from friends and relations, replying to their invitations, commiserations or rebukes arising from my change of address. I must have dozed off because the sound of the telephone gave me a severe shock.

'What? What's that?' I said, seizing the receiver.

'John Griffin?' I knew the voice but couldn't place it.

'Yes,' I said.

'It's George. George Sykes.'

'George! Yes, hello.'

'Can I come and see you?'

'What, now?' It was eleven thirty.

'Yes, now.' He sounded very determined.

'You sound very determined.'

There was a sort of grunt the other end.

'Yes,' I said. 'Do come. I'll make sure the courtyard

door is unlocked. What will you drink? Whisky and soda?' I knew the bar would be closed.

'Brandy'll do me,' he said gruffly.

'Brandy it shall be,' I said to myself, since he had rung off.

I was waiting in the little parlour with a gas fire hissing away when I heard the yard door open, and the tread of nailed boots on the flagstones.

'Come in, come in,' I said. 'It's rather cosy.'

He was dressed as he had been earlier that evening, in muddy cavalry twill trousers, a darned green pullover and a brown tweed jacket with leather patches at the elbows. The only splash of colour was a scarlet silk handkerchief spilling out of his breast pocket. He looked tired and unhappy.

'Like one of these?' I offered him my cigar case and to my delight he extracted a Monte Cristo and pinched off the end. I took one too, lit up and tossed him the matches. I had already procured a half-empty bottle of Hine from the bar and a soda siphon. With the remains of a bottle of Scotch that I kept in my bedroom we were well set.

'What's up?' I said. He wasn't exactly a friend, but we had been at school together and his wife worked with me so it wasn't unreasonable that he should look to me for advice, however little I wanted to give it.

'You and Mary,' he said stonily. 'It's got to stop.'

'Eh?' I was so startled I nearly dropped my cigar.

He raised his voice. 'Do you think I'm a complete fool? I know what's going on.'

'What's—?'

'Oh, come on, John,' he interrupted me. 'I don't particularly blame her. I know I'm rather a dull bird, and she's so intelligent. And headstrong. She's always liked her own way. Of course I see why you both get on. She's always been more your type than mine.'

'But . . .'

'Does Barbara know?'

'Barbara . . .' It obviously wasn't the moment to bring him up to date with the state of my married life.

'It must have put her nose out of joint.' He actually laughed, albeit not very mellifluously.

'George,' I said firmly. 'Hold on one minute. I'm devoted to Mary, she's a wonderful person, but we are not having an affair.'

He smiled, but it was nearer to a sneer. 'Do you think I don't know the signs? Mary coming home with her face glowing and then having a headache if I go near her. Unable to sleep unless alone. Jumping six feet in the air when the telephone rings. Working late for you every Thursday night, and now some Saturdays. Don't be frightened. I'm not going to attack you. But I want you to stop, because of the kids. It's murdering them.' He helped himself to the brandy. A good two inches.

'Have some soda,' I said, shoving the siphon towards him.

'Damn the soda!' he exploded.

I got up and walked around the room, trying to decide what to say. Now I knew what she meant that lunchtime in the pub about half telling him.

'Let's get one thing straight,' I said eventually. 'If Mary is having an affair—'

'She is. I know it.' There was an unexpected calm certainty in the way he said this, the result, no doubt, of many hours of anxious, jealous calculation. How much pain must lie behind that reasoned assertion? I would have liked to share my own grief with him, but instead I had to preserve the party line.

'*If* she is,' I persisted, 'it's not with me. There has never been anything like that between us.'

He looked up, wanting to believe me, already considering other possible candidates. What an irony! How I wished I was indeed guilty as charged.

'Before you pin the blame on Gaskin,' I said, 'reflect that if you were wrong about me, you may have been wrong about Mary.'

'No,' he said. 'When you've been as close as we have, you know. Believe me.'

I did.

'I mind,' he said. 'Of course I mind, though less than I would have expected. But the agony is the kids. Robin's started wetting his bed, Rosie cries at the least little upset. Now the nanny's given in her notice. And Mary doesn't seem to care. Oh yes, she talks about the children. You'd think they were her whole life, but when she's actually with them she's so preoccupied she might as well be asleep. Last week she drove the Volvo slap into the bullpen. She was only going slowly, but the foreman said she looked in a complete trance. Robin was in the back and he had an awful nosebleed. Even then, Mary was more concerned about being late for you.'

Last Thursday I had been away in London. I grunted and drew on my cigar. Much of Mary's uncertainty seemed centred on her children. Resenting her love for Terry, it was just a small step to scoff at her professions of putting them first. If she did that, I might argue, why stray at all? And parents often acquire a disagreeable habit of presenting their children as alibis for their own caprice. But really I knew this to be unjust. She loved her children and I strongly suspected that it was an imperfectly buried sense of guilt which sent her mind scampering this way and that, seeking relief in a decision no sooner made than rescinded.

'Robert Head?' mused George, interrupting my thoughts.

'Oh, *really*!' I said. 'Don't be absurd!'

'Well, she's having it off with someone,' he said grimly.

'Have you talked to her about it?' I asked.

He dropped his eyes and his face drooped.

'No,' he said. 'She's not as easy to talk to as you might think. She's so quick-tempered, so quick off the mark. I don't find it . . . oh, I don't know. We don't talk really. She snaps my head off. I sulk. I have more fun talking to Bert the herdsman than I do to Mary. At least he listens.'

I felt a wave of sympathy for him. His marriage must have seemed the beginning of a perfect life; a beautiful wife, nice children, a comfortable house surrounded by its own countryside. And yet it had turned sour. It would be no consolation to tell him that he was not alone, although Barbara and I had the relief that there were no children to damage.

'Farm flourishing?' I asked by way of a diversion from the gloom into which we had fallen.

'Yes,' he said brightening. 'Berington Dynamite won the championship at Peterborough *and* the Royal. And the barley yields are tremendous. It's all malting, you know. Very high premium. In fact . . .' He caught sight of a stifled yawn. 'I'm sorry, John. It's after one o'clock. I know you've got a busy day tomorrow.'

'Oh?' I was planning a day off to look for a new house.

'Yes, Mary was telling me. Trent Hall and so on. Sounds fascinating.'

'Yes,' I said grimly. 'It's going to be a busy day.'

He rose and, surprisingly, he put out his hand to shake mine. 'Thanks for listening,' he said. 'And sorry about the misunderstanding.'

'Don't mention it,' I replied. 'Just so long as you know.'

'Good night.'

I saw him out of the door and locked and bolted it behind him.

I checked with my diary. It *was* a blank day.

Lucky Terry.

CHAPTER SIXTEEN

I spent the next weekend walking round Berington peering into the windows of the various estate agencies. By lunchtime on Monday I had found a nice little house to let on Castleton Street, just up from St Amedroz church, with a walled garden and a big drawing room. By teatime the formalities were complete and I got back to the office in time for the chairman's summons for an emergency board meeting that evening. I took the train to London and reached our building with five minutes to spare. We settled down at the table, Elizabeth passed the chairman his glasses and he banged his gavel.

'Here we are,' he said fruitily. 'Item one. Basil van Zwanenberg's letter in today's *Telegraph*.' This was news to me.

'You know,' said Lord Darlington, leaning forward, taking off his bifocal spectacles and massaging his nose, 'you know, it reminded me of Potty Caldwell.' As Lord Darlington never usually spoke at meetings, we concentrated on a new departure. 'Potty was an extraordinary man. Indeed,' he said, warming to his subject, 'he didn't look unlike Basil. He was very tall and wore those very loud tweeds you don't see so often nowadays. Anyway, he had a good job in the City, with Penrhyn's, I think it was, or Masterson Accumulated. Whichever. He was married to my cousin Deirdre and they lived out near Sunningdale. Yes, it was definitely with Penrhyn's. He'd been taken on straight from school. Some uncle had suggested it, old Peter Penrhyn liked the look of him and there he was, set up for life. The McEwens were building that railway in the Andes, and Penrhyn's were up to their neck in the finance and everyone still remembered what happened with Barings. I think Lord Revelstoke was a non-executive director, if they had such things in those days. I wonder. Anyway Potty was sent out on a boat to check up on the local procedures – how the money was secured, who calculated the exchange rate, what receipts were issued and by whom. The usual stuff. But, you see, Potty's boat got diverted and put into Barbados. There was some trouble with a couple of Lascars. And who do you suppose was the first person he met on the quay? Deirdre's Aunt Mabel, who lived out there!'

The chairman took off his glasses and laid them patiently on the table in front of him. Lord Darlington paid no attention.

'She'd inherited a fortune,' he went on, 'and had run off with a half-pay major in the Indian Artillery. She'd seen a picture of Barbados and had always wanted to live there. After a few months the half-pay major jumped ship, if you see what I mean, taking most of her jewellery, most of the family stuff anyhow, and quite a wadge of cash. She used to carry it in a money-belt. Big notes tied up with elastic bands and those ribbons you used to get from Marshall and Snellgrove at Christmas. Deirdre's Aunt Mabel was delighted to see Potty since they'd both hunted with the Woodland Pytchley, so he stayed with her for a week, one thing led to another and the next thing Deirdre got was a telegraph asking her to send him his diamond studs and saying he wasn't coming back. He sent the same message to Penrhyn's, not mentioning the studs, of course. So you see he had to buckle down and get a job.'

I risked a glance at the chairman. His face was a study.

'Deirdre's Aunt Mabel didn't want to leave Barbados,' continued Lord Darlington. 'She had a big bungalow in the St James parish, right on the beach with a garden all round it, lots of palms and some rather sickly spruce that she'd had sent by Hilliers to remind her of Strathpeffer. Potty wasn't much good at the sugar trade, so he became a clergyman. I don't think they enquired too closely into his antecedents. I mean, they couldn't have, could they, seeing as how he was still married to Deirdre while living with her aunt, who was, by the by, still married to the half-pay major, who had turned up in San Francisco with a Cuban belly dancer. But he preached a cracking sermon and the natives loved him. He was always making jokes and the point was this: he had a first-class singing voice. Really professional. Not any old sort of hand-me-down amateur stuff. He could hit the right note. So there he was, singing and preaching, living the life of Riley when the war came. Well, of course, that really put the kybosh on things. No more cheques from England, general rallying of the Empire.'

'Ted,' said the chairman.

'Yes?' Lord Darlington didn't like being interrupted.

'Basil van Zwanenberg's letter?'

'What about it?'

'That's what we're here to discuss.'

'I know, Alan,' said Lord Darlington with heavy emphasis. 'I'm trying to explain.'

The chairman gave a wan smile. 'So?'

'So Potty came back, put up at Boodle's and sent his name to the War Office. Immediately all hell broke loose. The papers got hold of it. Deirdre demanded a divorce; the half-pay major, who was now a brigadier in Palestine, had to be recalled; the diocesan board were in really hot water. It was a bad show, I can tell you. You can imagine.' He looked round at each of us.

'Thank you,' said the chairman after a pause. 'Any other comments from anyone?'

I toyed with the idea of trying to tell them the one about the actress and the giraffe but thought better of it.

'I suppose you *have* all seen the letter?' he went on.

We shook our heads.

'Elizabeth.' The chairman's tone was distinctly dangerous. 'Could you photocopy this and distribute it?'

'Right away,' she said and scurried out of the room.

'What happened?' said Ralph to Lord Darlington, nudging me as he did so.

'Ralph!' The chairman's face was getting dark.

'Sorry.'

'Here we are,' said Elizabeth, hobbling back in.

We read the letter.

'Sir,' it said, under the heading 'Declining Standards in the Art Market'.

As one who has spent more than fifty years in the international art market, I should like to draw your readers' attention to the problems arising from the recent explosion in the prices paid for major works of art. The commission generated from these is so great a prize that there is some evidence of a sharp decline in the normally accepted practices adhered to by the reputable auction houses in this field.

In particular, the colossal prize to be won from the rumoured sale of a great ducal collection may be being fought over with manners more reminiscent of pre-war Chicago than modern-day Mayfair. To be constructive, may I, as an old man with a little experience, propose a conference of the parties involved, under an independent chairman, to draw up a code of practice to take us boldly, but honourably, into a new century.

Yours etc. Basil van Zwanenberg.

'He very courteously sent me a copy in the afternoon post,' explained the chairman. 'Which is why I was able to summon you here, John. This is aimed at you, I'm afraid.'

Me?

'At me?' I said, feeling for my cigar case.

The chairman smiled blandly and passed me an ashtray. 'Fighting through Mrs Englefield wasn't exactly the method of a *preux chevalier*.'

What had happened to Terry's five-point plan? I wondered to myself. Terry himself was sitting very quiet at the end, filing his nails.

'Yes, I thought that was a bit below the belt,' added Lord Darlington, examining the wall behind me. 'Not quite the thing, do you see?' he added helpfully.

Ralph Tritton was about to speak when the chairman banged on the table. 'We mustn't bully poor John. He did what he thought was right. We all make minor errors. He has my full support, as always. But what is our response?'

'May I speak, Alan?' This, in the softest of tones, from Terry.

'Yes, Terry, please.'

'Could you pass this to the chairman?' Terry said to Jack Bonas, who was taking notes beside him.

Jack was looking very frail, with odd pink patches showing on his grey skin. He hadn't shaved very carefully.

A crumpled piece of ruled paper was solemnly handed along the line.

The chairman scrutinized it. 'It is by way of being . . . ?' his voice trailed away.

'Signed instructions from Lionel Bridgwater, committing the whole of the Gimpal collection to us for immediate sale.'

'No guarantees?' asked Bonas hoarsely, and broke his pencil. On a big sale like this, we normally guarantee a minimum return and cut our commission. Just getting a major sale does wonders for one's morale, with a matching deterioration in that of our competitors.

'No guarantees,' purred Terry.

'No reductions?' Ralph sounded incredulous.

'No reductions.'

'You mean ten per cent from them, ten from the buyer?' It was almost a gasp from Bonas.

'That's the size of it.'

'My dear boy!' The chairman was beaming. 'This is a triumph!'

'I suppose it *is* legal?' put in Ralph drily.

'Oh, yes,' said Terry. 'Now he's out of St Seraphina's the ownership passes beneficially to him, subject only to his continuing to remain uncertified.'

Ralph raised his eyebrows.

'I have a legal opinion coming in the post from Withers,' Terry went on. 'They've had sight of the

127

original trust deed. I'm just giving you their verbal response.'

The chairman was scribbling away. 'I'll clear this with the PR department, but how's this for a draft?' he said. 'Press release, today's date. "Merrywethers are proud to announce that they will be offering the entire Gimpal collection of Old Masters over the next few months after preliminary examination in New York and Paris. They are aware of the newspaper correspondence initiated by a former employee but see no reason to respond." The pro can flesh it out.'

'First class,' said Terry.

'Hear, hear,' said Lord Darlington.

'That's the stuff to give the troops,' murmured Ralph in my ear.

'What?' said the chairman.

'I agree,' said Ralph. 'Very succinctly put, Chairman.'

'Thank you,' said the chairman, mollified. 'I always knew we'd get this one, and it's nice to be proved right. Now item two. John has had a modest success of his own. He has secured the sale of contents of Trent Hall, the Spencers' seat.'

'No more skullduggery, I hope,' muttered Lord Darlington.

'John?' The chairman turned in his throne to look at me.

'No,' I said, forcing a smile. 'Mrs Spencer used the Berington office for years. She was always a Merrywether client.'

'That's good,' Lord Darlington said, but he seemed unconvinced.

'Tell us about your other little plan,' said the chairman.

I explained about the sale of the estate.

'What do you all think?' There was a world of disdain in the chairman's voice. I immediately knew my cause was lost. The Gimpal sale was such an overwhelming victory and I was so far out of favour that any suggestion of mine was doomed for the dustbin.

'I'm against it,' said Jack Bonas, shaking his head.

128

'Madness,' said Lord Darlington. 'Stark staring insanity.'

'I'm sorry,' said Ralph, smiling at me apologetically. 'It's not our job. We're specialists. This would be a diversification too far. It's not as if we need the money now.'

I conceded defeat. Terry winked at me. It was no comfort; rather the reverse.

'Oh, by the way, John!' called out the chairman as I was leaving the room.

'Yes?'

'I want you to take the sale tomorrow.'

'Tomorrow?'

'Yes. It's just some middle-range Old Masters. I thought I'd take the day off. You lead too protected a life in the provinces!' He laughed cheerily.

'Fine,' I said.

'Enjoy yourself!'

'I will,' I promised.

CHAPTER SEVENTEEN

The atmosphere in the room was beginning to crackle. More chairs were filling up. Earnest men with catalogues were glancing covertly about, trying to spot competitors, two of our girls were checking the telephone links and another was adjusting the electronic currency chart to the morning's exchange figures. As the bidding advances, the last bid is shown automatically in five currencies: sterling, dollars, yen, Deutschmarks and Swiss francs. I could see the chairman sitting quietly at the back doing *The Times* crossword, presumably here to check on his country protégé. Elizabeth came hurrying over.

'Have you heard from the Getty?' she asked.

'No,' I said, 'but I can see Lester Liddy behind dark glasses in the sixth row. He'll be bidding for them, I imagine.'

'Mr Warren rang just now.'

'What?' Warren was director of the Getty. I knew they worked all hours, but it would be three in the morning in California.

'Here.' She handed me a slip of paper. It said simply, '$13 million for Lot 17.'

I checked the catalogue.

'Portrait of a young man. School of Batoni.' The reserve was £4,000, with an asterisk, which meant I could exercise my discretion to accept a bid of up to 10 per cent lower.

'Is this a joke?'

'Have you ever known Mr Warren *joke*?' It certainly was an improbable idea.

'Are you sure it was him?'

She glared at me. 'Of course I'm sure!'

I thought for a moment. 'It's very irregular. Call him back.'

'Call him?'

'Yes, call him. You've got ten minutes.' The large hand of the clock had just reached its zenith, and the conversation in the room suddenly died.

I climbed on to the rostrum and struck the wooden top with a nice thud of my gavel.

'Good morning, ladies and gentlemen, and welcome to this morning's sale of highly important Old Masters.' I beamed expansively. No-one shouted back. So far, so good. 'Lot one, on my right.'

A porter held out his hand and shouted, 'Here!', pointing at a large seascape by Salomon Ruysdael, looking deceptively good against the crimson silk wall. The reserve was £60,000, taking into account its two holes and lurid over-cleaning. I had already checked. We had no bids on paper.

'May I have a bid, please? Twenty thousand? Who'll give me twenty thousand?'

Everyone stared at their laps.

'Thank you! Twenty thousand. Twenty thousand bid. I'm bid twenty thousand.' What an obliging chandelier! Now it was the turn of the radiator at the back. 'Twenty-five, madam? Twenty-five, twenty-five thousand bid. Any advance on twenty-five thousand?'

One of the dealers raised a weary hand.

'Thirty! Thirty thousand on my right. Against you, madam.' I smiled encouragingly at the radiator and two men turned round to see who this enterprising lady might be. All they could see was a thick mass of spectators, any one of whom might be the bidder.

'Thirty thousand, ladies and gentlemen, for this very fine seascape. Thirty thousand bid. Thirty-five. Thank you, sir. Forty? Forty it is. Forty thousand . . . Fifty? It's against you, sir. Fifty bid . . . Sixty . . . Seventy. Seventy thousand bid. Are you all done? At seventy thousand pounds, it's going to be sold. Any more offers? Are you bidding, sir?' This to an earnest young man who was scratching his ear. Hastily he dropped his hand and furiously shook his head.

'Going for the first time at seventy thousand pounds. This is your last chance.'

I banged the gavel. 'Sold. Gallico's,' naming the Bond Street dealers who had bought the lot, unaware no doubt that it came from the stock of Wartheims, their immediate neighbours.

'Lot two, the Fuseli over there in the corner. Can we start at a hundred thousand pounds?'

One of the clerks passed me a note. 'No reply from Warren's home number. The office has an answering machine on. What now?'

'Who'll bid a hundred thousand pounds?' I knew that Wartheims had been sniffing round, presumably for a client. Their man was sitting in the front row and there was a long-standing arrangement that he was bidding if his catalogue was upside down and both hands were in his pockets. His hands were in his pockets, but his catalogue was facing up. His face was impassive.

'A hundred thousand pounds for this exciting double portrait. Will someone start me off?'

I gazed expectantly round. The top paper bid was £85,000 and the reserve was £250,000. What was more, we had underwritten the sale, guaranteeing the reserve to get the business of three other masterpieces to come. Even then, we were only on half commission.

'Eighty-five thousand then,' I said. 'Eighty-five thousand I'm bid. Eighty-five, eighty-five thousand.'

'Over there!' whispered a clerk.

'A hundred thousand!' I said triumphantly, catching the nod of an elderly man with a white goatee beard.

'Ninety thousand!' he shouted back. 'Ninety thousand is what I'm bidding.'

There was a ripple of laughter, and I saw the chairman look up.

'Thank you very much indeed, sir,' I said. 'Ninety thousand is the gentleman's bid. Ninety thousand pounds.'

Another hand went up.

'May I take *that* to mean a hundred thousand? *Thank* you, sir. A hundred thousand . . . a hundred and ten, and twenty, a hundred and forty . . . and sixty . . . eighty.' There were two bidders now. I simply turned from left to right. Like a spectator at Wimbledon. 'Two hundred thousand, two hundred and twenty, and forty, and sixty . . . eighty. Three hundred thousand, three twenty . . . Three hundred and twenty thousand, ladies and gentlemen. Three forty. A new bidder. Against you, sir.' The dealer on my left shook his head. I glanced at his erstwhile opponent. He ignored me. Then I saw my old friend from Wartheims. He was positively glaring at me, but the catalogue was still face up. He looked down and turned crimson.

'No more bids, then? At three hundred and forty thousand pounds for the first time.'

There was a clatter as the catalogue fell on to the ground. He pulled his hands out of his pockets and put it back – face down. I waited for him to thrust both hands into his pockets. He did.

'Three hundred and sixty thousand,' I said without looking at him. But the man behind him had spotted all this and raised a hand.

'Three hundred and eighty thousand. A new bidder. Four hundred thousand . . . four twenty-five, and fifty, and seventy-five . . . five hundred thousand, five hundred and fifty.'

The Wartheims' man took his hands out of his pockets and stood up. One glare at the man behind and he walked out. Oh, dear. I banged the gavel.

'Sold for five hundred and fifty thousand pounds. Michael Green.' The chairman winked at me.

Phew!

Someone was tugging at my arm. It was Elizabeth, pale and angry.

'What shall I *do*?' she hissed.

'Ask the chairman,' I said. 'Lot three, the Reynolds portrait behind me. Lady Theodosia Wharton and her

Nubian boy. Who will start me at a hundred thousand pounds?'

We bowled along, mostly exceeding our reserves, nothing spectacular, but all the time the potential disaster of lot seventeen was drawing nearer. The chairman materialized below the rostrum.

'This is supposed to be my day off,' he grumbled.

'Well, I'm glad you're here,' I said. 'Has Elizabeth explained?'

'Yes,' he said. 'You'll have to bid it up to that. What do they think it is?'

I looked across at the picture. School of Batoni was a compliment.

'Must be something there. Perhaps it's underneath,' he said. 'Take the bid. Hope for the best.' With that he walked out of the sale room.

'Lot sixteen,' called out the porter. It was a nice little Monnoyer flower piece. Reserve £56,000.

'Now then,' I called out. 'Jean Baptiste Monnoyer. Flower painting, dated 1691. From the Fitz-James collection. Forty thousand pounds? Am I bid forty thousand?' Three arms shot up on my left.

'Thank you, madam,' I said to an imaginary figure on my right. 'Forty-five thousand,' I said to the middle arm on my left. And so on.

'Sold for a hundred and seventy-five thousand pounds. Gruber.' I banged the gavel. 'Lot seventeen.'

'Over here, sir.'

The faces turned to the portrait. This is ridiculous, I thought. It's not even worth its reserve.

But the bidding was fast and furious. I started at £5,000 and we raced past 40. By 70 it was down to two, my paper bid from the Getty director and an old man in the back row. He appeared to be enjoying himself enormously.

When we reached £400,000 the room began to buzz. I saw the great bald dome of Pico Zust, the legendary Swiss expert, cross the room above the rows of heads like some great Renaissance cathedral on the move. He stopped in front of the painting, carefully screwed in the monocle that I, like everyone else, knew to be plain glass, and stared into the bulbous eyes of Batoni's sitter. Then he turned and walked back to his seat.

The ping-pong match with the old boy in the back row continued.

'One million, against you, sir.'

He smiled and nodded.

'Who is he?' I whispered to Elizabeth who was standing, white-faced, beside me.

'That's Mr Gallico. You wouldn't know him. He never bids himself these days. The usual buyer's in the second row.' The mouth of the man who'd bought lot one was agape with mystification. Suddenly I saw the light. It was some sort of sting. But on we sped, adding millions to the price.

'Six million,' I said. 'Against you.'

Mr Gallico raised a nonchalant hand. Someone gasped.

'Six million two hundred thousand.' I looked round, and paused. The silence was oppressive. 'Six million two hundred thousand,' I repeated. 'It's your bid, sir.' I smiled reassuringly at Mr Gallico, whose own smile was beginning to falter.

'Six million two hundred thousand.'

Elizabeth nudged me furiously. 'Go on,' she whispered. 'You can go to seven.'

I ignored her.

'For the last time, then, at six million two hundred thousand pounds. Your last chance.'

Mr Gallico's face had turned green. He tried to stand up, one hand plucking at his collar. He opened his mouth.

Bang! I brought down the gavel with a terrific blow.

'Sold! Gallico's. A new world record, I think.' Somewhere in the room I heard a loud raucous laugh. Something was amusing Pico Zust.

'What are you doing?' hissed Elizabeth.

'It was a con,' I said. 'Dirty tactics. You'll see. I thought

I'd make him pay the maximum. It'll be his own picture, but it's cost him a million in commission.'

'I hope to God you're right,' she said. 'The chairman's orders.'

'I hope I am too,' I said. 'Lot eighteen. Settle down, please.'

CHAPTER EIGHTEEN

'It was cleverly done.'

The chairman, Ralph and I were sitting round the board-room table, digesting the news that the call from Mr Warren had indeed been a hoax.

'Gallico and Garrisons acting in concert. Is that your theory, John?'

'Yes,' I said. 'I picked up some hint of that last week.' And suddenly I had a sickeningly clear recollection of an evening at the Tate with my old friend and rival Charlie McGregor winding up his speech with an hilarious imitation of Spike Warren.

'Well, thank God you did. But these are high stakes. We'd have had to shell out over five million pounds if we'd bought the picture on behalf of a nonexistent client.'

'As it is we've made a million from commission. John took a big chance, Alan,' put in Ralph. 'What would you have said if the American bid had been genuine?'

Alan looked up and smiled. 'I'd have fired him,' he said genially. 'We pay you to be on your toes, John, but don't think I'm not impressed.'

'Or grateful?' persisted Ralph.

'Very grateful,' said the chairman, still smiling.

'I doubt if others would have been as sharp,' murmured Ralph.

'What is this?' The chairman's smile vanished. 'A conspiracy?'

'Whose picture was it?' I asked, to deflect them.

'People I've never heard of,' the chairman replied. 'A family trust. The Harting Hampden Property Company registered in the Canaries. It's been entered for ages.'

'Hmm.' Ralph was stroking his chin. 'Maybe Basil was right. It *is* getting dirty, and some people would say we started it. No criticism of you,' he said, leaning over to pull my sleeve. 'You were doing what you were told.'

'What about John Best pushing the sale to his mistress's husband?' complained the chairman.

'That's done all the time,' said Ralph. 'Anyway, solicitors! We all know about them. We're supposed to be above that. We started it, but now they're joining in.'

I hadn't thought of it like that.

George and Mary were in London, staying at the Connaught. As he was attending a City livery dinner, I had bravely asked her out to dinner. I picked her up in a taxi and took her to St Quentin's. We sat in the corner, by the kitchen door.

'How's everything?' I asked, ordering some mineral water for her and whisky for myself.

'George is im-*possible*,' she said. 'I try to pretend, but it's really useless. It's like being married to a brick wall. He expects me to have sex, as he charmingly puts it, at every sort of unearthly hour regardless of how I'm feeling, and then doesn't speak to me for the rest of the day.'

I made a sympathetic sound and ordered some claret.

'I'm going to tell him I'm leaving,' she added.

I put my glass down. 'Are you sure?' I asked.

'Of course. I've got to *tell* him, haven't I?'

'Yes, but—'

'He'll get it sorted out by his solicitors. He'll be infuriatingly generous.'

'Won't he mind?' I was curious, as well as shocked.

'Naturally he'll mind,' she said sharply. 'I do everything for him. Run his house. Cook his meals. Answer his letters. He'll mind very much.'

'I don't suppose,' I said tentatively, 'I don't suppose those are the things he minds most about.'

'Then you don't know him very well,' she said.

'But he loves you.' That was the impression I had – a very strong impression, in fact.

'Yes,' she said complacently. 'I dare say. But as he can't show it, that's not a lot of good, is it?'

She was in a delightfully self-assertive mood, I thought, watching her chewing hard on a defenceless scallop.

'What about the children?'

'What about them?'

'Will they come with you?'

'Of course. Children should *always* be with their mother. Terry's been an angel. He's so understanding. He's found a house where they can have the top floor to themselves.'

'Going home at weekends?' I enquired, fascinated.

'That will be their home,' she said indignantly, 'George has never taken much interest. Anyway Robin goes to St Oswald's in September. It won't do him any harm to have some tuition in London first.'

'It seems rather drastic.'

'Oh, you're such an idealist, John,' she said, her wide lips unusually straight and hard. A physiotherapist once told me that there are over a hundred muscles in the face which determine the expressions. Here, beside me, Mary's face had changed from the soft receptive charm that it usually held into an impressive mask of independent power, almost savagery. I found I liked this side of her even more.

'Yes,' I said. 'Perhaps I am. It's because I am hopeful. Because I believe that good triumphs.'

Her laugh was jagged. 'Passion triumphs, my dear friend,' she said. 'That's the truth of it.' We sat in uncomfortable silence.

'Well,' I said. 'You once loved George.'

'Never,' she interrupted. 'I never loved George. I thought I could, or would. But I never did.'

'No?' I wanted to kiss her, to forget our pain, to comfort her, to comfort myself. I felt utterly useless. Her great brown eyes turned inwards and she reached over to take a sip of my whisky.

'Yes,' she said, and this time there was sadness in her voice. 'We were happy at first, very happy. But I was so young. Only twenty-three when I married him. It was such a thrilling adventure. Joining the adult world. Escaping my mother.' She paused, and then said, with a heavenly reminiscent smile, 'We were blissfully happy, like two schoolchildren. I ought to have known it couldn't last.' Her severe expression had returned. 'He's selfish, you see. Such an empty egotist.' She'd said the same of Terry not so very long ago.

'What if the dream of Terry goes the same way?' I murmured, as if inconsequentially.

She put her knife and fork down with a clatter. 'Men are such fools! All of you.' She was almost shouting. Had I touched a nerve?

'Simone de Beauvoir,' I said, suppressing my own anger, 'says that women have a fatal propensity for putting their men on a pedestal and then complaining when the adored one becomes insufferably conceited.'

'Simone de Beauvoir,' she snapped back, 'wasn't such a wild success herself, judging by Sartre's memoirs.'

'But didn't she write those herself?' I was getting out of my depth.

'What a touching scene!' It was Terry, looming over me like a tidal wave of Harrods hair oil and Eau de Gorille. 'Mind if I join you?'

Angrily I budged up on the banquette to accommodate him. It didn't help to see the two blondes at the next table nudging each other and giving him appreciative looks. I suppose I should have guessed Mary would tell him where she would be.

'You look gorgeous,' he said to Mary, leaning over to kiss her neck and inhaling deeply with his eyes appreciatively closed. 'Have you heard the good news about this young lady and me?'

'Yes,' I said, trying to keep a neutral tone and probably failing. 'I've heard.'

'Have you told the children, love?'

Love! *Love?* Ah, but here was good news, a chink of light in the night of despond. She was shaking her head.

140

'No, darling,' she was saying. 'I don't want to upset them all at once.'

'But they must know,' he said. 'Our plans . . .'

There was a delightful air of uneasiness playing about his temples.

'You must leave that to me.' She smiled, but firmly, removing her hand from under his. I was beginning to be reconciled to the assertive Mary, this new but vastly attractive creature. 'After all, they are my children, I understand them.'

'Of course, of course.' He was backing off, and none too soon to judge from the way her hand was brushing back an imaginary strand of hair.

Naturally I left Terry to take her back to her hotel, and drove north reaching my new home as St Amedroz' clock struck two.

CHAPTER NINETEEN

It poured with rain the whole of the next day and through the following night. The water beat upon the roof and against the window panes. Lying awake, I could hear it gurgling down the pipes and dripping on the balcony outside, collecting in bubbling pools on the leads and seeking out little cracks to trickle into the building.

As I lay there, staring into the darkness and reflecting on the past few days, I remembered a book of my nephew's, the tale of an elephant's family adventures. The endpapers of the book had shown endless lines of elephants, each following the next, each one's trunk holding the other's tail. Was that not an allegory of human life, where one man leans hopefully towards the woman of his choice? Just as she strains remorselessly towards some other preferred companion, so he, disconsolate, can feel behind him the less welcome tread of one who is willing him to turn back towards her. Occasionally we see our friends turn and combine, but for how long, and how accurate is the public picture, when many, like Mary, practise so assiduously the publication of misleading information? The pride that leads people to conceal their sadness behind a grand façade of apparent happiness can also serve to trap them. For when they try to emerge, they often find the spectators unwilling to accept a less attractive view.

With the dawn came the memory of Lord Tottenham's invitation. This afternoon, I must pack and drive, not to Wedderburn Woodhouse, but north to his other house, Tottenham, in Derbyshire. I crawled out of bed, put on the kettle and then dialled Mary's number.

142

'Yes?' It was George.

'Hello. Sorry to ring so early.'

'John? I'm always up, as you know.' He sounded very low. 'We're trying to pick up some sugar beet over by Whaleys Bridge. This rain is murder.'

How interesting. 'I suppose so,' I said.

'And it's murder on the sugar content. We averaged less than 18.4 per cent last month. Murder! That's what it is. Murder.'

'George!' I said, hopping from one foot to the other as the chill of the kitchen floor began to penetrate. 'Is Mary about?'

'I don't know.' His voice was more guarded now, even surly. I suppose he didn't much like being reminded that she slept in a separate room. 'I haven't heard her yet. I have to get the children's breakfast most days.'

'I want to ask her to do something this afternoon.'

'She'll be with you, won't she?' he said.

'Eh?'

'You're taking her up to Derbyshire.'

What? I had to think quickly. 'Oh, yes. George. Of course.'

'Well, aren't you?' He now sounded distinctly aggrieved. She might have told me if I was to be cast as all-purpose alibi.

'Yes, yes,' I babbled. 'Essential she comes. It's a great chance for us – the Tottenham silver. I hope you don't mind.'

'I never mind business,' he said. 'I do mind some other things. Ah, here she is.'

There was silence. Presumably he had put his hand over the mouthpiece, then: 'John?' How I love her voice. It's warm, soft, reassuring.

'I'm so glad you're coming to Derbyshire,' I said in a starchy way.

'Yes,' she said, falsely enthusiastic, 'I'm rather looking forward to it. And George is being angelic. It's Rosie's pantomime and I feel awful about leaving her.'

143

'And *thank* you for telling me,' I said.

'The valuations? Yes, I've got them here.' She was positively cooing.

'Damn your valuations! I admire your nerve.' Suddenly I was angry.

'Dear John,' she said. 'You know how Gaskin adores you.'

I slammed the receiver down. So that was why Terry had been so keen to invite me. They had calculated they could have two nights together with a perfect alibi: me!

The tea was too strong and too hot. I banged the cup down and ran a bath. I had just got in when the telephone rang. I grabbed a towel and answered it.

'Yes?'

'Don't be angry with me.'

'I suppose you're alone now,' I said.

'Yes, thank God.'

'The perfect husband is taking your children to school.'

There was a long silence.

'You've changed a lot,' she said at last.

'So have you,' I snapped.

'I knew you'd mind. I tried to ring you last night. Where were you?'

'I unplugged the telephone.'

'How sensible!'

'What have you rung about?' I asked.

'You may be my boss,' she said, 'but you're also my best friend.'

'What's wrong with Terry?'

'He doesn't understand me like you do.' She was speaking slowly, thoughtfully.

'It's because I understand that I'm angry. I don't like being your alibi. This is the second time. It makes me feel rather dirty, if you must know.'

'What if it were the other way round?'

I laughed. It was a direct bull's-eye. 'Terry's naturally dirty,' I said. 'It wouldn't register with him.'

'That's a horrid thing to say.'

'But it's true.' She didn't reply. 'Isn't it?' I insisted.

'Not in the way you mean,' she said. 'Now I must go and have a bath. I'm sorry if I've upset you.' She blew a kiss down the line and I was left, dripping and cold, staring at the wallpaper. I walked to the office.

'I didn't know you played golf,' said Robert. He still treated me with a disagreeable subservience whenever we met in the office corridor.

'I don't,' I said, leafing through a sheaf of sale notes.

'Your wife delivered some plus-fours this morning. Pretty jazzy tweed.'

He was a nondescript man, with regular features and a weak chin. He had his tongue slightly out, like a warm dog, with the same playful hopeful look of expectancy. Shall we make friends? Was that what he wanted? Anything was better than the cringing self-pity of the last two weeks.

'No. I'm shooting in Derbyshire tomorrow.'

'Well done! The Tottenham silver?'

'The Tottenham silver.' I walked on, cursing their silver and their gold and every other blessed artefact in the Tottenham household. Why couldn't they just send the whole lot to Christie's and leave me in peace, with Terry off my back? And, indeed, off Mary's.

I carried the suit back to the house, packed and drove north after calling in at the bank to collect my guns. There was no rain now, but the sky was heavy. North of Chesterfield I turned off the motorway and immediately the road began to twist and turn as the countryside grew wilder, with outcrops of rock and trees stunted by the fierce winds and less fertile soil. Soon I saw a turning with a signpost: Tottenham four miles. And then the tall Victorian planting, the slicker fencing that heralds a large estate. The lodges were immediately at the end of the village street. It was getting dark now, and as I turned the corner of the stable block I found two chauffeurs standing gossiping beside their cars. I was just winding down my window to ask which door to use when the rain returned, not gradually but in a terrific burst and clatter, drenching them where they stood so that they had to run sideways, clutching their caps on their heads, to reach the shelter of the stables' arch. In my car the noise was violent as the rain hammered on the roof above, bouncing off and streaming down the windows and blowing in great swathes across the gravel. Once I reached the hall of the house, the violence of the storm was muffled by the heavy brown curtains already drawn against the twilight.

Along a central table lay an untidy heap of coats, mackintoshes and umbrellas, discarded casually by the guests as they had arrived. The dripping coats of the last two arrivals had been flung on top of this pile, and there was still a steady sound of dripping as rain ran to the edge of the table and fell into puddles on the floor. On the massive chest by the stairs an altogether different line of clothing, recently pressed and carefully folded, with boots, shoes and galoshes in meticulous order, signalled the presence of other guests.

Down the stairs came a sudden burst of laughter as a door was opened to bring out a tray of dirty glasses.

'What name shall I say, sir?' enquired the butler, a tall man with a massive stomach imperfectly contained by his waistcoat.

'John Griffin.'

'Ah, yes,' he said. 'You're in the mauve room. They're having a drink in the library. Shall I show you the way?'

'Thank you.'

We proceeded up some inside stairs hung with glowering Tottenhams and their fragile-looking women, overlooked by a set of stuffed heads – stags, gazelles, an eland and a warthog – before he flung open a pair of double doors and called out my name.

'Come in, come in!' shouted Lord Tottenham, his great black beard giving him the portentous air of an Old Testament prophet. 'You know everyone, I expect.'

I kissed Mary, smiled tautly at Terry, shook hands with Lady Tottenham, Mrs Bracy, Colonel Bracy and was then seized in an agonizing grip by Melissa Wyndham, doyenne of decorators, heartbreaker to the London intelligentsia, the thinking man's Garbo.

'My dear Griffo.'

'Mel! What are you doing here?'

'Chasing Lord Tottenham,' she said, kissing me on both cheeks, 'I just die for those whiskers. Aren't they heaven?' she asked, appealing to Lady Tottenham, who was balancing precariously on her two sticks.

'Yes, my dear,' she replied with a smile. 'They are very nice in their own way.'

Melissa let out a shriek of laughter.

'Mr and Mrs Englefield,' boomed the butler as Antoinette, followed by Rupert, swept into the room. The others turned, while I put out a hand to steady myself against a table. There was a delicate crack as the vase toppled over and smashed, spilling its flowers and water on the carpet.

'God in heaven!' said my host. 'He's only been here five minutes and already he's smashing the place up. No, no! Leave it, leave it! Stubbs will deal with it, won't you, Stubbs?'

The huge butler advanced with an impassive expression, scooped up the pieces into one vast hand and retreated. Did I imagine the muttered oath?

'You know each other?' Lord Tottenham said.

Antoinette put out her hand, with a tense smile, and took mine. Clearly she was as shocked as I was.

'We met at the opera,' I said. 'Hello, Rupert.'

He gave me a dazzling smile and shook my hand warmly.

'How very, *very* nice to see you again. Mel, darling! You're looking even more dangerously glamorous than usual.' He had turned away even while addressing me and I was left with Antoinette.

'Did you have a good drive?' she asked with cool equanimity.

'Yes, thank you.' I looked at her face. On second viewing, it seemed rather less angular with its broad smooth forehead and huge almond eyes. Her mouth was small, but her lips were rich, deep and slightly pursed, so that one was drawn into them by the vivid concentration of natural colour in an otherwise pale, translucent complexion. This vertical effect was cancelled by the swelling of her cheekbones that gave a deeper dimension to the façade.

'Finished?'

Her voice cut through my reverie.

'I'm so sorry,' I murmured.

'Quite.'

Mary came across.

'This is Mary Sykes,' I said.

'Antoinette Englefield.'

They shook hands, then Antoinette moved away to be kissed by Melissa while a young man in a tail coat brought us some champagne.

'What's the matter?' Mary said, looking at me anxiously.

'Just a bit on edge.'

'I'll say. I've never known you break things.'

'Stick around,' I said. 'It'll probably get worse.'

Somewhere in the house a gong was beaten with dreadful ferocity.

'I'm afraid you've upset Stubbs,' said Lady Tottenham, making her way painfully towards us. 'He can be very temperamental.'

'I'm most terribly sorry,' I said. 'It was very clumsy of me.'

'Nonsense,' she said. 'It was awfully in the way. If you come up in the lift with me, I'll show you your bedrooms. You're both on the top floor.'

Dinner was an interminable feast. I sat between Mrs Bracy (stone-deaf) and Melissa (who never stopped talking to Lord Tottenham on her other side) so I was able to amuse myself by valuing the contents of the room, particularly the celebrated silver, some of which was on display. Anything was better than letting my eyes stray across the table to where Mary and Terry were exchanging infuriating looks of languorous admiration, while Antoinette, on Terry's left, stared at some spot on the wall behind Mrs Bracy's wig.

It's no good trying to describe my mental state. What with the Englefields and Mary and Terry, I really had to concentrate on something neutral. To try to deaden my warring thoughts, I valued every spoon, every sauce boat, every salver. My careful examination was abruptly interrupted.

'You can't take it with you, Griffin!' my host shouted down the table. 'The padre says that to me in church. But I think he'd do better to keep an eye on you.' There was a general roar of laughter.

'Really!' said Melissa as we left the dining room. 'You were positively dribbling over those candlesticks. Your friend Terry was secretly pointing you out to us. Very shaming, I thought.'

After dinner I found myself on a sofa between Mrs Bracy and my hostess. I never meet people of that age without reflecting what priceless experience they conceal beneath the humility that our cruel times teach to the very old.

'Do you like music?' asked Lady Tottenham, propping her sticks against a Boulle table loaded with porcelain boxes.

'*Who?*' bellowed poor Mrs Bracy, who was pretending to scratch her head while actually trying to adjust her elastoplast-pink hearing aid.

'Music, er, singing, you know. Madrigals,' said Lady Tottenham raising her voice a little.

'Not much,' was the uncompromising reply. I shook my head cautiously, not wanting to swell a chorus of discontent to what was obviously an attempt to make conversation, but equally unwilling to venture into unfamiliar territory.

'Well, I'm off,' said Melissa abruptly, kissing my cheek and then enveloping our host in a tight hug. 'Good night, you delicious old bear.' He caught my eye and blushed.

It was only then that I noticed that Mary and Terry had already slipped away.

Forcing myself to concentrate on other things, I picked up the latest copy of *Country Life* and took the lift to my bedroom.

What fools we make of ourselves. What utter fools! I was sitting in the armchair in my bedroom, drawn up near the fire, warmed and cheered by its noisy presence, when I saw the tall cupboard move slightly. There was a rhythmic vibration. The wall bracket tinkled. And then from next door, a cry. Oh heavens! That cry.

I found myself sinking on to my knees, then leaning forwards until my forehead touched the carpet, my whole body racked with an intense pain that seemed centred on my stomach. I would have done anything to have escaped such agony.

And I must have stayed like that, in that ridiculous position, for hours. Because when I recovered I was still crouched on the floor, cold and stiff, and with silent tears wet on my cheeks. And yet, when I thought about it in the half-light of the dawn, it was too ridiculous. Mary wasn't mine and never had been. Why should I resent her finding joy in Terry's arms? I'd just rather not listen to it, that's all.

The view from my bedroom window was spectacular. That side of the house faced due east, right across the great lake to where the sun was beginning to rise beyond the hills in the distance. The sky was a violent red, but streaked with blues and greys, and I could just make out some duck flighting in behind the island. When nature gives us such a sight, who can be bothered with a rosebed, or even another man's mistress?

Presumably such a house was always cold. My room was nearly thirty foot square. The radiator by the window was boiling hot, yet the ambient temperature was scarcely above freezing. The corridor to the bathroom was damp and icy, unwarmed by the pink and yellow watercolours. The bathroom with its stained sink, musty lavatory complete with chain and cracked enamel bath on stumpy little legs merely reinforced this air of permafrost.

I was too cold to even *think* of a bath. In the forecourt, two Land Rovers had been drawn up by the steps. Now another swung round the colonnade and was parked beside them.

Downstairs the corridors were full of noise. Excited dogs ran backwards and forwards and in the back I could hear the methodical sound of guns being unpacked and assembled with the accompanying rich smell of oil and wet mackintoshes, for outside a thick driving rain was again beating across the hills and even the fir trees near the house seemed misty, almost as if smoking, in the concentrated haze of glowing water.

In the dining room, its dark brown panelling hung with pictures of lurid deeds of slaughter, a matching haze of cigarette smoke thickened an atmosphere already heavy with burnt toast and bacon fat.

Mary, who had entered just ahead of me, was the only woman in the room. One or two of the men made perfunctory efforts to rise as she walked hesitantly over to the sideboard, but the others were slumped in front of plates piled high with fried eggs and black pudding – still half-asleep as the sun's thin gleam pierced through the rain to cast an eerie yellow light down one side of the room. Terry was already there, attacking his breakfast with gusto.

Mary seated herself at the table and started scratching away at the toast with a teaspoon. She gazed at the painting opposite. In the picture which had attracted her attention a bear was dying, one hound was tearing open the back of its neck while two others were burrowing between its hind legs, their mouths full of blood and gristle. But it had not died unavenged; at one side, another dog lay dead, its belly gaping. I watched the scene from just inside the doorway, before walking up to the table.

'Hello, John. Did you sleep well?' said Terry, finishing a sausage.

'Yes, indeed!' I smiled at him, deliberately ignoring

151

Mary who leapt up as if to kiss me. 'Those sausages look wonderful. Is that black pudding?'

To evade her, I made a wide detour round the back of the sideboard.

'I don't want to sell that sideboard!' roared Lord Tottenham who had come in during this manoeuvre. 'No point in looking for signatures on that one. My father made it himself. Is he always like this?'

He had addressed his remark to Mary. She had been watching me, I think, but now started and turned to our host.

'Oh, yes,' she said. 'He's always to be found underneath the tables.'

'So long as he's not underneath the beds, eh?' This was Terry's contribution and was followed by a slight pause.

Colonel Bracy and Melissa Wyndham came in together, laughing, and I was able to help myself to breakfast in peace.

'Will you sit here?' Mary murmured as I passed her, but I had caught Melissa's eye.

'Are you coming out?' I asked her.

'Of *course*!' she said. 'I want to see how you cope with the Avenue drive. Darby says the birds are almost all out of shot.'

'Darby?'

'Colonel Bracy and I have decided to end our days as Darby and Joan.'

'If she'll have me,' put in her delighted new suitor, oblivious of his wife's furious expression as she stood in the doorway buttoning up her massive tweed jacket.

'I heard that,' she said triumphantly.

'Ten minutes!' Lord Tottenham, having wolfed down some porridge, was tapping his wristwatch. 'Ten minutes and we're off. No stragglers!'

Outside the rain had stopped again, and the clouds seemed to be departing. I managed to get a seat in the first Land Rover with Colonel Bracy and Melissa. I had been introduced to my loader, a thickset grizzled character called Fox. He had a pencil-thin moustache and a firm handshake.

'You've got everything?'

'Yes, thank you, sir. You won't be needing your cartridge belt, will you?'

'Yes, please,' I said. 'I like to have it just in case.'

He looked rather offended, but most loaders run out of steam in a really busy drive, and I prefer to have my own source of ammunition handy.

There's an almost military sense of purpose as the cars set out for a shoot. It comes from watching too many films, maybe, but I like the feel of the convoy, the green vehicles, one after the other, weaving their way through woods or over hillsides, a companionable spirit of organized adventure.

We left the forecourt, with its peaceful statues and symmetrical lawns, turned left by a temple and plunged through some tangled woodland, overgrown with brambles, and down a steep incline. On our right lay the remains of a walled garden, now partially collapsed and planted up with Christmas trees. Looking back, I could still see the central tower of the castle riding above the trees, a symbol of order in a rural wilderness. Then down again through more belts of trees and then into a wide valley with great grassy banks rising up on either side to the half-bare beeches hanging down from the ridges.

The air was deliciously sharp and in the distance I could hear a cock pheasant calling. Twice it called, and then there was a fluttering of wings.

Lord Tottenham produced a small pack of playing cards and offered them round. Terry took his and turned it over. Four. I drew the three and Colonel Bracy the deuce. The two neighbours who had joined us in the forecourt drew the ace and the five respectively, leaving Rupert Englefield at six.

'We number from the right, move two at each stand. I'm not numbering,' Lord Tottenham said. '*But*,' he added, 'I shall stand behind you at the Avenue drive in case they're too good for you lot!' With that he marched off up the valley to meet the beaters, leaving us to take our places marked out by numbered pegs.

Number three peg was a little way up the left-hand bank. A level place to stand had been cut out of the turf, and the grass was littered with spent cartridges, some blue and some maroon.

'What happens here?' I asked Fox as he handed me a gun.

'It's loaded,' he said first. 'They've blanked most of the kale fields into this wood above us,' he went on. 'But the rearing pens are behind. You'll do all right here, but most of the birds break right.'

'Why's that?'

'It's the lie of the land. You can't see them, but there's a thick belt of firs in front of us over the hill. *Over!*' His bellow took me by surprise. I flung up my gun. There was nothing there. To my right there was a shot. A hen pheasant had slipped out of the trees and was planing over the colonel's head. He missed and fired again. She flew on, one leg dangling uselessly.

'Smithers'll get her. He's got his spaniels in Coronation Copse behind. Over you, sir.'

This time a cock pheasant, cackling with misplaced bravado, rocketed upwards from the trees. I fired and missed and Terry shot it dead before I could fire again. It landed with a terrific thump at our feet.

'Bloody poacher,' muttered Fox, obviously disgusted. But there was no time for discussion. Someone on the flank blew a whistle and the first flush of birds, thirty or forty, burst into view. We fired steadily. Birds were everywhere, rising and weaving above us, lifeless or kicking around us. We could hear the beaters now, tapping the tree trunks with their sticks, calling out raucously as the last birds rose despite a shout from a keeper to stay quiet. Then two long blasts on that same piercing whistle, and the first drive was over.

'Forty-one,' Fox said.

'I make it forty-three,' I said defensively.

'You can't count those last two hens. I reckon you shared those with the colonel. See? He's picking them up already.'

Sure enough, the colonel had given his gun to Mrs Bracy and had beetled out to seize two twitching birds that lay halfway between us. He was careful not to look in our direction.

'I think we can let him have those,' I said.

Fox snorted.

'Why are you so angry with me?' An arm slipped through mine. It was Mary, who had walked out to join us. The affection in her voice was too much for me to resist. I squeezed her arm against me and smiled at her.

'Life,' I said. 'I'm angry at life.'

'But why?'

Fox had moved discreetly away and was tinkering with a cartridge bag.

'Come and stand with me for the next drive,' I suggested.

'All right,' she said. 'I'll go and tell Terry. I'd promised to stand with him. But it'll be fine,' she said quickly to cut off my protest.

She ran down the line. I saw Terry's head turn sharply towards me. Then she came back.

The second drive was simply a return from the woods behind, so we had very little distance to move. Indeed Fox and I, now at peg number five, were standing only a few yards from the original number one of the previous stand. The ground was littered with mauve cartridges. A short little man with three brown Labradors moved into position behind us.

'That's a good sign,' said Fox. 'If Archdale stands behind you, that means the birds are coming this way. You'd better put your gloves on.'

I stared.

'It'll be hot work in twenty minutes,' he said. Then deferring to Mary, he stepped back, turned away and stood apart.

'Well?' she said, smiling confidently at me, her face

peeping out from underneath a fur hat. She looked superb.

I shrugged. 'My room is next to yours.'

For a moment she didn't understand, and then she flushed a rich scarlet. It was so painful for me to see her conflicting emotions that I too turned half away, shifting my gun from across my shoulder to under my arm, opening it as I did to check that it was loaded. Then I turned back to her.

'I'm sorry,' she said, and then she giggled. 'Was it very noisy?'

'No,' I said. 'I hadn't realized I would mind so much.'

'Mind?' she said, and her eyes flickered across my face.

'Yes, *mind*,' I said savagely. 'I mind. Is that so very odd?'

'Over *you*!' An anguished yell from a beater on the flank. I jerked up my gun and fired a despairing shot that took the tail feathers out of a low cock that had whirred out of the hedgerow above us.

'*Sharpen up there!*' A jovial cry from Colonel Bracy. Fox moved over to change guns. His eye held an unspoken rebuke.

'I'm so sorry,' said Mary. 'It was my fault.'

'Don't worry, miss,' said Fox. 'There'll be plenty more where that one came from.' In the far distance, we heard the faint notes of a horn.

'Is that the hunt?' Mary asked.

'Yes, miss,' said Fox. 'They always come this way on a Thursday. They won't bother us here, though. His lordship's one of their joint masters. He kennels the hounds at Long Tottenhope. It'd be as much as their lives are worth to disturb a shoot.'

There was a scattering of shots down the line.

'Watch it,' grunted Fox. 'Here they come!'

He was right. We fired and changed and fired and changed. When the guns got too hot even for my gloves, Mary found a scarf in the pocket of her coat and wound it around the barrels of my second gun. It was difficult to aim, but it kept us in business.

'They look more like starlings,' said Mary. 'Oh, poor thing.'

I had shot one through the body. It flinched, flew forward and then suddenly towered vertically upwards in a last frantic search for air and light before plummeting dead on to the turf behind us.

'I'll go and get that one,' she said as the whistle blew to announce the drive was over.

'That was better,' murmured Fox. 'Suits you having that young lady near you.'

We had a picnic lunch in a big timber hut further up a second valley. I found myself next to Rupert Englefield, who was savaging a chicken leg.

'Lucky our host deals only with Christie's, eh?' he said through his mouthful.

'Ur?' I had scalded my tongue on a mug of hot soup.

'I mean with us, and you and your two lovebirds there'd be no survivors if we were fighting over the silver here. Double guns, too!'

'No, indeed,' I said.

He leaned towards me confidentially. 'I had you marked down as a bit too solid for this work,' he said in a low voice.

'Oh?' I said, startled.

'Yes,' he said. 'But what you pulled off the other day. Bridgwater pictures. That was rather good. When you're fed up with Alan, give me a ring. Or just tell Antoinette. I think we could use you in St James's Square.'

I looked at him. His eyes met mine. They had a strange yellow tint. I didn't need to be clairvoyant to understand that he was thinking about my part in publicizing his wife's affair. *And* in his losing the Bridgwater picture sale.

'I'm sorry if there was any upset,' I said.

He raised one hand. 'That's OK,' he said. 'It comes with the rest of the pieces in this particular game.'

'As a matter of fact,' I added, 'I rather enjoyed the Batoni caper.'

His eyes never changed expression. 'Well, you can't

have it all your own way,' he said. 'There's always the next time.'

'*Good God*,' bellowed our host from the doorway. 'Are you going to eat all *day*?'

We started to repack our lunch boxes.

'There are *two more drives* – for anyone who's interested.' He disappeared again and the sound of a Land Rover engine sent us scurrying out into the afternoon sunshine.

CHAPTER TWENTY

The next morning I left Tottenham Castle with no greater progress towards securing work for Merrywethers than a vague invitation from my host to drop in at Wedderburn Woodhouse, his estate near Market Plumby, which was eagerly reinforced, with much wagging of her head, by his wife. I rather got the impression that the shooting season saw her marooned there while Lord Tottenham swanned about the Home Counties demonstrating, as a Victorian judge once put it, his deep and abiding love for all God's creatures by slaughtering as many as came within range of his shotgun.

I drove straight to Trent Hall where more than twenty cars, all provided and paid for by Merrywethers, were drawn up on the gravel in front of the house, emblems of the pressure we were under to keep our employing company in business.

'I'm very glad to see you, sir.' Horrod was looking ruffled.

'I'm sorry,' I said. 'It must be a nightmare for you. I hope my colleagues are behaving themselves.'

'Oh, yes, indeed, sir.' He had obviously never anticipated otherwise. This visitation was made up of the experts and photographers for the cataloguing. What would he make of the porters, especially Terry's chums from the Wedge and Whippet?

'No breakages?'

'No, sir, but Mrs Farmar is rather concerned about meals, sir.'

'Good heavens!' I said. 'We'll eat in the village. No-one expects you to cope with this lot.'

'We have prepared a cold luncheon for today, but the

159

cook feels it is not quite how Mrs Spencer would have expected us to look after our visitors.'

'Please, Horrod,' I said, 'tell the cook that we're extremely grateful for anything. As she's gone to the trouble today, we will wolf it down with great enthusiasm. But this could go on for days. From tomorrow we'll eat at the Oxfordshire Arms.'

'I think Mrs Farmar will be very relieved,' he said.

Inside I found Ginger Corbett fussing over some pictures with one set of photographers. From the flashes that intermittently lit up the stairwell, I knew others were at work above.

'You naughty boy!' Rodney came downstairs, his pockets full of papers. 'Now!' he said, taking me by the arm. 'To work! You never told me there were some rather tasty pieces here.'

'I told you about the commode.'

'Yes, that! *Very* shouty. But the Jacob chairs in the bedroom overlooking the fountain. You didn't spot those.'

'Oh, dear,' I said. 'Anything else?'

'Yes!' he said, delighted to score more points. 'Have you never heard of Charles Cressent?'

'Of course I have,' I replied. 'I love his work.'

'So?' He stuck his tongue into one side of his wrinkled-up face, and watched me with big malicious eyes.

Cressent, the great ebeniste, the master of rococo ormolu. Commodes? No. Clocks? No. There were two nice ones but both of a later date.

'A barometer I haven't spotted?'

'Mm-mm.' He shook his head. 'Oh dear, oh dear. What *do* we pay you for?'

'Not that chandelier?' There was a rather grimy gilt metal chandelier in one of the staircase wells.

He beamed. 'Yes, indeed. Slow but sure. The only known example was for St Germain. It was referred to in a report of a sale in Strasbourg by one of the Rohans, oh, 1860s . . . '63, I think. I'm almost certain this must be the one. Lovely stuff!'

'John!'

Jack Bonas, looking grey and tired, was leaning over the railings of the first floor balcony.

'Hello, Jack,' I said. 'What a nice surprise.'

He gave a slight smile. 'I just wanted to have a look,' he said. 'I haven't been to one of these since Castle Howard. I must say, this is a magnificent collection. Come up and meet my wife.'

I ran up the stairs, raising a hand in greeting as Mrs Farmar crossed the hall below me, carrying some books with a wooden box poised on top.

'Hello, Mrs Farmar!'

She tried to look up and nearly dropped the lot.

'My dear, this is John Griffin.'

Mrs Bonas never came to the office gatherings, and I could see why. She was short and pale and very nervous, with a distinct tic in her left eye. And yet it was easy to see that she must once have been very striking.

'How do you do?' I said, shaking her hand gently since her grasp was so faint.

'Jack says you're the old-fashioned one,' she said. It was a startling voice, very deep.

'Oh?' I said, rather nonplussed, shooting a nervous glance at my accuser. He was looking decidedly off-colour.

'Yes,' she went on earnestly. 'He says you stand up for the old values. The things that matter to him – to us.' When she looked at her husband, it was with pride, but also concern.

'Well, I take that as a great compliment,' I said, not sure whether I had lived up to it recently.

There was a shattering crash behind a door at the end of the corridor, a curse and then much muffled giggling.

'Now what have they done?' I said and strode to the door. The laughter died as I swung it open to reveal two of the china department girls on the floor desperately picking up the pieces of an Imari vase.

'Oh, Mr Griffin,' said the younger, a willowy girl with long fair hair and thin pink lips. 'It was my fault. I dropped it.'

'On my foot!' said the other, Suzanne, a dark girl who sometimes took notes at committee meetings.

Then they both burst into helpless laughter.

'It's so awful,' said the willowy girl, wiping the tears from her face. 'I know it isn't funny.'

'It could have been worse,' I said, helping them to pick up the rest of the pieces. 'Just put them in a carrier bag and mark it "Insurance Claim".'

'You're right about Giambologna.' The chairman walked in, causing utter consternation to the two girls. 'What a find! Hello, Victoria,' he said, catching sight of the fair girl. 'Destroying the masterpieces?' They fled.

'She's just my type,' he said, winking at me. 'I've had my eye on her for some time.'

I reminded myself that the redoubtable Lady Moorea was six foot tall with thick black tufts of hair and a laugh like a rhinoceros. If that epicene blonde was his type, to what atavistic urge had his wife appealed?

There was laughter downstairs. Mary and Terry had arrived. There had been no sign of them at breakfast at Tottenham, although to be fair I had had to leave early to get here in good time.

'Hello, my dear.' The chairman shook Mary's hand warmly after she had bounced up the stairs. 'John's been telling me how hard you work for us. Which I knew already, of course.' She flashed her eyes at me in a charming sidelong smile. I gave a grunt, hoping she wasn't the chairman's type, too.

'Mr Bryant's looking for you,' she said to me. 'He's got a policeman with him. They want to review arrangements on the day.'

I left them together and went outside to where Bryant, our chief of security, was drawing something in the gravel with a shooting stick. He was a thick square man with tight grizzled curls and no sense of humour.

'This is Inspector Lonegan,' he said.

'Hello,' I said. 'We've met on the St John Ambulance committee, haven't we?'

'Yes, indeed, sir.' He shook my hand. 'Mr Bryant knows what he wants.'

'What can I do to help?'

We spent the next two hours planning the complicated task of delivering many million pounds' worth of portable goods to up to a thousand potential customers in a marquee without losing any on the way to some enterprising thief. We had already decided to price the catalogues that gave admittance at a hundred pounds the set to restrict entry to manageable proportions.

'And make a nice profit,' Ralph had put in sourly.

'Nothing wrong in that, is there?' the chairman had asked, raising his eyebrows.

'Oh, no,' said Ralph. 'It's only that my old sister can't pay that just to come and look.'

'Then your old sister will have to stay at home, won't she?' laughed Terry.

Ralph had looked steadfastly at the table.

Once the policeman had gone, I went to check the arrangements with Mrs Farmar and spent half an hour walking round the grounds with Major Blood, the agent, agreeing the costs of local staff for car parking and admiring the views.

'Professor Spencer says you're going to handle the estate sale as well,' Blood said, fishing for information.

I intended to explain that my board had vetoed the idea, but something stopped me. I had had another idea, which I was keeping to myself.

'We're talking about it,' was all I added.

'Will it go as a whole?' he asked anxiously. What the poor man really wanted to know was whether he would have a job at the end of it. No doubt he had family commitments.

'I know it's ridiculous,' I said, 'but I'm not sure of the exact extent of the land.'

'Oh, come on,' he said cheerfully. 'Hop in and I'll drive you to the estate office.' He gestured at a muddy green Land Rover standing outside the stables. We rattled off down the back drive, over a cattle grid and

163

through some smartly painted farm buildings. A pair of gates, crowned with the Spencer leopards, and we were back in the village street.

'Here we are,' he said as he jerked to a halt outside a low red-brick building with long arched windows. 'Come in and I'll show you.'

We were met with a blast of hot air as he opened the heavy glass door.

'Mrs Spencer liked a tropical temperature,' he said.

There were two elderly typists in the outer office, very smart in their knitted cardigans and matching scarves.

'Mrs Spencer-Brandt rang you,' said one.

'What?' cried the major. 'From Sydney?'

'Yes,' she said. 'You're not to ring her back. She will call you later.'

'I suppose you know the daughter,' the major said wryly as we entered his inner sanctum, a shabby room that smelt cosily of pipe smoke and coal.

'Never laid eyes on her,' I answered. 'She'd emigrated long before I knew Mrs Spencer.'

'I shouldn't say this,' he said, 'but she's a bit of a thorn in my side. Always asking for accounts. That sort of thing. The husband, Brandt, is some sort of farmer. Likes to question what we do here, although it's no earthly business of his. Not till now.'

On the wall, between the sizzling fire and the windows on to the street, hung a long map dated 1827. The outer edge was a faded yellow, but the centre was coloured in poster paints. It showed the Trent estate to be shaped like a pyramid, sharp at the top and swelling down to a broad flank along the bottom, bounded by a river. To the left of the coloured section was inscribed, "Ld Berington's Land", and to the right, "Sir Hy Castleton's Land". And thus, give or take an occasional change of Christian name, it remained to this day.

'What's that river?' I asked, peering at the squiggled script.

'The one in the middle? That's the Wyvern. Badly

polluted, these days. I used to fish for trout there thirty years ago. Not now, though.'

'No,' I said. 'At the very bottom.'

'Oh *that*,' he said, in a disparaging tone. 'That's the Passen. It's more of a drain.'

'And how much land lies between the two rivers?'

'How much?' He screwed his eyes up and examined the map. 'Let me see.' He pointed at a green patch with his silver propelling pencil. 'That's Agar's Farm, nearly eight hundred acres now. Then you've got Rigby there, the Grimsby brothers at Dyke Farm, Stoke Spencer itself, the Obelisk Farm (that's old Mr Rootham), the Hundred-acre Wood, the Jubilee plantations and the Old Millhouse woods. It must be four thousand acres, though I can give you it in detail tomorrow. Got a buyer?'

'Not yet,' I said. 'What's the rent-roll, very roughly?'

'The village is mostly let to old employees. We don't charge them much. It's probably two hundred thousand pounds per annum. That includes the Millhouse shooting. It's let to the Popes, who run it as a syndicate.'

'And the total estate?'

'Eight thousand five hundred and sixty acres,' he said proudly.

'More than I remember,' I said, surprised.

'We bought some land off General Castleton last year. Private sale. He didn't want it made public, but Mrs Spencer gave him a fair price. They were always good friends.'

CHAPTER TWENTY-ONE

Back in Berington, I parked happily outside my new home. Three bays wide, three storeys high in a crisp grey stone that matched the whole street, I was becoming very fond of it.

I let myself in, switched on the kettle and walked through the little hallway that led to the garden behind. Though no more than forty foot square, contained within its variegated brick walling, it had a delightful air of secure peace, with its weeping ash in one corner shading a rustic wooden bench, and a sturdy magnolia in the other. The three walls were fronted by a border, now rather overgrown. It won't take me long to clean that up, I thought, as I hurried back to the kitchen to answer the door.

Inspector Lonegan stood there.

'Hello,' I said. 'Come in.'

'Thank you, sir.' He stepped in gingerly, pulled off his transparent plastic mackintosh and laid it on the chair by the door.

'May we talk?'

'Of course,' I said, leading him into the little sitting room where I had just begun to settle myself in by buying books, a compact disc player and some recordings from the shop opposite.

'I received this when I got back this evening,' he said, passing me a typewritten letter.

'Mr John Griffin,' it read, 'of Merrywethers, Sixteen High Street, Berington, is conspiring to defraud purchasers of antique goods sold through his firm.'

It was signed, in type, 'A Friend'.

I read it twice and handed it back. Those bloody valuations. Still sitting in the safe.

'Thank you for showing me,' I said.

He laughed. 'We get a lot of this sort of thing,' he said. 'We don't take them very seriously, not if we know the people concerned. But you've got an enemy, and I thought you ought to know.'

'That's very decent of you,' I said.

He was watching my face carefully. What on earth could he read there?

'It's not true,' I said.

He nodded enthusiastically.

'But there's a germ of truth in the general background.'

'Meaning?' He was trying to look unconcerned, but his eyes were sharp.

'Meaning that I was suspicious of something in the office. It wasn't anything I could have brought to the police,' I added hastily. 'I think it's subsided.'

'Sure you don't want to talk about it?' he said with a deceptive air of sympathy.

I decided on a pause, followed by assertive self-possession. 'No. It's really not firm enough. It was just a risk. I'm entirely satisfied that I knocked it on the head. I couldn't be justified in unleashing an investigation into a vague suspicion that I am now satisfied was unfounded.'

He stood up. 'Right,' he said. 'You know where we are.'

'Yes,' I replied brightly. 'That I do.'

After he'd gone, I sat for a long time in silence. Something was stirring in the back of my mind. Anonymous letters are said to be a woman's weapon, but that didn't seem likely in this case. Mr Kemble? Yet he was the guilty one. Robert Head? It's not unknown for people to accuse themselves, even obliquely, to try to assuage the pain of guilt. Or could Mary have told Terry, giving him another means of discrediting me? Or Mrs Gaskin? Mrs Gaskin! Truly, the worst feature of this sort of subterfuge is the suspicion that poisons everyone around it. Why would dear old Mrs Gaskin, kind, hard-working and thoughtful, suddenly take up the poison pen? And yet, and this was the uncomfortable part of it: what the letter said was not far from the truth. I had done nothing to alert London, or to trace the earlier transactions, because I wanted to keep Robert as a pawn to be used if I needed him. I had felt I had some justification for not disturbing the past. No-one had queried the valuations. Robert might even have been accurate. Why deliberately seek scandal and ruin his career on a suspicion? But then, he had more or less admitted his guilt. It was a dilemma.

I got up and poured myself some whisky.

My next job was to call Professor Spencer in Cambridge, to keep him in the picture.

'Bernard?'

'Yes.'

'It's John Griffin.'

'Oh, yes.' He didn't sound exactly enthusiastic.

'I thought you'd like to know how it's going.'

'Yes,' he said. 'I hope it's not being too much of a bore for you.'

Hardly, I thought. Our biggest sale of the year so far!

'We're set for the twentieth of next month,' I said. 'There'll be four days. Will you be staying in the house?'

'Heavens, no!' He sounded shocked. 'I've g-got far too much work to do here. I may come over for lunch one day, nothing more.'

'We need to meet to discuss reserves,' I said, 'and to give you the valuations. You must think about tax liability.'

'Talk to Dangerfields,' he said. 'They handle that.'

'Any particular partner?' I said, fearing the worst.

'Yes. John Best.' (I knew it!) 'He always handled Mum's things. You'll like him. He's a good man. I was very sorry to see that thing in the papers today.'

'What thing?'

'Oh, in Horace Walpole, that g-gossip column, you know.'

I walked to the station and bought the relevant paper. Immediately under the columnist's by-line was a big photograph of Best with his wife, a plump pretty woman, arm in arm at a garden party. The entry was headed 'OUCH!'

News has reached me that Lady Best, wife of society solicitor Sir John Best, has barred her husband from their Hampshire estate and is suing for divorce. Brendy, as she is known to her cronies, has had enough of her diminutive hubby's sympathetic ways with female clients. Latest reports link him with a blonde beauty loosely, oh very loosely, connected with the auction trade. When I ran Sir John, the third baronet, to earth at No. 6 Court at the Old Bailey, he refused to talk about his wife's change of locks. 'It's people like you who keep our litigation partners in school fees,' he told me. The irony is that until he became senior partner of Dangerfields last year, he was head of their matrimonial department, more accustomed to extracting settlements than to paying for them himself. Naughty boy!

Poor Antoinette.
I screwed the newspaper into a ball and flung it into a council bin.

CHAPTER TWENTY-TWO

I spent the next day at Trent Hall again, asking the office to make an appointment at Dangerfields for Monday morning. I came home to find a message on the ansaphone that Sir John Best would see me at eleven and one from Barbara saying she had gone abroad for ten days. I spent a hectic Sunday gardening and house-painting, surprising myself at my enthusiasm, and arrived in Gresham Street with a clear head at five to eleven.

'Mr Griffin?' The guard at the front desk looked me up and down and then handed me a pass. 'They're expecting you on the sixth floor.'

When the lift opened there was another guard standing there, accompanied by a short dark girl with a serious expression.

'This way, please.' She tried a shy smile, and led me down a narrow corridor into a big glass room, furnished with heavy black furniture.

'Sir John will be with you in two minutes. Would you like some coffee?'

'Yes, please,' I said. 'Black, no sugar.'

She disappeared.

'Well, well, well.' The dapper little man who I remembered so clearly was standing in the doorway. 'This *is* a surprise.'

Ever since the professor had named his lawyer, I had been trying to suppress any thoughts on the subject. I am doing my job, he is doing his. If there is a problem about his private life, it is because that is how he chooses to live it, not because I told my chairman that we were losing a sale because of sexual favouritism on the part of a trustee. If the chairman chooses to broadcast the news, my share of the blame is pretty small. And yet – of course I was sorry, particularly about his family. But also glad. Glad that we had got the work.

'Good morning,' I said. 'It's very kind of you to see me at such short notice.'

He shook my hand. 'I particularly wanted to meet you again. We hardly had the chance to get to know each other when you managed to get into Bridgwater.'

'No,' I agreed, watching him with, I hoped, an impassive and professional air.

'And yet,' he went on, 'you've become quite a feature in my life lately. Telling tales to Alan, doing my job for the Spencers. You're quite a busy bee, Mr Griffin.' All said with the broadest of grins.

'I'm sorry,' I said, and meant it.

'Oh, none of that,' he said. 'I will admit that I'm feeling rather sore about Antoinette. She won't return my calls.'

'You did well with your picture,' I said, unable to resist a dig about their unsuccessful hoax. His smile faded. 'The Harting Hampden Trust portrait. The accounts department tell me that Gallico's paid on Friday. You must be very pleased.'

'Oh yes,' he said smoothly. 'That was a gratifying result.'

The girl came back with two cups of coffee. 'That's yours, Sir John,' she said, pushing one towards him. 'The one with sugar.'

'Thank you, my dear,' he said and waited until the door had closed behind her. 'Enough pleasantry,' he said abruptly. 'Let's talk about business.'

'Would you rather deal with one of the other directors?' I asked. 'Given our recent connections.'

He stared at me. 'Oh, no, John – if I may. You quite misunderstand me.' He stood up again and walked to one of the broad windows overlooking the street. 'I won't deny that you have recently played a very negative role in my life, but we can't allow the Spencers to suffer because of our private imbroglios. I won't deny either that I was pretty receptive to old Tony Gallico's idea that

171

he might sell the Trent contents instead of Merrywethers. But that was a business transaction. The Spencers would have gained forty per cent of his profits because of their stake in Gallico's. But neither of the Spencer children liked the idea. They thought you'd do it better. I expect they're right.'

'So what's the position on capital gains?' I asked, hiding my surge of relief as best I could.

He opened the file he had brought in with him. 'The estate was passed to trustees some years ago, as were most of the major contents of the house. We can claim a certain amount of indexation. Indeed, the land values have probably dropped. But there will be a big tax bill overall.'

'I've got an idea,' I interrupted.

'Go on.'

'I found a bust which I'm pretty certain is by Giambologna. If I'm right, it's not only unique but will cause a complete reappraisal of his last twenty years.'

'So?'

'So. First it is worth at least twelve million pounds. Second, it is inconceivable that we would get an export licence without a long delay. The V. and A. will turn cartwheels to get it. That will cost the estate a fortune in delayed payment and discouraged bidders.'

'And?' He was watching me closely.

'Let's use that as an in-lieu negotiation with the Treasury. We did the Greenwich family heirlooms last year, so we're well up on their current thinking. This is a rare case where I think we'd do better negotiating with them than on the open market. In any case, we need several months to research it.'

'It's a thought,' he agreed.

'We need a decision now, to exclude it from the main sale. Apart from anything else, I still haven't found a receipt or any record of how it came to be there. It isn't in the 1848 inventory, but it may not have been thought important enough. I found it on the back stairs.'

'I see!' He laughed and turned away again. 'What do your people estimate the probable proceeds of the rest?'

172

'Between forty-two and fifty-three million,' I said.

He roared with laughter.

'It's amazing, isn't it?' he said. 'One elderly don and an alcoholic in Australia. Neither of them has any children. What will they do with it? You've heard they want to sell the land as well?'

I nodded. I didn't want to discuss that at this stage.

'I think it's a shame,' he said. 'It's a lovely house. You'd think one of them would like to enjoy so many generations' worth of collecting fine art. What really amuses me,' he said, lowering his voice slightly, 'are those wonderfully absurd Sunday paper analyses. You know – the top hundred fortunes. Half of them are people you've never heard of, two or three go bankrupt the next day, and our clients – the people who really have money, like the Spencers – never appear at all. What a farce the whole thing is.'

I waited politely, hoping for an answer that would release me.

'Yes,' he said finally. 'Yes. Talk to the Treasury. And exclude it. I'm sure you're right. You know, I know I shouldn't discuss the Bridgwater matter with you, being an ex-trustee—' I raised my eyebrows. 'Oh, yes,' he said. 'I resigned as a trustee immediately, of course.' He chuckled. 'But really, Merrywethers looks set to beat their competitors out of sight this year. Be careful you don't overreach yourself.'

The last six words were uttered in a new and wholly different tone of voice. And with that, he disappeared into another room.

I lunched at my club. Hope stared past me when I walked in.

Afterwards I headed up St James's Street, enjoying the autumn sun on the way to Merrywethers. Having nothing better to do, I walked down the corridor to Terry's office. A spruce starchy woman with red spectacles was typing busily in the anteroom.

'Is the great man in?' I asked.

She looked at me with disdain. 'Who are you?' she said.

173

'John Griffin.' If it made an impression, it wasn't a favourable one.

'I'll have to see.'

She knocked on the inner door. There was no reply. She knocked again.

'What the hell is it?' He'd come to the door and flung it open.

She took a step back, shocked, as I was, by his angry expression.

'Oh, it's you, Johnny. Yes. Come in.'

'It's nothing important,' I said hastily. 'I was only dropping in to talk about the Bridgwater plans.'

'Come in,' he repeated imperiously, and slammed the door behind us. 'You're just the person I want to see,' he said. 'Sit down there, will you?'

I walked over to the window and stood looking down at the people in the street. There was an old lady with a wicker basket on wheels laden with parcels. As she reached the edge of the pavement, a young couple hurried over to her. The youth took her arm while the girl manoeuvred the basket across the road. They parted on the other side with broad, happy smiles.

'What have you been saying to Mary?' Terry demanded.

'What?' I hadn't been listening. 'To Mary?'

'She's being very elusive. I need her.'

I didn't want to listen to more of this. But instead of keeping my mouth shut, I said: 'Well, she's got her family to think of.'

'And me,' said Terry. 'She should be thinking about me.'

'Can't you talk on the telephone?' Why do I let myself get sucked into these conversations?

'I don't mean *talking*,' he said. 'She's supposed to be my mistress. I need her here.'

'Oh?' What a man! 'There's always the Wedge and Whippet,' I suggested helpfully.

He actually laughed. 'I know you mean to be offensive,' he said, showing his gums, 'but since I don't think you'll be with us much longer, once I replace Bonas,

174

I can afford to laugh. Poor old John. No wife, no job, no Mary. What *will* you do?'

I was just wondering whether I felt strong enough to pin him to the wall with the letter spike when there was another knock on the door. This time his secretary entered immediately.

'The Duke of Bridgwater's here,' she said breathlessly. 'He's just *outside.*'

'Terry? May I come in?' A slim young man, with dyed orange hair and an artificial suntan put his head around the door. His face fell when he saw me. 'Are you busy?' It was impossible to ignore the fact that he was wearing make-up round his eyes.

'No, no,' said Terry, cheering visibly. 'Come on in. Do you know my colleague, John Griffin?'

We shook hands. The girl was quivering with uncertainty and excitement.

'We can finish our discussion later,' I said and walked out, drawing the girl with me. 'Take them in some tea,' I suggested. 'Even a biscuit.'

'To think he owns the Giorgione!' she whispered.

'Not for much longer if Terry has anything to do with it,' I said.

CHAPTER TWENTY-THREE

When I got back to Berington, Mary had rung in to say she had 'flu. She was away for a week, and when she did return, paler and thinner, she deliberately avoided any conversation with me except on professional matters. I respected her reticence, but I could hardly conceal from myself the disproportionately devastating effect not seeing her had had upon me. I would like to have felt relief. Instead it was as if I had risen in a shuttered room, groping in the half-dark, and then had opened a shutter on to a garden lit by the morning sun. To close the shutter again on that flaming scene was to find myself returned to a darkness so complete that I drew deeper into myself, recognizing that part of the fault lay with my scalded eyes. In any case there was much to do, in preparing for the Trent view days before the sale, that I hardly had time to think of anything else. I received a postcard from Barbara, saying she was going on from Florida to Los Angeles, so I assumed she had reconsidered breaking with Bertie. And why not? He had always seemed reliable.

At last we were ready for the Trent sale. The catalogue had been prepared, printed and circulated, and the status of the contents assured that they were well researched and documented. Indeed, Mrs Spencer had maintained her own highly detailed inventory which we had, naturally, largely reproduced. The relevant dealers and collectors had been identified and then alerted to what was on offer. The newspapers had given us generous coverage and the first day of the viewing brought potential clients in their hundreds, each clutching their valuable entrance tickets: our glossy brochures complete with Spencer family tree, colour photographs of the important items and scholarly little paragraphs, mouth-watering in their discreet praise, on each desirable lot. Some we estimated low, to encourage the faint-hearted, others high to tempt through exclusivity. Who knows what psychological process draws people into bidding so much more in the heat of an auction than they ever intended? We don't analyse them, we just bank our share of the proceeds.

The first person I saw was Colonel Chaucer, with Maisie on a lead.

'Hi, Griffin! We need you.'

I hurried over.

'Can you tell this man of yours to let me in?'

One of the security guards, with perfect courtesy, was pointing to a large sign which read, "No animals".

'Maisie always comes with me.'

'Of course,' I said. 'You're quite right,' I said to the guard. 'I made the rule, but Colonel Chaucer is an old friend of the family. It'll be all right.'

'If you say so,' he said glumly. 'What'll I tell the next one?'

'No animals,' I said. 'That's the rule. It's just that Maisie is an exception.'

'Thank you so much, my dear fellow,' said the colonel triumphantly. 'How's your foreign friend? Any sign of that thesis?'

'Any minute,' I replied. Which reminded me. I'd never heard from Hans. It was rather strange.

'I had you wrong,' he said. 'I thought you were trying to do a deal. I owe you an apology.'

'Good heavens, no!' I laughed. 'It's just that there are other sides to our work. I loved seeing that picture. It was a very pleasant occasion.'

'It's not that I don't need the money, you know,' he said suddenly. 'Everyone does. Oh, look, there's Mimi Port Talbot.' He pointed to a massive woman walking arm in arm with a tall young man with his hair all waved and quiffed. 'I heard she was in trouble with

177

the bookmakers. Excuse me. I must go and say hello.' He hurried off, dragging an unwilling Maisie who had been showing some interest in a police dog by the marquee.

'John!'

'Isabel!' I hugged her enthusiastically. 'What are you after?'

'Aha!' she said. 'That's what I want to talk to you about.'

She took me by the arm and led me off into the wilderness. 'You know that favour we talked about?' My heart sank. This area of the garden was all tall pines and rhododendrons. We followed a grass path that ended by leading up to a small ruined temple, now unroofed but with its façade intact, and a bench beneath the portico.

'Let's sit here,' she said.

'The favour,' I reminded her.

'Yes, my dear. There's a charming little flower picture I want.'

'Which one?'

'It's in the boudoir.'

'What?' I gasped. 'The Nicholson of the camellias?'

'The very one!'

'But that's estimated at eighty thousand pounds.'

'And what will Merrywethers' commission on the Gimpal collection be? Ten million? Twenty? I thought you always paid five per cent for introductions.'

'But . . .'

'Oh, I know I didn't introduce the sale, but you wouldn't have got it without me. And you said you owed me a favour. Anyway,' she continued, 'I've had an idea. Why not withdraw the picture and sell it to me privately?'

'I can't do that,' I said. 'We have to make the best price we can.'

'Oh, well,' she said. 'I was just trying to save you some money, that's all.'

'But, Isabel . . .'

'It was your idea,' she said. 'And that's the favour I want. I can pay thirty-five thousand. I can't compete with these millionaires.' She gestured at an imaginary army of

178

predators around us in the perfect silence of the glade.

'I see,' I said. 'I'll talk to the chairman.'

This wasn't what I had meant by a favour and she knew it. I stood up to leave.

'Thank you, darling,' she said.

We walked back in silence.

'Where *have* you been?' It was the chairman himself, his face red with exertion. 'I need to talk to you immediately.' He bowed to Isabel who waved and walked off. 'Jack Bonas died this morning,' he said abruptly.

'So suddenly?' I said. I sat down on an adjacent bench. It was quite a shock.

'It was very quick, his wife said. He was the last to know. Just think, it had been eating away inside him and he never realized.'

'Poor man,' I said, still taking it in. 'He'll be very much missed.'

'That's what I want to talk to you about,' said the chairman sitting down beside me. 'I've spoken to the others. I want Terry to replace him.'

'Are you sure?' I scarcely had control of my voice, even though his decision was the reverse of unexpected. It wasn't that I wanted the job particularly, I just didn't want more of Terry.

'Of course,' he said impatiently. 'I know you don't get on, but that's not the only criterion to be considered. He's got the best contacts and he's very efficient.'

I couldn't argue with either of those. 'He's very young,' I tried cautiously.

'Any other objections?'

'Not if you are content for Merrywethers to continue down the present track.'

'Meaning what?'

'Poaching other people's clients. Fighting dirty. That sort of thing.'

The chairman glanced at me. 'I'm disappointed in you, John,' he said. 'I thought you'd grown out of your misplaced squeamishness. This is a business, not a course in art appreciation.'

I nodded. I could see his point, but . . . 'Tell me this, then,' I said, and outlined Isabel's request. 'What shall I do?'

'Do?' he almost shouted. 'Withdraw the picture, of course. Give it to her for thirty-five thousand pounds and we'll sort the balance out after the sale. Get on with it now and let's have no more namby-pamby fooling about. I want you to make a success of your time with us.'

He stalked off. My time with them? It didn't sound like a long career. Even though I'd already clocked up sixteen years.

A portly man was coming towards me clutching his catalogue. He seemed vaguely familiar. I smiled a welcome. He bowed and immediately I placed him. The Tottenhams' butler.

'It's Stubbs, isn't it?' I said, walking up and putting out my hand. He took it rather reluctantly.

'Yes, indeed, sir. It's good of you to recognize me.'

'That was a wonderful shoot at Tottenham. I really enjoyed it. Do you often come to sales?'

'Oh no, sir,' he said. 'But I started here as pantry boy in between the wars. Lord Tottenham kindly gave me a catalogue. I got promoted to second footman here because I was the only one who could carry old Mrs Spencer, the late Mrs Spencer's mother that is, upstairs after she had her stroke. It was a rare bit of luck for a young lad, that was.'

'Was she very heavy?'

'She was a right hippopotamus, if you'll pardon my saying so.' He laughed, his whole face becoming younger as he relished the memory. 'Cursing and swearing, she was. Every night.'

'Are you going to buy anything?'

'I'm going to try for the club fender in the library,' he said. 'I spent so many years polishing it I'd like to have it now as a keepsake. Depends what it makes, though.' He wandered off.

The crowd was growing denser. The caterers from London had set up their own tent, striped yellow and white with glass-panelled doors and menus displayed at each doorway: *'Homard thermidor, confit de canard, loup de mer.'*

'Always thinking of your stomach, eh?' It was Rupert Englefield, with Antoinette on his arm. 'You must come and try Antoinette's cooking.'

'Please do,' she said, disengaging herself and walking on without smiling. Apparently it was his turn to break her rules, those shifting sands in which we all floundered. He hurried after her. I went in and sat down.

'Monsieur?'

'The duck and a glass of red wine, please.'

'Parfait.' The waiter simpered and left me to my angry thoughts.

'May I join you?' It was my old friend Charlie.

'Only if you speak English.'

He laughed and sat beside me. 'You're looking pretty grim.'

'I feel pretty grim,' I replied.

'I'm sorry to hear about Jack.'

'Yes, it's sad. He was a decent man.'

'I suppose Terry will be taking over.'

I looked up.

'Don't worry,' he said. 'I'm only guessing.'

'You're right,' I said. 'Ninety-nine per cent certainty.'

'Phew!' he said and then paused. 'John?'

'Yes?'

'I'm thinking of setting up on my own. This business is getting pretty rough.'

I decided not to ask any awkward questions.

'Would a partnership interest you?' he asked. 'Just a small business, dealing with people we know.'

'It's a thought,' I said carefully. A very tempting thought, given my present situation. But then again I loved the excitement of auctions, the cut and thrust of live entertainment. I saw it as the difference between life in the theatre and life on a film set. I shook my head. 'I'm not saying "no" out of hand,' I said. 'But I can't see myself as a dealer.'

'You like the thrill of the arena?'

'Perhaps.'

'I'll have the same as my friend,' said Charlie as the waiter hovered.

'What are you doing here?' I asked.

'Snooping,' he said easily. 'And learning. There are some good pieces here. That Cressent chandelier. You've got half the Versailles staff over there in the corner.'

'That'll please the waiter.'

'Or not,' he said. 'Depends if his French is real.'

Ralph Tritton joined us and then Mary. We ended up having a very convivial lunch, despite the news about Jack. Ralph was in sparkling form, teasing Charlie about his superiors, and Mary seemed entirely different from the morose creature who had moped about the office since her return. Terry was safely occupied talking to clients. Ralph took Charlie off to see a mutual friend at another table, so we were left finishing off our cheese.

'It's nice to see you smile,' I said.

'Yes,' she said. 'I've been very preoccupied, I'm afraid.'

'I'm sure you did the right thing.'

She stared at me. 'The right thing?'

'In staying with George.'

'But I'm leaving him,' she said. 'As soon as possible.'

'But Terry said—'

'I wish Terry wouldn't discuss our affairs with the whole world.'

I sat silenced.

'I don't mean you,' she said, putting her hand on mine. 'You've been so kind to both of us.' Yes – calculating John Griffin had been rather a success.

'Well, well!' It was Antoinette. 'You two look nice and confidential.'

I stood up, knocking over my chair.

'No,' she said. 'Please don't move. I can only stay a moment.'

She took the chair beside Mary, away from me. 'How are you, Mary?' she said, giving her a full and enthusiastic smile. 'It is so nice to see you again.'

'And you,' said Mary, recovering her poise. 'Are you going to buy something?'

'No,' said Antoinette. 'We're just here to show the flag. If Merrywethers make a mess, Garrisons can pick up the pieces. We often have.' This with the same guileless smile at, or rather past, me. 'You must come and dine with us when you are next in London. Both of you.' Then she stood up and walked away with the same smooth movements that I had first noticed at Covent Garden, the top of her body held so erect that it seemed almost detached from the legs that one knew must be moving beneath her long patterned skirt.

'Oh, dear,' said Mary. 'I'm afraid she got the wrong idea.'

'Not necessarily,' I said before I could restrain myself. 'She knows you're married.'

'What's that supposed to mean?' she said sharply.

'Don't married women spend their time promising to run away with people and then changing their minds?'

'I think you're being perfectly beastly.'

'Only now you've changed your mind again,' I said. 'Isn't that so?' I was beginning to be able to predict her sudden changes.

'Yes,' she said. 'Poor Terry. He needs me.'

'He certainly does,' I said.

'Well then,' she said, getting up, 'I'd better go and tell him, hadn't I?'

'John Griffin!'

I turned to see a familiar weather-beaten face smiling at me from behind a table laden with elaborate puddings. I hurried round to greet its owner, a short man with receding red hair dressed in a bulging beige suite with a light Burberry raincoat thrown over his shoulders, the universal badge of an Upper East Sider visiting Europe. Logan Basant was our (my) main East Coast interest. According to Terry's Target Unit, he had $81 million a year to invest in fine art, being the surplus income of his Basant Institute, an ingenious device to buy immortality without losing the advantage of tax deductions whenever

183

the heir to Basant Chemicals might be summoned to his sparkling white neo-classical mausoleum on the hill of Basant University, Vermont. Our forefathers endowed collegiate churches complete with resident choristers praying daily for plenary absolution for their benefactor; today it's a museum of fine art that placates a magnate's nagging fear of oblivion.

'I didn't know you were planning to be over here,' I said, shaking his hand.

'I wasn't,' he said, 'until I saw your catalogue. Then I just couldn't resist it.'

'Bidding?'

'I think I'll have a go at the Winterhalter. Unless you advise against it?'

This was the one thing I liked about Logan. He really enjoyed discussing his potential acquisitions and didn't signal any distrust that I might talk him into buying something just because we were desperate to get it shifted.

'Certainly,' I said. 'But you'll be bidding against Dusseldorf and probably the Ermenonville. They are here in force.'

'I reckon I can cope with them.' Logan smiled complacently. 'What about the Lawrence?'

'Not worth it,' I said. 'Tim Clifford wants that for Edinburgh. He'll get an export ban clapped on if you outbid him.'

'Should you be saying this?'

'No,' I admitted, 'but just between ourselves, concentrate on the Winterhalter, and maybe the Winckelsman commode to go underneath it. They should be together.'

He nodded, and seeing a rival in the distance moved hurriedly away.

Ralph Tritton was very unhappy about the Nicholson flower painting. 'We can't take it out now,' he said.

'Talk to Alan. He was most precise.'

'And sell it at less than half price to your friend?'

'It's not my idea,' I protested.

'You must have suggested it.'

'She suggested it. I asked his advice.'

184

'It's the same thing. I don't like it.'

'We do pay private commissions,' I pointed out. 'She's right about that.'

'I never liked that anyway,' he said. 'We never used to. The whole thing smacks of dishonesty.'

'It will be if we don't square the account with the executors,' I agreed.

'But how will we know what the value would have been?'

'That's a question for probate.'

'Even so, I don't like it.' He stamped off and I went to the office we'd set up in the billiards room to alert the chief porter.

I found Isabel in an upstairs bedroom examining the embroidered silk curtains. 'It's all fixed,' I said. 'You can have it for thirty-five thousand.'

'You angel!' she said, kissing me. 'Can I take it now?'

'No, you can't,' I said. 'And keep your voice down.'

'Are we criminals?' she asked with a chuckle.

'More or less.'

'I've also got my eye on that sideboard. I'm only joking,' she added quickly, seeing my expression.

Terry came storming up. 'Who gave permission for that bloody spaniel to come in here?' he demanded.

'Since you're asking me,' I said calmly, 'you presumably know the answer.'

'Not only has it bitten Tony Sheepshanks on both ankles' (so far, so good, I thought) 'but it's deposited the most gigantic turd on the staircase. I should know. I trod in it.' Oh, Maisie, I thought. What does your heart desire? Lamb chops? A tethered cat? Your wish is my command!

'Terry,' I said confidentially, 'that dog belongs to Colonel Chaucer, and I'm three-quarters of the way to doing a deal with him. So one squeak out of you, managing director or no managing director, and I'll be asking you to explain it in detail to the main board. Geddit?'

He stared at me. 'Every dog has its day,' he said eventually. 'I can see you're in a rare state over this sale. Still, I like a bit of assertiveness in a man.' He turned away

185

while I was debating whether to punch him on his perfect nose.

'Have you seen the chairman, Mr Griffin?' It was the blond girl, Victoria. 'He wanted to show me something in the attic.'

'Nothing you won't recognize,' sniggered Terry, turning back. She walked away, scarlet in the face.

'That was pretty unnecessary,' I suggested.

'Silly little slut,' he said. 'So you've heard about my new appointment?'

'Yes.'

'And about Mary?'

'Yes.'

'Quite my day, in some ways. She'll have to take me as she finds me this time round.'

'Congratulations.'

'Don't be so hypocritical,' he said. 'I know you'd have liked both the job and the girl.'

'I've never tried to take anyone away from her husband,' I said primly.

'Ha!' he scoffed. 'Only because you know you wouldn't succeed. Marriage doesn't last. That hypocrisy's gone. And what are lovers supposed to do? Watch while someone else less scrupulous carries off the girl? What's your plan? Wait till the next man claims her and then step in? But that's no more moral than being first, is it? You shouldn't be in this game if you're going to neuter yourself with Victorian self-righteousness. You know what I really like?' he went on. 'I really like watching you lose!'

He threw back his head and bellowed with triumphant laughter. The other people in the room, self-effacing art lovers, quailed before such an exhibition of uninhibited high spirits. He gave them a merry wave and passed down the corridor, still chuckling.

CHAPTER TWENTY-FOUR

On the first day of the actual sale my post at the office included a fat little parcel. When I opened it, there were two boxes of Havanas and a note.

'In case you didn't see, my mother's dish made £63,000 at your London auction. Enclosed is a wholly inadequate thank-you present.'

The telephone rang. All I could hear was a series of guttural sounds. 'What? I'm sorry, I don't understand.'

'John Griffin?'

'Hans! I've been wondering what happened to you.'

'Oh, my friend. You don't know what it is to live in a world of petty bureaucracy. The minister says this, his aide says that. But I have got your money.'

'Ten million?'

He laughed. 'Let's be reasonable. I have six million. That is a colossal price.'

'If I can get it for you for that,' I said, 'you will have a bargain.' It was more than I had expected him to offer.

'No, John. Not a bargain. But six million sterling we will pay. Do you think you can get it?'

'Yes,' I said. You gain nothing by too much caution. 'Yes, I think so. It'll be a bit complicated. That OK by you?'

I heard a deep sigh of satisfaction. 'You get me the picture, John. I will worry about the complications.'

'Great,' I said. 'Now I must run. We have a sale on this morning.'

'Good luck,' he said.

The chairman, by tradition, always took the first part of our country house sales. It gave a sort of family feeling to the proceedings – something that our major competitors lacked. When I reached the marquee he was knocking down a Reynolds portrait for a quarter of a million to Colnaghis.

I saw a familiar face by the awning: the old man who had bid in the hoax. 'Hello, Mr Gallico,' I said. 'We've got just the thing for you.'

'Indeed?' His large, white face remained expressionless.

'Lot one six three.'

He looked at the entry and snorted.

'Portrait of Orlando, Second Viscount Trent. P. Batoni.' The same artist.

'This one's from his studio, we think,' I said affably. 'Must be worth ten million to you, Mr Gallico.'

He marched away.

'May I have a word?' It was the land agent, Major Blood, wearing a bright pink carnation in his buttonhole. 'So my people can spot me,' he explained. 'Would you like some coffee?'

'Yes, please.'

We walked to his office, stopping to chat to two of the security guards who were patrolling the shrubberies with a dog.

'Anything more on the sale of the land?' he asked.

'Not really.'

'I'll tell you why I'm asking,' he said, then paused.

'Please do.'

'Well.' He was obviously in a quandary. 'I don't quite know how to put this. Ah, here's the coffee.' One of the two severe receptionists stumped in, balancing a mixed set of crockery on a tray. The coffee pot, for example, was Minton, while my cup was a fine example of Crown Derby. We drank in silence.

'And so?'

'It's like this,' he said. Then it all came out with a rush. 'I've been approached, you see. He's an old friend. We were in Aden together after Suez. He's made a fortune – clever chap in his own way – patenting nerve gas. Anyway, Bob, that's my friend, he's interested in settling

188

down now and thought about buying this place. Not the whole show, you understand. Just the house and nice bit of land. For partridge shooting, and perhaps a stud. Of course he'd want to keep me on.' The major dropped his eyes.

'Why not?' I said. 'It sounds an excellent idea.'

'You mean you're not selling it en bloc to the Bridgwaters?' he blurted out.

'Good heavens!' I said. 'Certainly not. Whatever gave you that idea?' It had only been my pet scheme, comprehensively knocked on the head by the chairman.

'Oh, merely gossip,' he said, with a wry smile. 'I know I shouldn't listen, that was the whisper at the Rotary Club.'

'I should've thought they'd got enough investment in land,' I said reassuringly.

'Yes,' he said. 'I expect so. It's just that Naylor, their head man . . . well, he and I never did hit it off. I know I'd be out on my ear if they bought it.

'I'll tell you something else,' he said, 'I think Lord Berington would be interested in buying Ferry House Wood and the farms round it. It'd make a big difference to his shooting. He mentioned it to me a couple of years ago as a sort of joke, but I'm sure he meant it. And he wasn't best pleased when we bought the extra land from the Castletons. I think he wanted that for his younger son.'

'I see.' This was very interesting. I looked at my watch. 'Right,' I said, getting up. 'I'm on the rostrum in an hour. I must go and do my homework.'

Back at the coal face, bidding was going briskly. Robert told me we'd broken two records for artists, one for the Gainsborough group and one for an exquisite piece by Madame Vigée Le Brun.

'But the Canalettos bombed.'

'Unsold?' I said, startled.

'No, but well below estimate.'

'Any idea why?'

'Might have been the quality of the Guardi. It rather put them in perspective for the private buyers.'

'Now show me the seating plan, and the paper bids.'

It went smoothly. A couple of nice Romneys went to Agnews, a huge Hondekoeter was bought by Lord Tottenham, Antoinette put up her hand to bid for the Boldini portrait but was outbid by the Boston Museum of Fine Art. I wondered whether she was bidding for herself or for a Garrisons' client.

'Lot four twenty,' I called out. 'A flower painting, school of Bosschaert.'

The porter held it up. I had seen it hanging over the fireplace in the housekeeper's room, but it was severely blackened, presumably by smoke and poor varnish.

'I've got a telephone bidder on this,' whispered Victoria.

The reserve was two thousand pounds, what we reckoned we could dispose of it for through the trade if bidding was slow. There were no paper bids.

'Now then, ladies and gentlemen,' I said. 'Will you start me at five hundred pounds?'

Alan winked at me from the back.

'Thank you, sir. Five hundred I'm bid. Six hundred.' I nodded to Victoria. 'Six hundred. Any advance on six hundred? Seven hundred. Two bidders.'

We advanced up to three thousand. Victoria shook her head and replaced her receiver. The last bidder, a red face in the middle distance, was on his own.

'Three thousand pounds,' I said. 'Three thousand. Are you finished?'

The fat man put his hand up again.

'Three thousand pounds. Yes, sir. It's your bid. Three thousand. Are you all done?'

He stood up shouting. I suddenly recognized Mr Tredinnick.

'I'm bidding. Can't you see? Are you deaf or something?'

I leant over the rostrum.

'I'm quite willing to continue the bidding indefinitely if you insist on bidding against yourself,' I said. 'But that last bid of three thousand pounds is your own.'

190

'Oh,' he said. 'Well, why didn't you say so before?' He subsided. His wife hid her face behind her catalogue.

'Three thousand two hundred. A new bidder.' A woman in the corner had waved her scarf. 'Against you, sir, three thousand two hundred pounds.'

Mr Tredinnick wouldn't even look up.

'Three thousand two, three thousand two hundred. It's against you, Mr Tredinnick.' His face took on a look of furious concentration, as if he was transferring himself bodily to another location by sheer will-power.

'Three thousand two hundred. Have you all done? Three thousand two hundred.' I banged the gavel. 'Mrs Castleton,' I whispered to Suzanne, who was collecting the details. She sent one of the other girls off with the sales slip.

'Lot four twenty-one, a portrait of Mrs Leonard Spencer by Gerard Brockhurst.'

When it was Robert's turn to take over, I walked across to the caterer's tent for a cup of tea. The sun was very bright and the countryside looked superb in its autumn colours. On an impulse, I turned and went to our office. I rang the Passenham number.

'Colonel Chaucer?'

'Yes. Speak up, can you?'

'It's John Griffin. I'm just heading home and I wondered if I could drop in.'

'Of course, my dear boy. Come and have some tea. We've got muffins!'

Maisie was watching for me through a window, barking excitedly. How could she possibly have known that I had brought a chocolate dog biscuit for her?

'What's this? Bribery?' shouted the colonel. 'I was right about you all along, I'm sure you're not here just to feed Maisie,' he added shrewdly. 'Business first, then tea.'

'Right,' I said. 'Can we go out on to the lawn the other side?'

'Something subtle, eh?' he said.

We stood on the terrace looking over the water at the distant village of Stoke Spencer and its surrounding hills. The woods were soft and hazy, with the farmland showing up as reddish brown plough. Spirals of smoke drifted up from the little village houses clustered round the church. It was as idyllic a scene in this afternoon sunlight as you could hope to find anywhere in the world.

'Come on,' he said. 'Spit it out. You want my lovely girl.'

'I want,' I said carefully, 'to do a swap. One piece of beauty for another. You once said this wasn't a view, but someone else's land.'

'Go on.' The colonel's face was cold now, facing reality. If ever a man needed money, it was he. Yet he had hung on to that picture through all the lean years, refusing even to show it to anyone lest the price offered be too high to be rejected.

'The Dutch government will present you with the whole of the southern section of the Trent Hall estate, four thousand acres with a rent roll of nearly a quarter of a million, in exchange for your picture. Some of the land will have to be sold for capital tax purposes, no doubt. But this view would take her place. It would be your land, not someone else's. We would, of course, commission a copy for you as well.'

He turned away. His head bent over. Suddenly he was erect again, wiping his eyes with a vast red and white spotted handkerchief which he pulled from his sleeve. We stood for a long time in silence. In the distance I could hear the Stoke Spencer church clock striking four. There was a distinct chill in the air.

'I'm sorry,' he said at last. 'But I love her. I really love her. You'll have to take her now. I can't bear to think about it. Just take her and leave. And none of your bloody gimcrack copies. You're a bastard, Griffin, but the rest of my family will thank you.'

I walked slowly into the house and took the picture off the wall. Maisie watched me carry it past her without a sound. But as I put her rival into my car, she scampered back to console her master.

CHAPTER TWENTY-FIVE

Having got the picture safely stored in our strong room, I had to move swiftly. The next day I contacted first the professor, who was delighted with the plan, then Lord Berington who confirmed that his younger son's trustees would pay an arbitrated figure for the off-lying part of the Castleton land and for the Ferry House parcel, nearly three thousand acres in all. He also used Dangerfields, so most of the details were faxed through from Trent Hall after I had explained the deal to the chairman and Terry as managing director.

'You've got to hand it to him,' said the chairman. 'It's a nice piece of work. And no agents' fees. It's a bit of good news to set against the latest bank rate increase.'

'Yes,' said Terry, watching me through half-closed eyes. 'You've done very well, Johnny. Any news on Lord Tottenham?'

'Cor blimey!' shouted the chairman. 'Give the man a chance.'

'Just keeping him up to the mark,' chuckled my persecutor. 'We don't want any slacking.'

No, indeed.

Major Blood was overjoyed. Could his friend manage to buy fifteen hundred acres? Yes, he was sure he could. He'd have the offer in by the next day.

'Do you think Colonel Chaucer will want my part-time help?' he asked hopefully.

'I doubt it,' I said. 'His son is an agent up north. I'm pretty sure he'll move back now. Even if they have to sell a quarter of it, there'll still be plenty to do.'

All that day and the next the sale proceeded along its orderly, efficient path. No more records were broken except when two identically peroxided blondes tried to outbid each other for a dumpy sofa covered in old chintz, establishing an all-time world record for dumpy sofas.

The last day we were into oddments. The cars and carriages and garden ornaments in the morning, general fixtures and fittings in the afternoon. I had been keeping an eye open for the club fender. It was lot 2410. Robert was taking the sale and doing rather well. I stepped up beside him.

'I'd like to do the next half-hour and then go home. All right by you?'

'Of course,' he said abjectly. 'Whatever you say.'

'Thanks.' He stepped down and I took over.

Victoria was noting the results. She was wearing a new lipstick today and had painted her nails. She was also wearing a very pretty diamond bracelet. Evidently she had discovered that the chairman was her type.

'Tat for tit,' Rodney murmured in my ear as he passed.

'Any problems?' I asked her.

'Not so far.'

'Lot two four one o,' I said.

'The club fender. Over here, sir,' chimed the porter.

I had spotted Stubbs. He was standing at the back of the tent, his face already lugubrious with anticipated failure. The estimate was five hundred pounds, so he must at least be prepared to pay that much. There was no reserve.

'Ten pounds,' I said. 'Anyone bid ten pounds?'

Several hands shot up. My first job was to slow the pace. I crept up. Fifteen, twenty, twenty-five, thirty. There was nothing I could do until we got to about two hundred, but I was banking on thinning out the competition through sheer boredom. A hundred and sixty-five, seventy, seventy-five, eighty. On we crawled.

Stubbs still hadn't made any sign of trying to bid, but his eyes were watching me.

There were three bidders now, and no doubt several others yet to enter. I had to find a window of opportunity.

The next step was to slow the pace of the actual bids.

194

'A hundred and eighty-five . . .' I ignored the urgent signals of the underbidders. I hoped my elephantine manner would lull them into thinking they had all the time in the world.

'A hundred and ninety-five. It's a very nice club fender, ladies and gentlemen. Made for the house, I don't doubt. Very fine piece of craftsmanship. Two hundred. Thank you very much, madam. Two hundred bid for this exceptional artefact.' Two of the bidders started looking through their catalogues out of sheer boredom. The third was talking to her neighbours.

'Two hundred and five?' I said directly at Stubbs. He nodded. I banged the gavel. 'Sold for two hundred and five pounds. Stubbs.'

Victoria smiled at me. 'Friend of yours?' she said sweetly.

'Probably forgot to tip him,' said Terry. I hadn't noticed he had been standing behind me. 'That wasn't very ethical,' he said, an aggressive expression taking shape.

'Do you want the Tottenham silver or don't you?' I hissed on the spur of the moment.

He raised his eyebrows and smiled. 'Oh?' he said. 'Yes. I like it.'

I wiped my brow. 'Here!' I called to Robert. 'You can take over now.'

That night I rang the professor. 'Fifty-seven million pounds,' I said.

'Ridiculous, isn't it?' he said, laughing. 'And you think that bust will pay most of the tax?'

'Yes,' I said. 'I think it will pay the lion's share anyway. Most of the property passed into the trust between 1954 and 1973. There's quite a lot of recent indexation to claim, and of course the relevant tax was paid then. The land and the house should bring in another sixteen million. I reckon that, excluding the investments, we will be sending Dangerfields over sixty-five million pounds before Christmas.'

'You think I can afford a stocking, then?'

I laughed obediently.

'I'm sorry I didn't come,' he said. 'I just couldn't face it.'

'I entirely understand,' I said.

'But I'm delighted the Chaucers are getting Stoke Spencer. They were always kind to me.'

'Good,' I said. It's a rare transaction where everyone's happy.

Even Mr and Mrs Horrod were pleased to be retiring to Torquay.

Back to pot lids.

CHAPTER TWENTY-SIX

'John?'

'Yes, Mary.'

We'd been valuing the contents of a house where the elderly couple had died within days of each other after sixty-seven years of marriage. We'd stopped for tea in Market Plumby. I'd thought of trying to take her hand again, and discarded the idea. Life seemed set to carry on downhill. I was planning a long holiday, if the chairman agreed, preparatory to a new start, emotionally if not also professionally. That depended, I guessed, on Terry. Not a very safe foundation to build on.

'It's possible, isn't it?'

'What?'

'To be happy together.'

'For sixty-seven years, you mean?'

'Yes.'

'Yes,' I said. 'Or for a good long while, at least. My parents were. Your parents were. My brother and sister-in-law are.'

'But you weren't,' she said. 'And George and I aren't.'

'Cheer up,' I said. 'It doesn't mean we're pariahs. Perhaps we made a mistake, or we grew apart. Married too young. Luck plays a big part.'

'It's cliché time, is it?'

She was wearing a grey suit with a scarlet blouse that set off her colouring. The skirt, cut like a tulip, hugged her hips and she g.ve off a heady scent.

'How's your daughter?' I asked by way of a diversion.

She smiled, recognizing a change of subject. 'She's fine. A little broody perhaps, but nothing out of the way.'

'And your plans to move?'

'Proceeding slowly. I'm not telling the children yet.'

'Is that fair on Terry?'

'John.'

'Yes, my dearest Mary?' I said meekly.

'You have got to stifle these unnatural impulses to take Terry's part. Masculine trade unionism doesn't suit you any more than mawkishness.'

'I hear and obey.'

'Or satirical servility.'

'Do you think you might be rather difficult to please?' I asked with genuine interest.

'Yes,' she said. 'All women are. We can't afford the male luxury of self-deprecation.'

'No room even for a sense of humour?'

'Not about ourselves.'

'I've always thought,' I counter-attacked, 'that that was the only true test of a sense of humour. Any fool can laugh at someone else's misfortunes.'

'It takes a real fool to laugh at himself, you mean?' she snapped.

She was angry so I backed off, too tired to face what would have been unusual for us, a real row. Let Terry cope with this, I thought. He has the compensations to go with it.

'Are you worried about the children switching so abruptly from one man in your life to another?'

'That's it!' she cried. 'If only Terry would let us move in by ourselves.'

'Into *his* house?' I asked, amazed.

'Where else? You'd think he'd be pleased. After all, he says he can't live without me.'

'That's because he believes you want him too.'

She dropped her eyes, then she took my hand. 'Could you suggest it to him, John?'

'Me?'

'You've been such an angel in listening to us both he might accept it better from you.'

'I can't think why.'

'Because,' she said, 'he respects your judgement. You may not like each other, but in many ways you are rather alike.'

There was a pause.

'Please?' she persisted.

I forced my gaze up from her lap to meet her eyes. It was impossible to decipher her expression. I nodded with great reluctance. 'I'll talk to him,' I said. 'But don't expect too much.'

'Thank you,' she said. 'Can you drop me home? I mustn't be late for Rosie's dancing class.'

I left her at their farm gate. Later I rang Terry at his home, feeling a complete idiot as I did so.

'I've been talking to Mary.'

'I wish you wouldn't interfere,' he said angrily.

'I know. I'm sorry. But I've got a suggestion.'

'Which is?'

'Let her move into Ladbroke Grove with the children on her own. Give them time to readjust. You know how important they are to her.'

'What's it got to do with you?' he said.

'Nothing,' I agreed. 'But it's good advice.'

'Well, keep it to yourself,' he said. In the background I could hear another voice. 'I'm sorry to interrupt you,' I said. 'I'd hoped to catch you alone.'

'Some of us have work to do,' he said. 'I've got Lionel Bridgwater here. We're planning the sale.'

There was muffled high-pitched laughter, then he rang off.

CHAPTER TWENTY-SEVEN

As soon as I reached the office the next morning Mrs Gaskin bustled in.

'Thank goodness you're early,' she said. 'I wanted to warn you.'

What now?

'It's Robert Head. He's in a terrible state. He was outside the door when I arrived. He must have been there some time because he was shaking with cold.'

'So?'

'It's something he's had in the post. I said you wouldn't be here until nine thirty, so he's gone off to see his solicitor, he said. He'll be back any minute.'

A door slammed.

'That'll be him now, I expect,' she said.

It was. Robert burst in through the door, his face mottled, pale green and twitching with some uncontrollable emotion.

'Thank you, Mrs Gaskin,' I said. 'Come and sit down, Robert.'

He contained himself until she had left the room and then exploded.

'What's this?' he shouted. 'What the *fuck* is this?'

He thrust a thick envelope in my face.

'Calm down,' I said. 'And let me look at it.'

It was a summons. 'Thorpe v. Merrywethers' I read.

'When's it for?' I scanned the details. 'Today! When did you get this?'

'I don't know,' he said. 'I haven't been looking at the post while the sale was on. I opened it this morning.'

Then I remembered. Robert's four files, still hidden in my safe. The fraudulent valuations I had been meaning to

200

put right. And the name on the top file had been Thorpe.

Frantically I dialled the London office.

'Who deals with litigation?' I asked the operator. It was years since I'd been involved in any active contest of this sort.

'Mr Bonas,' she said, then added, 'Well, his office. Shall I put you through to Judy?' There was a series of clicks.

'Judy Wells.' I had a vague picture of a tall woman with short brown hair and glasses slung round her neck on a ribbon.

'Judy, it's John Griffin here.'

'Oh, yes?' she said.

'Do you know anything about a court case? Thorpe versus Merrywethers.'

'Yes. Mr Bonas was dealing with it.'

'Can you give me any details?'

'Mmm. I've got some papers here. Most of it's with the solicitors.'

'What's the dispute?' Even though I knew. I was now feeling as worried as Robert looked.

'Some dealer who bought something on an agreed valuation. You know the sort of thing.'

'Why in heaven's name wasn't I told?' I asked quietly.

'To tell the truth,' she said, 'I don't think Mr Bonas took it very seriously. He just told Truscotts to see them off.'

'But . . .' It was no good. 'Can you give me Truscotts' number?' I desperately thumbed through the papers. The Isleworth court, eleven a.m. We'd never make it. I scribbled down the number and hung up. 'Come on,' I said. 'Let's get there.'

I ran back to my house to get my car but it was ten to twelve when I parked outside the court house. There was a girl from Truscotts waiting anxiously on the steps. I'd been able to ring through to get a message and I knew that Mr Truscott would be in court.

'Hurry up,' she said. 'They're well on with us. The previous case folded early.'

Robert and I sat on a cold green bench in the corridor.

We'd agreed that the only thing to do was to stick with his valuation whatever it was and plead ignorance.

'You won't rat on me?' he asked miserably.

'No,' I answered him. 'I promise I won't.'

Mr Truscott, an elderly man with freckled skin, hurried out.

'Is it too late to settle?' I asked.

'Settle?' he said. 'I've been *begging* your people to settle. Jack Bonas wouldn't even take my calls. They've got a mass of people in there. Dangerfields are acting for the defendants.'

'Dangerfields? In a case like this?'

'Sir John Best, no less.'

I began to realize what I might be in for. 'Just go in and settle.'

'On your authority?'

'On my authority.'

The court usher came out. 'Mr Head.'

Robert followed him.

'Do something,' I said to Truscott, who was clearly dithering.

'I can't go against my instructions,' he said obstinately.

'Look,' I said. 'I'm a main-board director, and I'm instructing you to stop this case. Please do it.'

'I'll have to speak to Mr Burton.'

'Mr Burton?' I exploded. 'What's it got to do with Mr Burton?'

'He's managing director now, isn't he?'

'Ring him then, but for heaven's sake be quick.'

'This isn't my fault, you know,' he said truculently. 'There's no need to be offensive.'

'I'm sorry,' I said. 'But it's vital. Ring him, please.'

'Very well,' he said. 'But it's very irregular.'

Got it in one.

The court usher came out again. 'Mr Griffin!'

'Me?' I stood up, astounded. 'But I've not been summoned.'

He looked at his list. 'Yes, you have, sir,' he said. 'And you're here. This way, please. The judge is waiting.'

I stared round wildly for Truscott. There was no sign of him.

'If you please, sir.' The usher was becoming restive. I followed him into the hot little courtroom. Sir John Best was sitting in the second pew behind two men in wigs. He winked at me. I tried a smile. I shouldn't think it was very convincing.

'Raise your right hand, please.'

I took the oath. Robert was sitting in a chair at the back of the court, his face even greener than before.

I turned and faced the judge, a youngish man who was watching me closely. One of the two men with wigs, fat and with a broad welcoming smile, stood up.

'Mr Griffin?'

'Yes.'

'Mr John Griffin?'

'Yes.'

'You're a director of Merrywethers, the defendants in this action?'

'I am.'

'A main-board member?'

'Yes.'

'May I show you this valuation? It's exhibit one, Your Honour.'

The judge inclined his head and made a note.

It was Robert's valuation, countersigned with my signature at the bottom, valuing a pair of terracotta figures by Clodion at £65,000. Not out of the way; if they were by Clodion, that is.

'That is your signature?'

I looked at it closely. 'It is.'

'Could you explain to the court the procedure your company adopts in these matters?'

'Certainly.' I ran them through the need for private sales, the system for valuation and our office etiquette.

'So you wouldn't necessarily see the pieces yourself?'

'No.'

'In fact you didn't inspect these particular figures?'

'No.'

203

'Have you ever seen them?'

'No.'

'You're sure?' He advanced menacingly.

'Yes. At least . . .'

'At least . . . ?'

'It's possible that I've seen them somewhere. But very unlikely. It's not my field.'

'It's not your field,' he repeated slowly. 'So you left the valuation to your colleague Robert Head?'

'Yes.'

'Who is qualified to make such valuations?'

'Yes,' I said, trying to smile at Robert. He looked as if he was going to faint. 'He's highly qualified to do so.'

'Highly qualified? Indeed?' The man's eyebrows were raised in polite scorn. 'I see!' He walked away from me, then turned abruptly: 'And you have every faith in his probity?'

'Of course.'

'You're on oath, Mr Griffin.'

I could feel my heart beginning to pump too fast. 'I'm aware of that.'

'I'm glad you are. I'm going to put that question again, because I want to help you.' His smile was chilling. 'At the time that you signed this valuation, you had every faith in his probity?'

I relaxed. This was help, indeed. 'Yes,' I said confidently. 'I can swear to that.'

'You are swearing to it,' he said. 'Now, has anything happened since to cause you to doubt that probity?'

I paused.

'You are on oath, Mr Griffin. Kindly remember that.'

'I'm sure Mr Griffin is aware of it,' put in the judge, giving me a welcome space to catch my breath.

'I am infinitely obliged to Your Honour,' said the barrister, who was looking anything but.

Best sat up straighter in his seat and stared at me.

'No.'

'Are you aware of the penalties for perjury?' snapped the judge.

'I am, Your Honour,' I said, trying to keep my voice steady.

'I have here a tape recording of a conversation between you and Mr Head in your office,' said the barrister, trying not to sound too smug. 'I'd like to play it to you.'

But his last words were drowned in uproar. The other barrister was on his feet demanding something and – worse – Robert was also standing up and shouting, 'You bastard. You *bloody* fool!' at me.

The judge's gavel banged again and again on his desk. Two ushers were hustling Robert out of the room. Mr Truscott had hurried in and was frantically hissing something in the other barrister's ear.

'Clear the court!' cried the usher.

The girl took me by the arm as I left the witness box. 'We're going to wait in the corridor.'

'Will you keep your head?' I hissed at Robert, when we were outside together.

'But the recording!'

'It's a bluff. It's got to be.'

'You mean you didn't tape our conversation?' he whined.

'Of course not. What's more, I actually checked the telephone the week before. I'm risking a prison sentence to protect you, so pull yourself together.'

Mr Truscott came out again, his face scarlet with anger and the freckles showing up as purple.

'This is the last job I do for Merrywethers,' he said. 'I've never been involved in anything like this before.'

'Did you speak to Burton?'

'Yes. He said to settle. We'll have to pay in full and my fees will reflect the damage this has done to my firm.'

'No doubt,' I said coldly.

'But it may not end there. The judge is out for your blood. Our man's putting up a terrific fight. I don't think they can use the tape. We're claiming it's illegal.'

'What tape?'

'Whatever *your* standards may be,' Mr Truscott said, working himself into a terrible rage, 'you don't find

Queen's Counsel claiming evidence that doesn't exist.'

'Queen's Counsel! For a damages dispute?'

'I told you they're taking it seriously.'

The usher returned. 'Mr Griffin.'

Not since the days of waiting outside Der Führer's study in the sure knowledge that his knobbed cane was being flexed ready for me had I felt so afraid.

I returned to the witness box.

'Mr Griffin.' Everyone else was seated. The judge was staring at me with great distaste. 'I have every reason to believe that you have recently committed a serious crime in this courtroom. Deliberate perjury, to be precise. Since we follow the practice of the law, and even though the proof of your crime is inadmissible by virtue of its being obtained illegally, there is nothing to stop me referring this to the Director of Public Prosecutions. Your learned counsel has suggested, with no shadow of proof as far as I can see, that you were acting honourably in protecting a subordinate. It seems to me just as possible that you were hoping to secure a dishonourable and deceitful success for your firm in this law suit, which I understand now to have been settled with full costs in favour of the plaintiff. After careful thought, I have decided not to pursue the matter, but I will not disguise my shock and disgust that a man in your position should conduct himself in so disgraceful a manner. Because of reporting restrictions your behaviour will go unheard, but I intend to take this opportunity, before my colleagues' – his glance took in the silent seated men, all of whom, including Best, were watching me intently – 'of asserting that such conduct makes you wholly unfit to hold the senior position in a respected firm that you currently hold. Leave this court!'

I walked out, collected Robert and we drove northwards in silence. Having made an appointment to see the chairman the next day, I switched off the car telephone. I had no wish to hear Terry's opinion on the subject, though nothing he could say would be more severe than my own self-judgement.

CHAPTER TWENTY-EIGHT

I spent the rest of the day indoors, in my new home, reviewing the last few weeks. I didn't much like the attitudes I had begun to take, the manipulations I was finding it easy to orchestrate. I could claim, if I wanted to, that I had felt myself forced into shoddy dealing because of the need to keep my job, but I found that I did not want to abdicate responsibility for my own standards in this way. If the job was taking precedence over my standards, it was time that I changed the job. It seemed a long way from studying Masaccio in Florence, secretly accompanied by Barbara, the image of Botticelli's Primavera with all the alluring grace of youth. Where was she? I wondered. Pursuing her immature lover on the Pacific Express? Was she as lost as I? John Griffin the Avenger seemed rather a poor fool to me.

The telephone's discordant jangle interrupted my reverie.

'Yes?'

'Fifteen all.' It was Antoinette.

'How do you mean?'

'Don't you understand? You're very simple,' she said, with a smile in her voice. 'Today was my revenge. You can't think I wasn't entitled to it. Rupert thought you got off lightly.'

'Was it your idea?' I asked, intrigued.

'You don't think poor old John Best could have thought it up on his own?' She laughed scornfully. 'He's such a booby!'

'But . . . ?'

'Perhaps you'll be more careful next time,' she said.

'Wait!' I said. I could feel she was about to ring off. Silence for ever. 'Wait!'

'Well?' Her accent was already more pronounced, anticipating her exodus.

'You're right,' I said. 'I deserved today. As a matter of fact, it's helped. I'm going to resign.' This wasn't much of a gesture. Terry would surely have grounds enough to dismiss me.

'Oh, don't overdo it,' she said. 'As soon as John played me the tape, I knew you would protect your crooked colleague. You're too emotional, my friend.'

'But how was it done? I actually checked the office.'

'I know. You should have seen us listening to the tape where you took the telephone to pieces. John was crying with laughter.'

I made no reply, though I couldn't repress a smile myself.

'Well, there you are,' she said. 'But I like you. Now we're even, let's meet for lunch in London.'

'Will you be alone?'

'Perhaps.' She laughed. 'We'll see.'

She rang off. I stared into the receiver, then put it down – very slowly. At least I was solvent, healthy and under no further threat of public disgrace.

'What a mess.'

I was at head office, sitting opposite a three-man tribunal: the chairman in his throne, Terry on one side watching me, Lord Darlington on the other staring into space.

'I take full responsibility,' I said.

'But why didn't Jack tell *one* of us?' intoned the chairman.

'Sick man,' muttered Lord Darlington. 'Sick man.'

Terry nodded energetically, then he leant forward licking his upper lip. 'Will you resign, or do we have to dismiss you?' The chairman was looking at his hands, but Lord Darlington's eyes were now fixed on mine. His expression was one of intense excitement.

'Of course I resign forthwith,' I said without hesitation. 'And I'm grateful for your allowing me to do so. This whole business has made me look at myself, and I don't much like what I've become.'

'I've never noticed any difference,' muttered Lord Darlington. I laughed.

'It's hardly a laughing matter,' said the chairman, 'Ralph says he will resign with you if you go.'

'That's uncommonly generous of him.'

'It jolly well is,' said the chairman, 'considering the terms of his pension agreement.'

'Don't worry,' I said. 'I'll talk him out of it.'

'I've accepted Robert's resignation as of this morning,' put in Terry. 'And we're reimbursing the four clients identified by Mrs Sykes.'

'Good, good.' murmured the chairman absent-mindedly. He was toying with his pen. 'John, I don't like to see you go in this way.'

'Thank you,' I said. 'But it's unavoidable.'

'Yes,' he said. 'But you must work your two weeks' notice as per contract. That's right, isn't it?' he appealed to Lord Darlington.

'Quite right.'

I suppressed another laugh. 'Because?' I asked.

'Because of tidying up in preparation for the Bridgwater sale. Terry's going there this weekend. He needs your support. And they're asking for you in New York. Will you do it?'

'Naturally,' I said, 'if I can have tomorrow and Thursday off. I want to visit my brother.'

'Agreed.' He waved his hand majestically, adding, 'You know how important this sale is for the future of the company.'

I did indeed. With the bank rate up again, money was pouring out of Merrywethers in unsustainable torrents.

I nodded. And escaped.

I rang my brother.

'John?' he said. 'Is that you?'

'Yes,' I said. 'Can I come home?'

'Of course,' he replied. 'When shall we expect you?'

'Tomorrow teatime.'

The following afternoon the weather broke and the Northumbrian sky grew prematurely black as gusts of piercingly cold wind began to sweep across the ploughland, shaking the trees and beating the spiky saplings in the hedges. In Hanging Wood the great beeches began to sigh and crack as the wind took hold of them and tugged and buffeted at their foliage, sending great spirals of the last remaining leaves, brown, green, blue and orange, landing gently on the forest floor. In the anthill that I was watching so intently all was normal. The endless seamless heaving of that integrated world of pine needles, earth and ants continued in its ceaseless labour with the columns of its grimly methodical forces passing and repassing on their expeditions far into the forest. The weather to them was like the universe to man, a vast, mysterious setting that bracketed their tiny world and whose great effects one may observe and comment on without ever feeling individually involved.

I was well wrapped in a thick green shooting coat over several pullovers, and my feet were warm and comfortable in boots my brother had lent me. As the cold increased, I began to rub my hands vigorously together.

Just in front of me, as I sat with my back against the tall pine, the earthworks of a badger sett commanded the dell like some ancient prehistoric fortress. It required little imagination to picture these massed excavations, with their banked-up escarpments and air of solid permanence, as the setting for the ancient tragedies of mythology – the battleground for Achilles and Hector, or Tristan and Mark. The wind died down, and I felt a spot of rain. It gently brushed my nose and gratefully I lifted my face towards the purple glow of the sky that I could just make out through the branches above.

Suddenly I felt, rather than saw, a movement and very slowly brought my head round to face the sett. A large badger, her coat ruffled and dusted with soil, had emerged and was sniffing the air, her heavy head motionless. Almost immediately three other smaller heads appeared a few yards on her right. They must have come out already, I thought, out of sight under the rim of that earthbank.

I was amazed at their beauty, by the vivid exotic air that their fierce black and white stripes gave them in the soft, subdued colours of a wood at dusk. And as they moved about, grunting and sniffing, their great coats swaying as if barely connected with their busy scrabbling feet, I watched fascinated, a spectator of the primeval world of nature washed clean of human complications.

Then there was a new clarity in the air and as I sniffed, some sense awakening, some memory stirred, and it began to snow. Great white flakes, softly, silently, heavy and peaceful, came falling across me and already it was settling, firm, shining, beautiful. I felt my whole body contract into one vast shivering burst of natural joy, in which memories of childhood, the primitive instinct for the seasons and my own sharpened senses combined with natural vigour and animal spirits to produce an intense, almost overpowering, sense of supernatural awe.

But now it was night. As the snow settled on my shoulders it blotted out the sounds of the wood: the sudden cry from a bird at roost, the eerie snapping of twigs, the flutter of the last returning pigeon seeking sanctuary. Picking up my torch, I made my way reluctantly back along the glistening path, down past the old millpond and across the stream where the brambles were assuming strange new proportions and already the water was running higher. By tomorrow it would have retaken most of the reedy banks – the annual territorial assertion of its power as it welcomed reinforcements from the hills above, cascading down the mossy drains and swelling the stream to a spate of foaming, peaty water that would surge and beat against the stone bridge by the old abbey mill as it had done for centuries past.

The sound of my feet crunching through the snow towards the main road was oddly comforting, reminiscent, perhaps, of long childhood walks with my father,

211

whose sculpting skills produced magnificent confections: snow palaces with wings and porticoes, or huge snow beasts with horns and long snaking tails.

What are my worries, I thought as I laughed in the face of the blowing snow, licking away the icy flakes with my tongue, when the world continues like this? And it was with a much lighter heart that I started the long climb up across the park to the lights of the house.

CHAPTER TWENTY-NINE

When I returned to Berington after lunch and let myself in through the door of my little house there was a single letter on the mat. It was from my club. I paused only to put my sister-in-law's flowers into water before opening it.

'Dear Mr Griffin,' it said.

As Chairman of the House Committee, it is my unpleasant duty, in accordance with Rule XIV, to ask you to consider offering your resignation forthwith, following your unfortunate appearance in court. This would preclude our having to convene a sub-committee to consider the matter less discreetly.
Yours etc.

It was signed: John Best.

Underneath, he had written in pencil: 'You will understand my deep personal regret at having to write to you in this vein.'

I laughed out loud. The old scoundrel! He must have had a hard time keeping a straight face in front of the club secretary.

I scribbled a quick response, resigning forthwith. Sad but not unreasonable under the circumstances, I decided.

Packing a suitcase, I drove south for my second visit to Bridgwater Park. The same man was on duty at the gate, but this time he was expecting me and as I drove on, admiring the same splendid view of the house across the valley, I noticed that the scarlet and silver flag was now flying high.

'You must be John Griffin.'

'Yes, Duke.'

'Oh, Lionel, *please*.' He was still wearing make-up, but the hair was shorter and dyed a paler shade of gold. 'Terry says you're the best man they've got on assessing the market.'

I was unexpectedly flattered. I had been half prepared for a hostile reception. Certainly not for praise from Terry.

'It won't be hard with these pictures,' I said. 'They are among the finest remaining in private hands.'

He smirked and, taking my case, handed it to the old man who had shuffled across the hall to join us. 'Mr Griffin's in the Chinese dressing room.'

The old man nodded and made his way painfully back towards another doorway.

'Come and have a drink. Terry and Mrs – um, is it Sykes? – are here already and some friends of mine called Tredinnick.'

The dreaded couple with the tapestry.

'Ah.'

'I think you've met them. Mimsie is a goddaughter of my mother's.'

I wasn't looking forward to meeting her other half again. I followed him through a series of rather austere rooms into a small sitting room.

'Oh!' I couldn't restrain my response to the pictures – twelve Tintorettos, 'The Parables', hung two deep and so close to each other that it was almost as if the room were frescoed.

'Not bad, eh?' He seemed remarkably normal, I was beginning to think, apart from the squeak and the face.

'How are you?' Mrs Tredinnick had been standing in front of the fire talking to Terry and came over to shake my hand. She had such a charming smile that it completely dominated her otherwise dowdy appearance. It radiated a universal kindness and warmth. 'I thought you were marvellous taking the Trent sale.'

'Oh, thank you.' Like most men, I am secretly thrilled by any flattery, however ill-deserved. Did I say secretly?

I suspect that it was written over my face in blazing Technicolor.

'Puffy gets very nervous bidding, I'm afraid. It's all those people – he's shy, you know.'

'Really?'

'Oh, yes.' She laughed, a surprisingly loud sound from such a comparatively small frame. 'I know he doesn't seem that way. He's terrified of being dominated. That's why he pretends to be so fierce.'

Mary came in, followed by the object of our conversation. He looked just as aggressive as when I'd last seen him bidding against himself at Trent Hall.

'Hello,' he said, thrusting his chin out and shaking his stomach within its waistcoat. 'Working weekends now, are you?' He thrust down his hand but this time I was prepared, and advanced mine at chest level. There was a distinct pause while our two hands hovered, mine about eighteen inches above his. Our eyes met. I smiled and reluctantly he raised his hand and took mine in a moist and flabby embrace.

'I hope Mary has been showing you the pictures,' I said.

'Oh, no,' he protested. 'I'm *very* familiar with them. Mrs Tredinnick has been advising Cousin Lionel on the rehanging.'

'Splendid!' I said. 'I'm sure she would do that very well.'

'And why shouldn't she?' he blurted out, as if he had been certain of scorn.

'You quite misunderstand me,' I said truthfully. 'From everything I have seen of your wife, I believe she has excellent taste.'

Except in men? It was time to claim a hug from Mary. I tried not to linger over it.

'Did you have a good drive down?'

'I came by train,' she replied.

'By train? I thought Terry was driving you.'

'He decided to come early.'

'I'm the culprit.'

I'd completely forgotten our host, who had been stand-ing watching us. There was a motionless quality about Lionel Bridgwater that I found creepy, even threaten-ing. Now he walked forward and placed a hand on Mrs Tredinnick's arm.

'I lured Terry with the promise of a voyage of discovery in the muniment room.'

I caught Mary's eye. It glittered.

'Four clubs.'

'How much?'

We had settled down to bridge. I had drawn with Mary against Puffy Tredinnick who was playing with his wife. We were sitting round a card table comfortably drawn up in front of the library fire, Mary having double-jumped in hearts.

'Four clubs,' I repeated, for his benefit.

'Oh, dear,' said Mary, 'I always get in a muddle with this.'

Puffy held up his hand. 'No conferring, please.' He winked at his wife, but she was smiling reassuringly at Mary and chose not to notice. 'Well?' he said truculently.

'It's your bid,' I pointed out.

'Oh, no bid,' he said. 'No *bid.*'

'Four spades,' said Mary in a careful voice.

'*Four spades?*' shouted Puffy.

'No bid,' murmured his wife.

'Four no-trumps,' I said quickly.

'Meaning?' Puffy leaned towards me, his little blue eyes screwed up in uncertainty.

'Darling, you really shouldn't ask him,' said his wife.

'Look.' He turned on her. 'Do mind your own business, my darling, *please.*' She sighed.

I looked at my cards: four spades to the king, a void in hearts, three diamonds to the knave and six clubs to the king, knave. I was feeling aggressive.

'I mean to say, is that a conventional bid?' he insisted.

'You'll have to ask my partner,' I said, without raising my eyes.

216

He turned to Mary. 'Yes,' she said. 'Are you bidding?'

'No bid,' he said. 'Kings, eh?'

'Five diamonds.' Again Mary's voice was thoughtful, poised.

'No bid,' from Mimsie Tredinnick.

'Seven clubs,' I said.

'*DOUBLE!*' shouted Puffy triumphantly.

'Redouble,' whispered Mary.

'*REDOUBLE?*' he squeaked.

'No bid,' said his wife.

'No bid,' I chimed in.

There was a long silence.

Then Puffy folded up his cards with a snap and slapped them on the table.

'No . . . *bid*!' he said. 'I need a drink. Hey, Sanders!'

The tall, dark man had quietly entered to put some more peat on the fire. It smelt delicious and gave off a misty blue smoke.

'Yes, sir?'

'Some more of this ducal brandy.' Puffy was waving his empty glass.

'May I get you some more Cointreau, madam?' he asked Mary, but she shook her head, as did Mimsie.

'A little whisky, sir?'

I smiled a refusal. He took Puffy's glass and retreated.

'Your lead,' I said to Puffy.

'All right, all right.' He sniffed and threw out a card. The ace of hearts.

'Try that for starters,' he said, wriggling on his chair.

Mary put down her hand: the ace, queen, knave of spades, the queen and five small hearts, no diamonds, and four clubs to the ace. Unless one of them had all three missing clubs to the queen, it was a lay-down.

Oh, dear. I know I shouldn't have. But I gave a stage groan and then played a low heart from Mary's hand. Mimsie followed with the eight of hearts and I paused.

'Good God!' cried Puffy, impatient for his victory. 'Hurry up!'

I slipped out the two of clubs, pushing the cards across

to Mary who gathered them briskly into our first trick.

'*What?*' Puffy's face flooded with blood, turning the cheeks purple with stress. I played the ace of clubs from my hand. They both followed suit. Not daring to risk Puffy's further confusion, I played it out, Mimsie's queen of clubs falling on Mary's king on the second round.

'Seven clubs doubled and redoubled,' I intoned as I wrote. 'Two hundred and eighty. Grand slam vulnerable, fifteen hundred. Rubber seven hundred. Two thousand four hundred and eighty. And fifty for the insult!'

'Thank God we're not playing for money,' said Puffy quickly. 'Couldn't you do anything with your queen, darling?'

'Not playing for money!' cried our host who had entered unobserved. 'Of *course* you're playing for money. I never allow people to play for less than a pound a hundred. That was my grandfather's rule and it still holds good. You know that, Puffy!'

'Oh, yes,' smiled our unhappy opponent. 'Oh, quite.'

And yet he is really a nice man. Afterwards, when the women had gone to bed, Puffy and I settled down on the sofa and he told me about his company. Hard though it was to believe, he had started his working life as a waiter. He had begun drinking a lot of coffee, got the shakes and had had to break the habit.

'I was never more furious in my life,' he chuckled, lighting the giant torpedo of a cheroot that he had extracted from a rather flashy cigar case. 'I was physically sick twice a day, I could hardly see because of spots before my eyes. I got kicked out of Thierry's Brasserie. And all because of a social habit that got out of hand.'

He looked up with a momentary glare of angry memory.

'So I started a chocolate bar. My then girlfriend had rich parents and together we took a lease on a little shop in Notting Hill. We served the first hot croissants in London, or so I claim.'

'And now?'

'Now?' he said. 'Now we have forty-seven bars here, two in Manhattan and from next month one in Dallas.'

'Do you have a brand name?'

'Yes,' he smiled. He might even have blushed if his complexion could have accommodated a deeper hue. 'Chez Puffy.'

I wasn't sure whether laughter would be in order. He was surveying the glowing end of his cheroot with apparent interest.

'Very welcoming,' I tried. 'It has a nice sound.'

'I like it,' he said. 'It was Mimsie's idea. She's very clever.'

'I can see that.'

'And she puts up with me.'

We could hear Terry and the duke playing snooker next door. Occasionally there was rather high-pitched giggling and, once, a squeal.

'Bit of a shirt-lifter, your colleague,' Puffy said shrewdly.

'Mmm.' I didn't like to be disloyal to my managing director, even though I had only nine days to go.

'You have to work all the angles to get your sales up, I suppose.' He blew out a perfect series of smoke rings.

'You can say that again,' I agreed, getting up to help myself to another slug of whisky from the decanter.

'We have three principles,' he said. 'Good location, pretty waitresses, no coffee.'

'It obviously works.' I sat down again.

'Yes, indeedee.' I looked to see if he was pulling my leg, but no, he was obviously getting himself into the swing of the transatlantic diversification.

The next day was spent listing the Gimpal pictures for immediate sale, and deciding which ones to take to New York. I spent most of the day on the telephone, negotiating with our carriers and with Smith Villiers, our tame underwriters at Lloyd's. Terry and I, working together better now that the end was in sight, had decided to take just six pictures, the Giorgione, the Guardi, the Rembrandt, one of the Tintoretto set and an exquisite pair of Fragonard panels depicting a rejected suit followed by its sequel, a successful seduction. In both, the figures, wearing theatrical dress like the famous Louveciennes set, were surrounded by the same elaborate architectural capriccio, the garden of a ruined Renaissance palace based, perhaps, on Claude's 'Enchanted Castle'. Fifty million pounds to be packed up, crated and flown there and back to set up our stall, in traditional style, to lure the museums (and, of course, my special client Logan Basant) over to London for the sale.

'Have you been to see the cascade?'

Terry, Mary and I were hammering out the background release for the press office when the duke poked his little painted head round the door.

'No,' said Mary. 'Is it far?'

'Out through that door,' he said, 'down the avenue to the steps and follow your ears.'

We rose obediently.

'Oh, Terry.'

'Yes, Lionel?'

'I'd like to show you those engravings.'

'You go on, love.' Terry turned to Mary with his charming smile. 'We'll catch you up.'

As he spoke I noticed an insistent flicker in his right eye, an involuntary semaphore that signalled hidden chaos. Had I misjudged him after all? He passed a large white hand across his face and the eye reappeared, still now and staring straight at me. Hurriedly I looked away, pulling at my ear as if to show solidarity through a matching itch.

'Don't miss the grotto,' called out our host. 'The Neptune is by de Vries.'

The air was sharp and fresh and there had been a heavy frost, so that the grass crackled under our feet as we walked slowly down the broad avenue towards two gigantic statues that faced away from us, their bulging shoulders and straining backs gradually coming into focus as we advanced. We walked in silence, and after a bit Mary slipped a confiding hand under my arm. The wind was stronger now that we were out of the lee of the house and its sheltering plantations.

'What a view!'

We had reached the top of a steep flight of stone steps flanked by those two marble giants. Ten feet above us, their stony faces stared in titanic anguish across a deep valley towards dense, rolling beech woods, stark and almost bare of leaves but still beautiful in their mysterious shadows, lit here and there by a surviving patina of frost. Immediately below us we could hear the roar of a waterfall that plunged unseen into the broad, black water that snaked through the valley below. Again there were horizontal stripes of frost glimpsed through the trees, but also enriching the effect we could see the greys and whites of other figures, standing, kneeling, astride white horses rearing from their marble plinths. The whole valley glittered with frozen life, four centuries of sculpture assembled here, in a hidden valley, to startle and enchant the unsuspecting visitor.

I felt Mary shiver and turned instinctively to put an arm around her shoulder, but she shook herself free and moved a few paces apart, her face turned from me.

'Are you cold?' I asked, hoping she wouldn't want my coat. She shook her head, and moved another step so she was tight against the right-hand statue.

A great gust of wind shook us. Again I put out a hand and again she shook it off. But then she turned towards me and I saw that her face was streaming with tears.

Should I have felt sympathetic? I suppose so, but I was too full of anger – anger at Terry for his arrogant lack of even the most elementary attempt at discretion, anger at Mary for loving Terry, but most of all anger at myself for playing the pathetic and undignified role of Rakitin, the rejected suitor who stays on nevertheless.

She took a handkerchief from her pocket, blew her nose and then we looked at each other. Suddenly we were both laughing.

'I'm so sorry,' she gasped as we went down the steps. 'I just can't help thinking of Terry slavering over poor Lionel. Who do you suppose does what?'

'I'd much rather not know,' I said.

'Hello, you two!'

The Tredinnicks were sitting on a bench at the foot of the steps, both huddled enviably in thick thermal jackets, their faces scarlet in the wind. I was surprised to find myself delighted to see that Puffy was holding his wife's hand.

'Budge up, darling,' she said, making room for us, and we all sat for a few minutes gazing into the torrent that foamed out of a dragon's mouth beside us and fell headlong through massive rocks into a pool a hundred feet below.

'It comes from the lake on the other side of the house,' said Mimsie. 'Then it's pumped up again the other side of the old village. There – can you see that thatched roof beyond the boathouse?' As she spoke, we heard raucous laughter from above. Looking up, I saw the other two, fresh from the engravings, scampering down the steps.

We seemed an ill-assorted group, I thought; every prospect pleasing and man quite unarguably vile. The contrast between the glittering landscape and the imperfections of its largest animal inhabitants was uncomfortably acute.

'When do you get back from New York?' whispered Mary, out of earshot of our companions.

'Next weekend.'

'Give me a ring.' With that she stood up briskly and set off up the steps, passing the others without a glance.

CHAPTER THIRTY

We landed at Kennedy Airport with a considerable thump, shuffled our way towards the immigration inspectors, swore that we were innocent of importing any plant life and while the chairman and Terry went straight off in a limousine to meet the Getty group, I stayed behind with Bryant to see the containers through customs. He was travelling in the security van, so I picked up a cab. It was filled with the cloying scent of a coconut air freshener, and the bakelite division, criss-crossed with Scotch tape, held a stained sign announcing, 'Thank you for not smoking.' I held up a cigar in one hand and a ten-dollar bill in the other.

'Driver?'

'Yeah.'

'What does this tell you?'

'It tells me I just love cigar smoke,' she said with a grin, and took the note as I passed it through the plastic grille. Through the drizzle, the whole of the Manhattan skyline seemed to be smoking like Gehenna: the world's ashcan, an infernal vision of decay. It was a bleak sight as we bucketed through the potholes of FDR Drive alongside the Hudson River, both grey-black with no reflections, twin ribbons between the biscuit-coloured horizontally sliced mountains of apartment blocks, with windows by Seurat, mathematically monotonous dots.

We were staying at the Carlyle, on 76th and Madison. And just round the corner is our office, a converted brownstone which had once been home to the Draycott family. The first thing you see when you walk in is a luscious portrait by Sargent of his daughter-in-law, the chairman's grandmother, with her ivory skin made even more startling by the deep magenta of her velvet dress.

'John boy!'

'Peppard! Good to see you.'

Peppard Ault III folded his huge hand over mine and crushed it inwards. He's a big man, with great moon spectacles and a wide, cleft jaw. As president of Merrywethers Inc., our New York sister company, he brings all his impeccable Ivy League background into play in attracting business to our eager hands.

'Where's the merchandise?'

'Trundling across Triboro Bridge as we speak. Did you fix my meeting with Logan?'

My special client was one of the main reasons for my being there.

'Yeah. You're giving him dinner at La Goulue at nine thirty tonight. But first we're due at the Frick in, uh, fifty-three minutes. Spike Warren and the rest of the Getty crowd are hosting a cocktail party in honour of Joyce Bodeg. She's done such a great job there, don't you think?'

'That's nice,' I said. 'I'd better go and change.'

'You do that. Shall I get Diane to send a car to pick you up?'

'Thanks, Peppard. I think I can just about walk from there.'

'Suit yourself.'

'And tomorrow?'

'Press call here at seven thirty. Breakfast at the Pierre at eight. Diane's sent a list over to the Carlyle.'

I walked back to the hotel, changed and spent a peaceful half an hour downstairs with a glass of iced bourbon to keep me company. It's a quiet room, all reds and pinks, the sofas upholstered in Turkish carpet, the chairs in red velvet and the walls appliquéd with softly coloured prints of flowers. While I sat and smoked, three young black girls dressed in browns and greys, hips emphasized, topped by hats with veils, came and sat down. The one facing me had scarlet lips that parted in a broad smile to show shining teeth. She had slender ankles and when her coat swung open it revealed the shortest of grey jersey skirts over long, svelte thighs.

'A penny for your thoughts.'

It was the chairman.

I laughed. 'Human beauty over works of art.'

'One endures,' he said, smiling, 'the other passes. What's that, bourbon?' He sniffed it. 'Mmm. Rather good.'

A waiter, smiling confidently but with his fists clenched, came over.

'How are *you* today?'

'Tired and thirsty.'

'You can order anything you like.'

'I'll have what he's having.'

'Coming right up.'

The chairman sat down beside me. 'I'm going to miss you, you know.'

'Me too,' I said, to be polite. And realized it was true. I enjoyed the hectic bustle of our market place. I just wish it could have been conducted with less deviousness.

'Fifteen years?'

'Sixteen tomorrow.' Yes, I had been working it out.

'What will you do?' he asked.

'I honestly don't know, ' I replied. 'I've had one or two offers.'

He raised a hand. 'I'm sure you have.'

'But first a few months off. I'm toying with the idea of going to Australia.'

'Wonderful continent,' he said. 'You could look up old Trentham. He hasn't bought anything for ages.' The waiter brought his drink, which he downed in one. 'Come on. Are you walking?'

'Of course.'

'Same here. We'll leave my car for Terry. He's still in the bath. I've told the driver.'

It was dark now, and the rain had cleared. Central Park glittered with little lights. Beyond it the stark skyscrapers of the West Side, with their strangely evocative outlines – Notre Dame ahead of us, St Denis on its left – sparkled in the crisp, clean night air. There was a striped awning outside the Frick Museum and two guards were chatting to a policeman. They paid no attention as we tramped in, gave our coats to a woman at the turnstile and headed straight for the Fragonard Room where I could already hear the familiar shattering laugh of Pico Zust splitting the air.

'Aha!' he said coming over to us. 'I have heard about your latest exploits, John. You are not a popular man in Bond Street.' His angular head, bald now for many years, was covered in perspiration.

'The Tischbein?'

'*The* Tischbein.' He roared with laughter. 'Hans is like a man with a new wife. He could scarcely bear to show me. Of course I had seen it, but I will tell you a secret, John.' He put an arm around my shoulders. 'I never spotted its significance. I admit it. Does that surprise you?' I nodded. (I'd like to have seen his face if I'd said no.) 'Yes, well,' he continued, 'nobody's perfect. And to prove my point, I will tell you another secret.' He bent his head towards mine. 'That is *not* a Giambologna.'

I stared. My precious discovery? The Trent Hall bust that was going to rewrite a whole chapter in the history of world sculpture?

'You don't think so?'

'I know so.' He was serious now.

'Because?'

'Because I bought it from the studio of Gustav in Antwerp and sold it to Mrs Spencer myself. Perhaps you didn't know Gustav was a sculptor before he learned how to paint.' He took out a crimson bandana, put it completely over his head, rubbed vigorously and removed it again. Two women next to us, who had been chattering shrilly about Palm Beach, stared at him open-mouthed. 'These pills, you know,' he said. 'Monkey glands. I'm a stag in the morning, but not so good in the evening.'

'You sold it to her?'

'Oh, yes, my friend. And for not much money. It is a brilliant imitation. Gustav had a great sense of humour.

226

He loved jokes. One day, he told me, someone will build a reputation on this little *jeu d'esprit*.'

'Not so little,' I said, laughing ruefully. 'And I was all set to write a monograph for the *Goethe Magazine*. The V. and A. have already started an appeal.' This was dreadful news. Not that I was concerned with it any more – other than pride and my faith in my judgement.

'Come over here.' He steered me towards my favourite picture in the whole world: 'Storming the Citadel', Fragonard's ravishing canvas ordered by Madame du Barry and then rejected. For years it lay rolled up in his studio at Grasse, forgotten by everyone but his family. A masterpiece of erotic beauty.

'I know. You know. No-one else knows. That sounds like a source of mutual profit.'

'What's this?' shouted the chairman. 'A conspiracy? What are you talking about?'

'I'm telling John about another Tiepolo that I think I have discovered,' said Pico smoothly. 'A ceiling in an old palace in Prague. You are losing him, my poor Alan. Perhaps he will join me.' He prodded my chest. 'Think about it, my friend.' And with that he disappeared again beneath his bandana, while I was dragged off by one of the museum trustees to meet Joyce Bodeg, the guest of honour.

At nine o'clock I walked back across Madison and down a couple of blocks to La Goulue, that reassuring whiff of France in the Upper East Side. The menu may be longer on swordfish than skate, but it is the one restaurant in New York where a real Havana cigar can be found masquerading in a box of unimpeachably Dominican origin.

As I turned down the street, I fell in beside Logan Basant who was peering short-sightedly at his pocket book by the light of the street lamp.

'It's this way,' I said, taking his arm.

He leapt backwards, pulling his arm away and falling into a sort of crouch while whipping what looked like a small aerosol out of his raincoat pocket.

'John!' he said, his face relaxing into a grin. 'You should be more careful of sidling up to a fellow in these damn streets.'

'I'm sorry,' I said as I waited to shake his hand once the aerosol was safely reinstated in what I now saw was a webbed contrivance strapped under his coat that presumably guaranteed swift delivery.

The table was booked in my name, but as soon as the head waiter saw Logan, a distinctive figure with his flaming red hair and bulging belly, he insisted on moving us from our comfortable corner table to one that held a perilous position between the desk and the main path through to the room behind. Then the wine waiter was in on the act.

'*Bonsoir*, monsieur. How are *you*?'

'*Très bien* – I guess.' Logan shook the proffered hand.

'I have some of your favourite – the Lafite 'eighty-nine.' The man winked conspiratorially. 'Shall I get it right now?'

'*Non merci*,' said Logan, to my relief. 'I am with this gentleman.' I got a very sparse glance – no doubt as one less likely to spend.

Logan and I had first met when I was called over to value some tapestries he was negotiating to buy from the Hammer Foundation. There was some doubt about their provenance and by the time the matter was cleared up we had become good friends. I liked his buccaneering approach to collecting – his fierce pursuit of personal preference plus a gimlet eye for investment value. He bought nothing earlier than Rembrandt and nothing later than Sargent. Somehow we had always got on well together, sharing the jokes and the excitement of chasing beautiful objects.

'Thank you for the draft catalogue,' he said, by way of opening our discussion over the clam chowder. 'What do you want me to buy?'

I laughed. 'You're a model client,' I said. 'There aren't many others who'd put it that way.'

'And?' He was a serious man in his own way.

'And.' I paused to think. 'Let's look at both sides. First any gaps you want to fill, then ones you might especially enjoy.'

'I've got three Tintorettos, including the "Susanna and the Elders" you sold me.'

'Yes. You mustn't dispose of that. These ones make an incomparable set, but unless you want to go banco on him I wouldn't push for them. In any case, I can't believe the Getty won't snap them up. They seem tailor-made for mopping up their problem over spending the income this year.'

'You'll sell them in separate lots?'

'I'm not sure.' This had been a major talking point between Ralph Tritton and Terry. As I would have left Merrywethers by the time of the sale, I had decided to keep out of it. The question was still unresolved.

'So tell me what you would go for if you were me.'

Two plates piled high with *gigot d'agneau aux flageolets* arrived, accompanied by a decanter of claret the colour of crushed loganberries. Logan took a sip after the waiter had poured it.

'*Magnifique!*'

The waiter smiled non-committally.

'What is it, John?'

'Ducru-Beaucaillou 1966.'

'Should I know it?'

'Well, I love it.'

He reached inside his jacket and this time brought out a little red notebook in which he carefully inscribed the name as I spelt it out.

'So?' he said, beginning to show impatience. 'The Giorgione?'

'Oh, no,' I said. 'You should buy the Fragonards, and if you're really feeling rich the Vermeer.'

'What Vermeer?'

'Aha!' I laughed. 'We didn't know there was a Vermeer either until last week. It has the nameplate of De Hooch. I can't be sure how they'll sell it because it's been accepted and catalogued as De Hooch at least since 1831, when the Hesse family sold it. Gimpal bought it from Charles des Laumes during the war. But I'm as certain as I can be, both stylistically and by content. We haven't brought it here because it's being studied by the Baarsen Institute in Amsterdam.'

'What's the subject matter?'

'Two women cleaning a piece of carpet that's had something spilt on it, milk or white paint by the look of it.'

He nodded thoughtfully. 'What about the Fragonards?' he then said. 'Are the girls pretty?'

'Have you ever known Fragonard paint a plain woman?'

But he didn't seem to be listening, distracted by something over my shoulder. 'Don't look now,' he said, 'but there's a fair bit of passion at the table in the corner behind you. She seems ready to eat him up here and now.'

'Tell me when I can turn.'

He watched, transfixed, and then, 'OK,' he whispered.

I turned and looked at the couple, who had abandoned their dinner and were amorously entwined side by side on the banquette.

I turned back, feeling my face becoming flushed.

'Do you know them?' Logan asked.

'Well,' I said. 'As a matter of fact I do.'

'Who is she?'

'She's my wife.'

That shook him. 'Your wife?'

'We're separated,' I said, 'so there's no angst involved.' I took a good swig of the claret.

'And the man?'

'That's the good news,' I said. 'He's a solid citizen.'

'She's paying the check,' he whispered.

'That figures,' I said glumly.

'They're leaving.' I shrank into my chair, but I needn't have worried. No doubt Barbara and Bertie had eyes only for each other because they didn't notice me. Then they were gone.

'I've never been married,' said Logan. 'The only two

women I really loved were married to other men.'

'Perhaps you've been lucky,' I said.

'Perhaps. I haven't given up all hope. I'm only sixty-five and I can still beat most of the Burlinghame Club at croquet.'

'No doubt that's the best test for surviving a California divorce. Some brandy?'

'Yes, please.'

It was midnight before we parted on the corner of Madison and 71st.

The next morning I sat silent while Terry fielded the barrage of questions from bleary-eyed journalists on the current state of the art market. Some snow had fallen, and we shuffled our way down Fifth Avenue to the Pierre for a working breakfast with Peppard Ault and his pale blonde assistant Diane, a tall girl with bee-stung lips and a carefree manner. Terry was obviously impressed by her and it rapidly became apparent that she was distinctly taken with Terry. To the extent that before Peppard and I had finished tabulating the probable bidders, she had taken his hand and insisted on leading him off to see an exhibition at Tiffany's.

That was the last I saw of him, because the rest of the day was spent in the crucial, if tedious, business of taking the regular clients who knew me, one by one, into the private room where Bryant had installed the six masterpieces and spelling out the merits of our magnificent merchandise. The next morning I took, by way of the chairman's farewell gesture, the Concorde flight home, a free man and alone.

CHAPTER THIRTY-ONE

It was a strange sensation walking up Charles Street towards Merrywethers two months later to view the Bridgwater pictures before their sale the following day. The streets were full of bargain-seeking shoppers and two television vans were parked outside the Merrywethers awning with fat bearded men in anoraks pulling cables this way and that, ready for the great sale.

Although I had spent most of this time abroad, catching up with friends in Florence and Munich, I had kept abreast of the publicity. The Vermeer had not been accepted as such by the art establishment, for it was barely mentioned on the saleroom pages. A man had thrown a knife at the Giorgione in Paris but it had been deflected by the new bulletproof lamination Bryant had been experimenting with. There had been profiles of the duke, of old Gimpal, and even of Ivana his one-legged mistress, miraculously still alive and living in a château in the south of France. The gossip columns had been busy, too: reporting a rift, now healed, between the Englefields, the approaching divorce of the Bests, a possible knighthood for the chairman and, this very morning, printing a picture of Terry and the American girl Diane coming out of a London nightclub, under the heading:

Transatlantic bid for saleroom high-flier.

'Terry Burton,' it went on, under the by-line of Horace Walpole, 'heavily fingered as a future chairman of Merrywethers and much in demand as the thinking girl's beefcake, is only too eager to knock himself down to gorgeous pouting New Yorker Diane Brubaker. And Diane (wait for it, folks!) is the only child of Baltimore bagel czar Sy Brubaker. Nice one, Terry!!'

Somehow I didn't think the duke would enjoy that.

In particular I had not called Mary, whom I assumed to be safely restored to family life. Whether she was or not, I was trying to kill off my increasingly painful love for her by enforced and total rupture. But night after night she returned to me, sometimes on Terry's arm, sometimes on mine. The dreams passed, but when I woke it was to find my mind flooded with sorrow. It was always she I first thought of when I woke, and as I tried to find sleep each night it was always she whose image crowded my tired brain.

'Nice to see you back, sir.'

I waved at the commissionaire and ran up the steps, two at a time.

'Have a care, John! We don't want you dying in the saleroom!'

Ralph, leaning on his stick, was standing beaming at the top of the flight with Peppard Ault beside him. 'Haven't you got a catalogue?' he asked.

I nodded. I had it folded in my overcoat and kept it there.

Lord Darlington came hurrying towards us, a red carnation in his buttonhole, but when he saw me he paused and then turned on his heel.

Ralph grinned at me, then raised his hand. 'Mary!' he called out. But of course I had already spotted her, moving quietly between the throng of patrons, bidders, sellers and just plain tourists who filled the corridors leading to the main saleroom.

'John.' She came running over quickly and then stopped, abashed.

'Yes?'

'You never returned my calls.'

'No.'

'Look, we'll leave you,' said Ralph. 'See you in the viewing room.'

They walked off leaving us standing by ourselves.

'Why?'

'I don't know. Have you left George?'

'Yes.'

'But—'

'I don't want to talk about it,' she muttered.

'All set for the sale?'

'Oh, yes.'

'And are you based here now?'

'No,' she said, smiling nervously. 'I've got your job.'

'The Berington office?'

'Yes.'

Impulsively I grasped her and kissed her on both cheeks. This was excellent news. And I had no regrets. Life moves on, and new horizons are more exciting than familiar landmarks.

'That's wonderful!' I said. 'That's much more like it. I loved the job. You'll be perfect for it.'

'Thank you,' she said. 'It *is* fun, although I've hardly got used to it yet. It's very different with you and Robert gone, but there are a lot of new people too.'

'Good,' I said. 'It's better if you appoint them yourself from scratch.'

A hand tugged at my coat.

'I reckon you're talking to the best work of art in this room.'

It was Logan Basant. I introduced them and slipped away, ignoring an angry glance from Mary, to catch up with Pico Zust whom I had spotted wearing an outrageous pink striped suit with brown and white correspondent shoes. We wandered round the three rooms, jostled by the crowds of sight-seers, examining the Bridgwater pictures. It would be the last time they would be seen together.

'He had an immaculate eye,' murmured Pico. 'Each one is a masterpiece, even this little gem.' We gazed at a tiny watercolour of a ruined temple perched on some vertiginous rocks.

'Tredenti?'

'Perhaps.' He mopped his brow. 'Have you considered what I wrote to you about?'

I smiled at him, the old villain! He had suggested a

partnership, based quite openly on exploiting the art market's weakness for new 'discoveries'. I would provide a respectable front for what I had no doubt was an inexhaustible supply of doubtful pieces.

'No, thank you. I'd love to work with you, but I need a rest from controversy.'

'No sense of adventure? Going soft?' His green eyes mocked me from behind his sodden handkerchief.

'Perhaps.' I shrugged and, relenting, took his arm. 'But I am very touched and complimented.'

He gave a snort and turned away.

It was raining when I came down the steps into Charles Street.

'Going my way?' Mary was standing there, with a large green Hermès umbrella.

'Which is?' Why was I so starchy with her? I think I was afraid of any more knocks.

'The company flat you used to use. I'm camping there at the moment. Come on, I'll rustle up some lunch. Jam sandwiches and a bottle of Beaune.'

'Sounds like heaven,' I said.

'Well, come *on*,' she said. 'I'll drive you. My car's on one of the four-hour meters round the corner.'

When we reached the flat, we climbed the familiar stairs together and while I opened the wine Mary prepared a fire in the sitting-room grate, lit it and began to lay the table, munching a sandwich she had found. Made more confident by a swig of burgundy, I decided to ask the question uppermost in my mind.

'Do you feel better for leaving George?'

She stayed silent, her eyes lowered. I took her hand, and turning it over, kissed the palm.

'Why didn't you kiss me before?' she said. 'The time when we went blackberrying?'

'That's easy,' I said. 'Because you were in love with Terry.'

'Ah,' she said lightly. 'And if I had been free?'

'I would have given you a present. A large basket of ripe blackberries.'

'Will jam do?' She leaned over and kissed my lips.

'Mary.' I gripped her arms and we stared at each other.

'I need you,' she said plaintively. 'You're the only real friend I've got.'

Friend! A word to chill a lover's heart. The universal codeword for denial. Can we just be friends? Please stay out of my bed!

'You've got to understand.' Her eyes were beseeching me.

'Understand what?'

'Why I had to leave George.'

'Of course I understand.'

'I'm frightened,' she said. 'It's such a big step.'

'Well then,' I said, hiding my impatience. After all, some problems have to be faced.

'But I'll tell you something else,' she said. 'When I thought of another year, another ten years, with poor George I thought I'd cut my throat.'

'Don't talk like that! You have the children who need you.'

'Exactly,' she said, rubbing one side of her head with her fingers.

'You know I love you,' I said. 'Don't you?'

'Well,' she said, looking first at the floor and then directly at me. 'Yes, perhaps I do.'

'Will you marry me?'

She smiled uncertainly, and again her eyes darted away from mine. 'But . . .' she said, then stopped.

'But?' I encouraged her, my heart racing at even the flimsiest hope of securing the regard of this woman whom I still loved so completely.

'But I'm not sure I'm in love with you.'

She hugged me, slipping both hands under my arms and pressing me to her. Of course I kissed her again, and this time I didn't let her go.

CHAPTER THIRTY-TWO

'John.'

  'Mmm?'

  'What time is it?'

  'Nearly seven o'clock.'

  'Evening or morning?'

  'Morning.'

She sighed and pulled me closer to her and I buried my head in her neck, breathing in her natural fragrance.

  'What's this?'

  'What do you think it is?'

  'But I've got to go to the office,' she murmured while clasping her arms tightly round my waist.

Disengaging myself with deep reluctance, I made her some tea. Across the landing I could hear the water running and then a snatch of song, something by Schubert, clear and with a melody of unbearable sweetness.

The telephone beside me gave its familiar drone and, without thinking, I picked it up.

  'Yes?'

There was a long silence. I had forgotten this was not my company telephone.

  'Yes?' I repeated, dreading the response I knew would come.

  'That's you, Griffin, isn't it?' It was George, of course, his voice grim and defeated.

  'Yes, George. I've just got back. How are you?'

  'So you're a liar as well as a crook.'

  'No,' I said. 'I stayed here last night because this used to be my base in London. I hadn't entirely got used to the changes. I think Mary's up if you want to speak to her. I can hear sounds off.'

'I bet you bloody can,' he said, but still in that sad, lifeless voice.

'I'll get her.'

In the bathroom, Mary was stretched out luxuriously in a bath foaming with scented bubbles.

'Come here.'

I knelt beside her and kissed her mouth, her eyes, her neck.

'George wants to speak to you.'

'Oh, God!'

'I shouldn't have answered the silly thing. I quite forgot.'

'Don't worry,' she said, emerging pink and slippery to my touch. 'I will explain. He had to have my number, because of the children.'

She put both her hands on my shoulders, and stared at me severely. 'Do you love me?'

'Yes.'

'Do you want to live with me, to see whether I am really what you think I am?'

'Yes.'

'You won't feel you've got to marry me?'

'Yes, I will.'

'You've got to say no.'

'No.'

'Into the bath then, and we'll talk while I get dressed.'

'I hear and obey.'

'That's how I like it.' She pulled a towel from the cupboard and wrapping it round her as I eased myself into the steaming water, said, 'Now I'll speak to George.'

Later I sat in the armchair, sipping coffee, while she studied her face in the mirror.

'I'm thirty-three years old,' she said solemnly. 'I have two children, a good job I do not intend to give up now that I've started it, and there is a patch of grey just here. Look!'

I laughed.

'You are nearly ten years older,' she went on remorselessly, 'you must be the worst life insurance risk in England, I don't suppose you've got much money and

238

you appear to run on an unsavoury mixture of tobacco and whisky.'

Try laughing at that! I nodded, a tiny suspicion of approaching sorrow lodging itself promiscuously in the centre of my brain.

'But,' she said, securing her bra with a deft snap, 'we love each other, and what's more we are true friends. Don't look so sad.'

'Did you talk like this to Terry?' I said disconsolately. 'What about his Eau de Gorille?'

'Ah, but I *adored* it! Each time I got a whiff I started to imagine him rootling about inside me.' She came and put a finger to my lips. 'But the past is past. I was utterly lost, and I made a rather dreadful mistake. I don't blame myself, and I don't think you do either. I needed someone really abrasive after George – and I certainly got it. Do you harbour a grudge because of what I put you through?'

I shook my head.

'What passed between us was the small change of any good relationship,' she said. 'And it helped me to know you better, to see how you coped with such a situation, just as I needed to find my own way.'

'And have you?'

'Oh, yes,' she said. 'I know what I want now. I want to be good at my job so I can earn your respect, but most of all I want to share my life with you. Can you put up with my grey hairs?'

'I *think* so.'

'That's good, then. I've told George I seduced you last night and that I'm moving in with you immediately.'

'With the children, I hope.'

'But, of course! Can you do your job from Berington?'

'Yes,' I said. 'But I haven't told you what it is.'

'Save it for later,' she said briskly. 'I'm going to be late unless you pull on some trousers and drive me there. I'll join you for the sale, then I must go home. From tomorrow home will be with you. George is taking the children for a week to his mother. That fits in rather well. It will give us time to prepare for them.'

CHAPTER THIRTY-THREE

The pavement outside Merrywethers was crammed with crowds of people attracted by the television cameras and the promise of celebrity bidders. I pushed my way through and was immediately accosted by Elizabeth. She looked tired.

'Thank God, John. There you are. The chairman wants to see you in his office straight away.'

'But . . .'

'No buts. It's urgent.'

I looked at my watch. There were twenty minutes before the sale began. We took the lift to the second floor.

'He's got one of the princes with him right now. Will you wait here?'

I sat down obediently and thumbed through my catalogue. Soon there was a bustle and half a dozen people came out of the chairman's office.

'Thank you, Sir. It's a great honour to see you here.' The chairman was in unusually oleaginous mood, bowing deeply over his visitor's hand. The royal group was moved off down the corridor, followed by the chairman who had ignored me completely. Then he came back.

'Ah, John. I'm rather *occupé* as you can see, but Terry and I wanted a word.' He ushered me along the corridor to Jack Bonas's old office door, now resplendent with a gilt notice announcing 'Managing Director', and knocked. There was a long pause and then a voice cried, 'Come!' (I couldn't believe he ever knocked before entering in the old days.)

Terry was sitting behind his desk with his legs over the arm of his chair.

'So!' was all the greeting I received, or wanted. He gestured to a low chair drawn up in front of him, while the chairman slunk off to the sofa by the window.

'A glass of champagne?' Terry was looking down at me with a slight smile.

'No, thanks.'

'It's rather good.'

'I've no doubt it is,' I said agreeably. 'But it's too early in the day for me.'

'Just as you choose,' he said, pouring a glass for the chairman.

'The company has prospered since your departure,' he said.

I nodded encouragingly. He seemed satisfied and went on:

'I'm still negotiating with the Treasury over ceding that bust from Trent Hall in lieu of tax. I believe it's a Giambologna.' Good luck to you, I thought.

'John gets the credit for that,' put in the chairman.

'Oh, no,' I said modestly. 'I was never at all certain of the attribution.'

Terry smiled broadly. 'Luckily we are,' he said. He was drinking Perrier water, I noticed, no doubt because he would be taking the sale.

'I had a call from Garrisons,' the chairman blurted out. 'They want to merge.'

'Surrender is the word,' cut in Terry. 'They're throwing in the towel.'

This was news indeed.

'There might be a place for a liaison manager,' Terry said. 'To oversee the changes, jettison the dead wood.'

'Ah.' As a piece of dead wood myself, no doubt I would be ideal.

'We thought you might be interested. Same salary, of course.'

Both men looked at me expectantly.

'We realize you've worked long and hard for Merry-wethers,' said the chairman, trying to inject a little warmth into the room. 'You deserve this. After today's sale we can pay back those bloody bankers and tell them to stuff it.'

'It's very kind,' I said, 'but I prefer matters as they stand.'

Terry snapped the folder on his desk shut. It was difficult to tell if he was pleased or not.

'It's a good offer,' he said.

'And I'm grateful.'

'I'd *like* to see you back.' The chairman came round to stand beside me. 'This Treasury negotiation isn't going as smoothly as we could wish.'

This time he had definitely overstepped the mark. Terry rose and went to the door.

'I don't think we should discuss details if he isn't interested.'

'I agree,' I said, and put out my hand to the chairman. 'But thank you for thinking of me.'

'It's a whole new vista for the company,' he said. 'You should be sharing in that.'

I shook my head. Terry bowed as I left the room, his hands firmly behind his back.

'Don't come peddling life insurance round here, will you?' he murmured, and shut the door.

'Well?' Ralph Tritton was standing outside in the corridor.

I took his arm. 'I'm sorry, Ralph,' I said, as we walked slowly down the stairs. 'I didn't want to leave. But now I'm free of Terry, I certainly don't want to return. My only regret is not to be working with you.'

He didn't reply, but led me across to one of the interview rooms where we drank some coffee in friendly silence. And then we heard, or felt, that hush that descends on the expectant audience when the auctioneer mounts the rostrum.

'Come on,' I said. 'We can't miss this.'

We made our way to the side of the Red Damask Room where I could see the other bidders. Logan Basant had passed us in the corridor, but had given no sign of recognition. Rupert Englefield raised a hand in greeting and then hastily dropped it, his head swivelling towards the rostrum. He must be feeling pretty sick that Garrisons weren't handling the sale. He certainly looked it. And there were other familiar faces in the crowd: Colonel Chaucer, Lord Tottenham, the grim face of old Gallico, an impassive Spike Warren, his titanic bulk spread over two chairs, and Melissa blowing kisses from beside Colonel Bracy. But the duke was nowhere to be seen.

Terry was already standing on the rostrum smiling confidently. Victoria and Suzanne were to one side by the bank of telephones and, the picture of health, the luxuriant Diane was sitting in the front row, her eyes feasting on him.

'She looks rather wonderful, doesn't she?' whispered Mary, appearing beside me and slipping her arm around my waist.

I grunted.

'It doesn't bother me,' she persisted. 'I lost that particular madness that morning at Bridgwater. It's as if it never was. Do you believe me?'

I looked steadily at her. 'Yes.'

Suddenly the television lights blazed on, filling the far end of the room with a scalding white glare and smearing thick black shadows along the frames of the nearer pictures.

'Lighting by Turner,' she whispered as Terry announced the first lot, speaking slowly and clearly into the microphone after first checking that the currency display board was working. His voice, chameleon-like, seemed to have acquired a mid-Atlantic twang.

'Isn't the duke here?' I asked Mary.

'No,' she said, looking around. 'He's been abroad, but he was expected back at Heathrow this morning. I think Terry is rather hoping that he'll miss that bit in "Horace Walpole".'

'I dare say he is,' I muttered.

It started smoothly. A Stubbs went to the National

243

Gallery of Wales, a Tiepolo to Gallico's, and the next three, a pair of Verandaels and a pretty little Watteau, to anonymous telephone bidders.

Then came the Fragonards. I watched Logan sit impassively while the bidding rose to £4 million. At that stage it was between a telephone bidder, fielded by Victoria, and Georges Mornand who regularly bid for the Louvre. When Victoria shook her head, Terry raised his eyebrows and put on his most calculating but charming smile.

'Have you all done then? At four million on my right, they're going to be sold.'

Logan raised a languid hand.

'Thank *you*, sir. A new bidder. Four point two million pounds.'

Logan was sitting immediately behind Georges so the latter could hardly turn round without seeming too obvious. He could not be sure, therefore, who his competitor was, although if he had done his homework he could guess. He nodded.

'Four point four million. Against you, sir.' This to Logan.

Logan raised his hand again.

'Four point six million.'

We moved so as to be able to see both their profiles. The angular Georges preserved a total impassivity. Logan, on the other hand, had a slight smile.

'It's against you,' said Terry, leaning down towards Georges.

The latter nodded, rather abruptly.

'Four point eight million.'

Logan's hand rose immediately. Victoria was still speaking into her telephone, but now replaced it with a rueful smile.

'Five million.'

Georges shook his head.

'Five million pounds for these two exquisite paintings. Any more? Five million for the first time.' No-one stirred.

244

Half a minute later Logan had landed the first of his purchases.

The Giorgione made £24 million and the Rembrandt made £18 million. So far so good. Although they were telephone bids, I strongly suspected Spike Warren of being the purchaser of both on behalf of the Getty Museum. I spotted just a glint passing between him and Lester Liddy, who was standing in the opposite aisle, after each final bid.

'Lot eight,' said Terry. 'Catalogued as De Hooch. There's been some controversy over this lot, ladies and gentlemen. Some speculation. But we're selling it as a De Hooch.' I half opened my catalogue. The estimated sale price was given elliptically as 'Refer Department', meaning that their expectations would vary according to who expressed an interest, but Victoria had said they thought that £1.5 million would be the top side.

Both Victoria and Suzanne were talking into their telephones and the chairman was carrying a mobile phone in one hand and his drink in the other as he hurried in and leant against the doorway.

'One hundred thousand bid,' said Terry, glancing at the paper bids on the desk in front of him.

'A hundred thousand pounds, a hundred thousand.'

Two hands were raised on different sides of the room. Slowly the bidding crept up to a million. Perhaps Terry was right to play it safe. We reached the estimate. Victoria's telephone contact was still in, so was the bidder on the left of the floor.

It continued to £2 million (a slight stir in the room, a little whisper going round).

'Two point two million . . . two point four, six . . .' The hand didn't rise again from the floor, but Logan's did.

'Two point eight million, thank you, sir.' Terry gave him an oily smile which was not returned.

'Three million.' Mr Gallico had put up a tentative finger.

'Three point six, three point eight . . .'

'Four million pounds.' This last bid was a sensation.

Spike Warren, who had been deep in conversation with Liddy, his roving buyer, suddenly waved his catalogue. Victoria spoke into her telephone and nodded to Terry. The television cameras, which had been switched off, suddenly started swivelling round the room.

'Four point six million, four point eight . . . Three bidders, ladies and gentlemen, for this charming Dutch picture. A very important piece. Five million. It's against you, sir,' he said to Logan, who was thinking hard. He did some sums on his catalogue and shook his head.

'Against you,' Terry said to Victoria. She also shook her head, and replaced her receiver.

'At four point eight million pounds, then . . .'

I raised my catalogue.

Terry stared at me.

I waved it in a friendly manner.

'Is that a *bid*?' Terry called out.

'I hope so,' I said, smiling at him in a cosy, companionable sort of way. He looked across at the chairman, who was talking into his mobile telephone.

'Five million,' I called out, in case he was in some doubt.

'Are you mad?' said Mary, tugging at my arm. 'It's not worth a quarter of that. Anyway, you haven't got the money.'

'Five million bid,' said Terry reluctantly.

The chairman had moved to his side and both were staring at me with hostile expressions. Ex-employees are not expected to bid against the Getty Museum. Was that it? I grinned at them. And off we went, spiralling up to £15 million. I hadn't realized £10 million could fly past so swiftly.

'Fifteen point two million.' Terry sighed with relief as Spike, who had been watching me, raised his hand. I raised mine. Terry's eyes locked on mine across the room. Then they dropped.

'Fifteen point five . . . sixteen million . . .' The room was entirely still.

'Sixteen point five . . . seventeen million . . . seventeen

point five million . . .' The cameras were on the pair of Americans.

Spike shrugged his shoulders as if to say, Let the fool have it if he wants it so much. And if he can pay!

'At seventeen point five million pounds for the first time. It's against you, ladies and gentlemen. The bidder is in the corner. Do you want it?' This last as a final appeal to Spike. He glared at the floor. Bang!

The chairman appeared at my shoulder. 'Where's the money?' he said angrily. 'Is this some practical joke?'

'Right behind you,' I answered his first question calmly, pointing to where Logan, beaming happily, was standing miming a champion's victory gesture.

'Good teamwork, eh, Alan?' he chuckled. 'I'm backing my new roving agent's judgement. He thinks it's a Vermeer, so do I, and so I reckon does Spike.' We looked across at the latter, who shook his fist at us with an equally broad smile.

'And now, ladies and gentlemen—' Terry was hammering furiously on the rostrum. 'Settle down, please. Lot nine, the unique set of twelve Tintorettos, the single most important lot of this decade. Who'll start me at ten million pounds? Ten million. Thank you, sir.'

'Thirteen million,' called a dealer in front of us.

The crowd was bubbling away so much that I had to move down the wall to get a clear view. Pushing on, I found myself next to the telephone desk below the rostrum. To my amazement, Victoria's face was bright red and she seemed to be pleading or arguing with whoever was on the other end of the line.

'Oh, no,' she was saying, 'you can't mean that.' She glanced up, saw me and put her hand over the receiver. 'For God's sake,' she said. 'You've got to help.' Me?

'What is it?'

'It's the Duke of Bridgwater. He wants to stop the sale.'

'*What?*' I took the receiver. 'Hello?' I said.

'Who's that?' snapped the familiar high-pitched voice.

'John Griffin.'

'I thought they'd got rid of you.'

'Well . . .'

'I *order* you to stop the sale. I am withdrawing my pictures. That unfaithful lump of *shit*! I give him the biggest
sale of his life. And he throws me over for a *cunt*!'

'I'm afraid it's rather too late,' I said.

'Twenty-two million,' Terry was saying above my head.
'Twenty-two million against you, sir.'

'Oh no it's not,' shouted the duke in my other ear. 'My
solicitors are on their way round now, and you'll be liable
if that *fucker* sells ONE MORE *FUCKING* PICTURE!'
His voice had risen to a shriek.

'What are you doing on that telephone?'

It was Terry. He had actually stopped in mid-bidding
and was glaring down at me from his rostrum.

'It's for you,' I said cheerfully, and handed up the
receiver on its extended cord.

There was an angry buzz around the room and I could
see Ralph anxiously waving to catch the chairman's attention. He had Sir John Best beside him, looking self-
important and even a little smug.

'You can't speak to me like that,' said Terry into the
telephone. His face was twitching like a windmill and
his mid-Atlantic intonation had been replaced by something from the north of Watford. 'You've no right to
say that. No right whatever.'

'Is this an auction or what?' shouted out the man from
Wartheims, and there was some clapping. By now Best
and the chairman had converged below Terry.

'He's mad,' I heard the chairman say. 'He's not respon-
sible for what he's saying.'

'If so,' replied the lawyer calmly, 'it would mean that
you had no authority for this sale, since your instructions
came from him personally.'

'But if we stop now, there'll be a terrible scandal.'

'If you go on, you'll be bankrupted by the damages. I
can tell you that with absolute confidence.' He waved
a piece of paper at Terry, who was pleading into the
telephone. 'This is a sworn affidavit withdrawing your

248

authority to sell his grace's property as of this moment. I must require you to cease this auction forthwith.'

For a moment I thought Terry might be going to hit him. Instead he just put down the receiver, stepped from the rostrum and walked out of the door beside him.

'Oh, God,' wailed the chairman. 'Our bankers! I've spent a fortune promoting this sale. They'll roast us alive.'

'Ladies and gentlemen!' It was Peppard Ault who saved the day. He leapt up on to the rostrum. 'We apologize for this interruption.' There was widespread laughter. 'We cannot continue with the sale' (some shouts) 'until we have clarified the instructions of the vendor' (more laughter). 'No doubt you will read all about it in the newspapers tomorrow.' It was a good approach. This time they laughed with him rather than at him.

Mary was beside me again. I felt her there, even before I saw her.

'How *embarrassing*!' she whispered.

Terry, his face taut and colourless, reappeared, adjusting his tie and pretending to talk calmly to Peppard as if nothing serious had happened. He rounded on me. 'Always trouble when you're about, Griffin. Nothing changes.'

'I'm sorry.' I bowed and smiled. I reckoned I could afford to be relaxed. 'This latest problem seems to lie more at your door.' He took a step towards me. 'However,' I added soothingly, 'if you're still in business after today, we will happily promise to restrict our bidding to the other auction houses.'

'Terry's only joking.' The chairman wheeled round anxiously and squeezed my arm. 'By the way, congratulations on your new job. It's an imaginative appointment,' he went on, trying to smile at Logan who was standing beside me. I wasn't used to the chairman's client mode. Not that it was particularly convincing as there was sweat running down his face, and his hands were trembling.

'It isn't if he goes on paying ten times the value of goods

in the face of established research,' snapped Terry. 'The Baarsen Institute were very specific about the pigments of that so-called "Vermeer".'

'Terry!' The chairman let go of my arm and moved away, propelling his managing director ahead of him straight into the purple face of the man from Wartheims.

'You took my bid!' he was shouting. 'You took my fucking bid. You can't stop an *auction* like that. Give me my pictures!'

'My dear Noel,' said the chairman, turning down his enraged client's collar which had risen askew in the confusion, 'come to my office for a large drink.' They disappeared.

'Wasn't the Vermeer rather a punt?' asked Mary. Logan looked at me enquiringly. Behind him I could see Rupert Englefield holding one hand to his ear while speaking rapidly into a portable telephone. He was grinning broadly. I reckoned the merger was off for the moment. Indeed, Garrisons might be swallowing Merrywethers before the month was up. Even though the commission earned on the pictures already sold was safe.

I shrugged. 'If you exclude the picture that pops in and out of the Beit collection depending on the current mood of the IRA, there are only three other Vermeers in private hands and this is a vastly superior painting to them. If I'm right, it's a bargain. If I'm wrong, and I may be, at least it raises the expectations on the other paintings by De Hooch.'

'And?'

Logan grinned. Behind us another shouting match was building up, punctuated by the flash of camera.

'What he isn't telling you, my dear,' he said softly, launching into the very story I had begged him not to explain to anyone, under any circumstances, 'is that he's also advised me to offload my own De Hoochs. He's put them in a sale at Christie's in New York tomorrow. He reckons we'll get most of it back in sympathy bidding. You know what the punters are like. One big price for a painter, and they're all scrambling.'

'Like sheep to the slaughter?' She didn't look too impressed.

'Or pigs to the trough.' He snorted, still buoyed up with the euphoria of a new purchase. 'Why don't I buy you two young people lunch? I've got a table at the Caprice. I want to drink to the future!'

Mary took my hand in hers, and this time I held on to it without demur.

'Yes,' she said. 'So do we.'

THE END

SWEET THAMES
Matthew Kneale

'RAW IN CONTENT, ELEGANT IN TREATMENT. . . RICHLY
ENJOYABLE'
David Hughes, *Mail on Sunday*

It is 1849. A major cholera epidemic threatens London. Working
unsupported by employer or public authority, Joshua Jeavons,
engineer, is completing his great drain plan for the capital.
When the deaths begin, he works even more furiously, driven
by a bold vision – a London freed of rotting sewers, cleansed
and reborn, and he, Joshua Jeavons, hailed as the discoverer
of the source of the killer disease.

Then his beautiful young wife Isobella, a paragon of female virtue,
suddenly disappears and Jeavons must turn his attention to new
and even more perplexing questions. Why her coldness? Why
her absolute refusal of his attentions since the first night of their
marriage? Could certain unthinkable accusations, made anonymously
against Isobella in a series of letters, actually be true?

Jeavons' search for the answers to the mysteries that surround him
leads to the shores of the Thames where only sewer-scavengers
thrive; to glittering Haymarket cafés where high-class prostitutes ply
their trade; and finally to the dangerous heart of London's slums.
What he finds there, amid poverty, disease and death, will shatter
his ideals and strike at the core of everything he has ever held dear.

'A PUNGENT, IMAGINATIVE THRILLER'
Suzi Feay,*Time Out*

'EXCELLENT . . . THE GRADUAL UNFOLDING OF THE PLOT IS
SUPERBLY DONE'
Mark Illis, *Spectator*

0 552 99542 8

BLACK SWAN

SERVING SUGGESTIONS
Michael Carson

'AN EXCELLENT COLLECTION FROM A MASTER'
Barry Seddon, *Manchester Evening News*

Aside from his well-loved novels, Michael Carson has established a
formidable reputation as a short-story writer, appearing regularly in
magazines, anthologies and on Radio 4's *Morning Story*. In *Serving
Suggestions* we find a selection of his choicest, his latest and,
quite simply, his most irresistible.

Flung far – from New York to Buenos Aires, from Merseyside to
Ras Al Surra – the stories spotlight, among others, missionaries
who unbend in the undergrowth, Imelda Marcos on her knees,
and a man wedded to his car in a Britain where Environmental
Correctness has gone Too Far. Devotees of 'Wobbles' Benson,
who debuted unforgettably in *Sucking Sherbet Lemons,* will
find him here in Catholic adolescent mode – pious in the face
of 'Methodists and other pagans'.

The stories range remarkably in mood, from the powerful drama of a
concentration camp survivor who suddenly casts aside the timidity
of a lifetime on a San Francisco bus, to a wicked black comedy
which suggests what to serve a neighbour who polishes her door
knocker with your husband's boxer shorts.

Serving Suggestions is a triumph, leaping from what is hilarious to
what is moving with incomparable grace. It is a celebration of the
versatility and craft of one of our very finest storytellers.

'SHORT STORIES ARE THE PERFECT MEDIUM FOR HIM . . . A
CARSON BOOK FOR PEOPLE WHO DIDN'T THINK THEY LIKED
CARSON'
Alkarim Jivani, *Time Out*

0 552 99586 X

BLACK SWAN

IN THE PLACE OF FALLEN LEAVES
Tim Pears

'CONSTANTLY DELIGHTFUL AND CONSTANTLY SURPRISING . . .
THIS NOVEL IS SOMETHING COMPLETELY NEW AND EXCITING'
A. S. Byatt

The summer of 1984, one of the longest and hottest of the twentieth
century: police and miners fight running battles; unemployment
reaches record levels; the nation's teachers are on strike.

In a faraway Devon village hidden in a valley, however, the world
has stopped turning and time is slipping backward. 'This idn't
nothing', Alison's grandmother tells her, recalling the electric
summer after the war when the earth swallowed lambs. But Alison
knows her memory is lying: this is far worse. She and her friend,
Johnathan, awkward son of the last of the Viscounts, think time has
stopped altogether, when all they want is to enter the real world of
adulthood. In fact, in the cruel heat of that summer, time is creeping
towards them, closing in around the valley.

Like the crooked landscape in which it is set, this poetic novel is
a tapestry: of past and present, memory and discovery, elegy and
hope. By turns moving and funny, *In The Place of Fallen Leaves*
is one of the most memorable and widely acclaimed first novels of
recent years.

'MORE PERFECT THAN ANY FIRST NOVEL DESERVES TO BE'
Jennifer Selway, *Observer*

'THE STRONG RHYTHMS OF THIS ASTOUNDING FIRST NOVEL
ARE AS HYPNOTIC AS A DRUM BEAT'
Penny Perrick, *Sunday Times*

0 552 99536 3

BLACK SWAN

MAYBE THE MOON
Armistead Maupin

'WONDERFUL, FUNNY, POIGNANT AND GUTSY . . . YOU CAN
FEEL THE AUTHOR'S HUGE AND HURT AND LOVING HEART
BEAT ON EVERY PAGE'
Anne Lamott, *Mademoiselle*

All of thirty-one inches tall, Cadence (Cady) Roth is a true survivor
in a town where – as she says – 'you can die of encouragement'.
Her early leading role as a lovable elf in a smash-hit American
film proved a major disappointment since moviegoers never saw
the face behind the rubber mask she had to wear. After a decade
of hollow promises from the Industry, she is still waiting for the
miracle that will make her a star. Through a series of bracingly
frank journal entries, Armistead Maupin tracks his spunky heroine
across the saffron-hazed wasteland of Los Angeles – from her
infrequent meetings with agents and studio moguls to her regular,
harrowing encounters with small children, large dogs and human
ignorance. Then one days a lanky piano player saunters into Cady's
life, unleashing heady new emotions, and she finds herself going
for broke, shooting the moon with a scheme so harebrained and
daring that it might just succeed . . .

Maybe the Moon, Armistead Maupin's first novel since his
bestselling *Tales of the City* series, is the tale of an outsider told
from the inside. It is a work that speaks to the resilience of the
human spirit.

'DELIGHTS, AMUSES, MOVES AND ANGERS YOU WITH THE
LIGHTEST OF TOUCHES. IT IS, AS MIGHT BE SAID OF CADENCE
HERSELF, A SMALL MASTERPIECE'
Simon Callow, *Vogue*

'*MAYBE THE MOON* WILL DISAPPOINT ONLY THE
ENVIOUS. RICH, MOVING, SEXY AND FUNNY, IT ALSO HAS
A PLEASINGLY ANGRY STREAK'
Patrick Gale, *Daily Telegraph*

0 552 99569 X

BLACK SWAN

A SELECTED LIST OF FINE WRITING
AVAILABLE FROM BLACK SWAN

THE PRICES SHOWN BELOW WERE CORRECT AT THE TIME OF GOING TO PRESS. HOWEVER TRANSWORLD PUBLISHERS RESERVE THE RIGHT TO SHOW NEW RETAIL PRICES ON COVERS WHICH MAY DIFFER FROM THOSE PREVIOUSLY ADVERTISED IN THE TEXT OR ELSEWHERE.

☐ 99550 9	THE FAME HOTEL	*Terence Blacker*	£5.99
☐ 99531 2	AFTER THE HOLE	*Guy Burt*	£4.99
☐ 99586 X	SERVING SUGGESTIONS	*Michael Carson*	£5.99
☐ 99348 4	SUCKING SHERBET LEMONS	*Michael Carson*	£5.99
☐ 99465 0	STRIPPING PENGUINS BARE	*Michael Carson*	£5.99
☐ 99524 X	YANKING UP THE YO-YO	*Michael Carson*	£5.99
☐ 99169 4	GOD KNOWS	*Joseph Heller*	£6.99
☐ 99195 3	CATCH-22	*Joseph Heller*	£6.99
☐ 99409 X	SOMETHING HAPPENED	*Joseph Heller*	£5.99
☐ 99538 X	GOOD AS GOLD	*Joseph Heller*	£6.99
☐ 99208 9	THE 158LB MARRIAGE	*John Irving*	£5.99
☐ 99204 6	THE CIDER HOUSE RULES	*John Irving*	£6.99
☐ 99209 7	THE HOTEL NEW HAMPSHIRE	*John Irving*	£6.99
☐ 99369 7	A PRAYER FOR OWEN MEANY	*John Irving*	£6.99
☐ 99567 3	SAILOR SONG	*Ken Kesey*	£6.99
☐ 99542 8	SWEET THAMES	*Matthew Kneale*	£5.99
☐ 99569 X	MAYBE THE MOON	*Armistead Maupin*	£5.99
☐ 99552 5	TALES OF THE CITY	*Armistead Maupin*	£5.99
☐ 99383 2	SIGNIFICANT OTHERS	*Armistead Maupin*	£5.99
☐ 99374 3	SURE OF YOU	*Armistead Maupin*	£5.99
☐ 99408 1	THE COVER ARTIST	*Paul Micou*	£4.99
☐ 99381 6	THE MUSIC PROGRAMME	*Paul Micou*	£4.99
☐ 99461 8	THE DEATH OF DAVID DEBRIZZI	*Paul Micou*	£5.99
☐ 99501 0	ROTTEN TIMES	*Paul Micou*	£5.99
☐ 99536 3	IN THE PLACE OF FALLEN LEAVES	*Tim Pears*	£5.99
☐ 99500 2	THE RUINS OF TIME	*Ben Woolfenden*	£4.99

All Black Swan Books are available at your bookshop or newsagent, or can be ordered from the following address:
Black Swan Books
Cash Sales Department
P.O. Box 11, Falmouth, Cornwall TR10 9EN

UK and B.F.P.O. customers please send a cheque or postal order (no currency) and allow £1.00 for postage and packing for the first book plus 50p for the second book and 30p for each additional book to a maximum charge of £3.00 (7 books plus).

Overseas customers, including Eire, please allow £2.00 for postage and packing for the first book plus £1.00 for the second book and 50p for each subsequent title ordered.

NAME (Block letters) ....

ADDRESS ....